I0658738

BAJA SILVER

BOOK 2:
SAM WHITE HOMELESS MYSTERIES

Timothy A. Brown

Cover Design by Chris Oliveria

NFB
NFB Publishing/Amelia Press
119 Dorchester Road
Buffalo, New York 14213

For more information visit Nfbpublishing.com

I dedicate this book to Cecile Martin,
my life partner for over thirty-five years, gifted poet,
editor, organizer, artist, mother and grandmother.
Your love and support are my light and inspiration.

Also by *Timothy A Brown*

SQUATTER'S GOLD
BOOK 1 SAM WHITE HOMELESS MYSTERIES

"Squatter's Gold a compelling, vivid
read whose underlying consideration
of social issues will linger in the mind
as much as its story of a struggle for
gold and new opportunities"
- MIDWEST BOOK REVIEW

PROLOGUE: APRIL 30, 1579
Present Day Cabo San Lucas,
Baja California Sur, Mexico

CAPTAIN FRANCES DRAKE reclined on the white sand beach in the shade of a palm tree, looked up at his ship, and barked, "Square away the starboard lines." He jumped up and joined in the line of ten sailors pulling a hefty rope to upright their ship. He was respected by his remaining crew for always being ready to jump into a task or a fight and his self confidence was contagious.

Sailors had offloaded precious cargo to release their ship from the beach at the night's high tide. They had careened (scraping barnacles and patching worm holes on the wooden ship's bottom) for two weeks on this sandy beach. They had gathered fresh water and traded for provisions of venison, oysters, and fish. They also traded Chilean wine for pearls with native Pericu' at this beautiful southernmost point of the massive peninsula between the Pacific Ocean and the Gulf of California.

Drake's mind wandered back to the sparkling afternoon two months earlier, when they had been hunting for the Spanish Galleon, Nueva Senora de la Concepcion. At three in the afternoon on March first, the crows' nest lookout signaled their target was three miles ahead. Drake had prepared his crew for a bloody battle, as the "Concepcion" was equipped with such artillery that its nickname was the 'Cacafuego' (Shitfire).

They were directly astern of the Spanish ship and well within sight, but instead of directly pursuing it, Drake implemented his plan, raising a Spanish flag and ordering wooden wine casks, filled with water and tied to the stern of their ship, to be cast overboard. The effect was like putting on the brakes and the Spanish captain then assumed it was another Spanish vessel. The Spanish crew were not expecting pirates on the Pacific side of the Americas. In fact, Drake was among the first.

Drake was surprised and delighted when the Spanish captain, Juan de Anton, assumed they were a friendly ship and did not attempt to run away. Instead, the "Concepcion" came about and pulled along side the Golden Hinde. Drake ordered de Anton to surrender, but he refused. Drake's crew opened fire with arrows and guns and stormed the decks. The Spanish did not resist, but hid below deck, and the Cacafuego was taken without an injury on either side.

The treasure they found would make Drake's legend (eighty pounds of gold, a man-sized golden crucifix, jewels, thirteen chests of silver coins, and 26 tons of silver bars). The gentleman pirate treated the Spanish crew and especially their officers well, feasting with them, giving them gifts, and eventually turning them free after the plunder was loaded onto the Golden Hinde.

Drake had left England two years earlier with five ships under his command. But his British galleon, originally "The Pelican," now renamed the "Golden Hinde," was all that remained of his expedition. Her deck was one hundred and two feet long with a twenty-foot beam and she was armed with twenty-two cannons. Drake's original complement of eighty men was maintained, as he had kept some of the best surviving sailors from other ships which had been broken up by storms or forced to return to England.

Drake had sailed south from Plymouth, England along the west coast of Africa, across the Atlantic to the coast of Brazil, around Cape Horn, then north through the Southern Pacific, attacking Spanish ports and ships along the west coast of South America. He had taken an arrow in the back from indigenous warriors along the way. It had not been life threatening, but still caused him discomfort.

Dubbed the "Gentleman Pirate," Drake was a privateer, supported unofficially by Queen Elizabeth I. He had come farther than any British ship and intended to be the first Englishman to circumnavigate the Earth.

The Golden Hinde was weighted down with pirated plunder. Drake's crew had sacked Valparaiso, Chile and taken a ship laden with Chilean wine (which the men enjoyed immensely while careening). Near Lima, they had taken a Spanish galleon and liberated twenty-five thousand pesos of Peruvian gold. Best of all, Drake had learned that another Spanish galleon, La Nueva Senora de la Concepcion, had just sailed for Manila and they had given chase.

Perhaps just as valuable as the amassed treasure, Drake had also captured the much more accurate Spanish charts of the Pacific Coast of North America, the Sea of Cortez and routes to the present-day Philippine islands. He was now meeting in private with his ship's officers, looking at the captured charts and discussing their next moves.

Drake began, "We can see from these charts that the Spanish route of return from Manila to Acapulco runs to the northeast of here, and our chances of intercepting another treasure galleon along this route should be excellent. A ship returning from the East should have a wholly different plunder - perhaps silks, china, spices, and more jewels. We need to sail north to cross the Pacific, as well."

The first mate jumped in. "Captain, as you know, she is quite laden already and sits low in the water. If we raid another treasure ship, we won't have adequate tonnage. In addition, we will need a full course of provisions to cross the Pacific, and according to these charts, it may be months before we are able to restock supplies."

Drake thought for a moment, looking at his hijacked Spanish charts. He had earlier thought about exploring the waterway marked as the Sea of Cortez. He spotted an island in this sea to the north, a three to four day sail from where they stood. "I propose we can explore this Sea and bury five to ten tons of our silver here, where there is a salt flat." His index finger touched the chart at a large island labelled Isla Carmen. "There are no Spanish colonies anywhere near on the charts, though we may find more native settlements.

"We can always return for the silver, just as we did with the plunder we took from the Spanish in Panama" (Drake referred to an earlier expedition) "when we marched overland with the treasure, but couldn't find our ships." The officers nodded agreement and they laid plans to bury a portion of their silver, then sail north to look for another conquest.

"ISLAND ho!" yelled the sailor from atop the center mast. Drake opened his telescope and saw the island he believed to be "Isla Carmen" from the charts. Roughly fourteen miles long and up to two miles in width, Carmen was far larger than the other four nearby islands. Two pairs of saddleback mountains towered along its spine, and a large lagoon on its northeast end was marked as a salt flat, on the chart.

Drake told his first mate, "We will bury our silver on the east side of the island and collect salt for our journey before we reverse course." He could see that the island paralleled the peninsular shore, which was over five miles away with jagged peaks like shark's teeth, two to four thousand feet high. He also saw smoke rising from several fires near the beaches, indicating a native settlement.

As the ship sailed along Carmen's eastern shore, Drake looked for a site to bury his silver. They came to a shear rocky cliff with red rocks in a familiar pattern. "Look, it's a red monkey," yelled one of the crew, and many agreed, laughing. Drake also spotted a small blowhole in the solid rock ledge at the foot of the cliff and decided to take a closer look. They lowered a rowboat, and four sailors rowed him toward the island.

Drake climbed out on the rocky ledge and leapt from boulder to boulder toward the blowhole. The tide was on the high side and the northern current drove the water through what appeared to be a tube in the rocks that was three to four feet across. It wasn't much of a blowhole in that there wasn't a fountain - more like a bubbling up - but the water rose a couple feet above the rocks when a swell rolled in at high tide.

Drake looked into the hole as the water receded down about five feet, and dropped a rock-weighted line that hit bottom at forty feet. He thought, this might work perfectly if we can drop a boulder or two down the hole and plug the tube it would be perfect and it's close to the water.

On the ship, the crew set to work using a complicated housing of wood, rope, pulleys, and metal crane to lift the 2.5 x 2.5 x 1 foot, eight hundred pound crates of silver bars out of the hold and into rowboats, then rowing the whole production to the island. A group of eight sailors used long iron bars to lever several three-foot boulders to the edge of the blowhole before rolling them into the tube. Satisfied the hole was blocked, they used the crane and pulleys to carefully lower each crate into the hole until fifteen crates with six tons of silver bars were stacked in the tube and the top of the stack was ten feet from the top of the hole. Drake then directed them to drop smaller rocks on top of the crates, covering them with a five-foot layer. The difficult work took all day.

Back at the ship, Drake marked an X on the chart where the silver was buried and in the margin wrote "Red Monkey Rock." The crew of the Golden Hinde later collected sacks of salt from the large lagoon, then put off to the south. The next afternoon, they passed a large bay marked "La Paz" on the chart. They were confronted by Pericu' who were menacing from their canoes and shores and wanted no contact with the outsiders, so Drake decided not to land, as they were well supplied to round the peninsula and head north in search of another Spanish treasure ship.

Drake and his crew did not find the treasure galleon they sought on their journey north along the coast of the Californias, nor did they return for their buried silver.

The Golden Hinde, in June of 1579, became the first English ship to land in present-day Northern California and Oregon. In northern California, they traded with the native Coast Miwok to provision their return journey, and were surprised at the abundance of beavers, otters, and other fur-bearing animals, as well as herds of elk and deer.

Well provisioned, they sailed north looking for a fabled northwest passage that didn't exist, but they may have made it as far as present day Vancouver Bay before giving up and heading back down the west coast of North America.

Following the stolen Spanish charts, they sailed southwest across the Pacific Ocean between Asia and Australia to the Mollucca Islands (present day Indonesia). Drake befriended and traded with the island's Sultan, adding spices to his cargo. He then rounded the southern tip of Africa at the Cape of Good Hope and sailed north through the Atlantic along the Western coast of Africa, to return to England.

On September 26, 1580, Drake sailed triumphantly into the port of Plymouth, although he returned with only fifty-nine remaining crew members. Half of his cargo of spices and Spanish treasure was turned over to Queen Elizabeth. The Queen's share added up to more than a year of revenue for the crown, and Drake earned his Knighthood.

All written accounts of Drake's voyage were committed to the Queen's "Secrets of the Realm," and he and his crew were sworn to secrecy under penalty of death. The queen could not risk this information falling into the hands of the Spanish. The Spanish crown was said to have offered 25,000 pieces of gold for the pirate Drake's death or capture. A later fire destroyed most of Drake's records from the historic expedition.

PART ONE

TRUTH STREET

CHAPTER ONE
GENDER, LOVE and BLOOD

Sacramento, California
11:45 p.m., Tuesday, September 20, 2005

"ADULT BOOK STORE" blared in red and gold neon letters as a three-foot image of a shapely woman in a pink negligee blinked on and off, on and off. Strobing colors blended into asphalt heat waves shimmering like a river. Twelfth Street's three-lane, one-way corridor flowed ten blocks south to California's state capitol building. The heat lingered in the last hours of a simmering Sacramento summer, eighty degrees at midnight.

Passing into autumn, the waning gibbous moon glowed big and bright, refracting off the confluence of the American and Sacramento Rivers ten blocks northwest. Within a six-block area, hundreds of homeless people slept on sidewalks, in alleys and on railroad property. Some slept on thin cardboard. The lucky ones had tents.

Outside the neon corner store were two denizens of the streets. One solidly built, short young woman with punky blonde hair, tight red shorts, and gold halter top stooped at the edge of the sidewalk, talking to a middle-aged white man through the window of a silver Mercedes sedan. In the store parking lot, a young man had just left a customer's car. Well, he/she looked like a tall, wiry, brown-skinned man with very long, shiny black hair but they wore a paisley skirt and smeared makeup. They recognized the young woman on the sidewalk as a fellow sex worker they'd seen a few times before and thought, That fucker, her pimp, won't be far away. If he flashes a knife or gun at me again, I don't know - I might have to clock his ass.

Next door to the adult store, through a chain link fence ringed with Trees of Heaven, sat Dignity Park, a private park for homeless people run by St. Frances Village. The park was empty because the Village was a day shelter only, with multiple services and a dining room where scores of volunteers fed hundreds of homeless men, women, and children a hot, nutritious lunch everyday. The Village's night watchman sat on a bench in Dignity Park, watching the sex workers and customers interact, with a pellet gun on his lap. The Village director paid him five dollars for every rat he exterminated.

At that moment, a 1968 brown Impala pulled up and parked on the A Street side of the adult store. He/she saw it and ducked behind a van in the small parking lot. A copper-skinned man of about thirty with curly dark hair and a thin mustache, dapper in brown corduroy pants with a yellow-collared shirt, slid out of the car. His demeanor was pompous as he strode down the hot sidewalk toward the punky-haired girl.

They thought, She looks more like a girl. I'd say she's about sixteen. She shouldn't be out here. This pimp is a prick. They watched as the pimp held out his hand, wanting money from the girl. She handed him a wad of bills and as he counted it, his face changed from smug smile to 'don't fuck with me!' He held out his hand again, but she shook her head, holding her hands out, palms up. He put the wad in his pants pocket with his left hand while his right became a fist, and he punched her on the left side of her head.

She didn't fall down, but she was stunned, as he had only slapped her before. He was groping her halter top and then her shorts trying to find more money, and she pushed him away. He hit her again with a right fist to her jaw and she went down.

They started moving after the first punch and was now bounding like a big cat toward the altercation. Just as the girl went down, they brought up a right fist from down low to land a vicious uppercut to the pimp's chin. The pimp's head popped up like a "rock-em-sock-em-knock-his-block-off" robot toy, and before he could recover, they landed a left fist to his nose, which dropped him hard. The pimp didn't move as blood poured down his cheeks. They kicked him in the ribs to check that he was out and saw the gun in his waistband. They thought about taking the gun, but they decided against it, then helped the girl to her feet.

The night watchman had witnessed the violence through the chainlink fence and parking lot, and was on his phone to the police. They asked the girl if she could walk and she nodded, taking his hand. The girl saw that Markus was out cold on the sidewalk and realized that she was in trouble, so decided to go with this stranger. They both heard the siren as they walked towards the village entrance on Twelfth and B Streets. The nightwatchman had seen them coming and had already called them a cab.

He met them at the Park entrance. "Hey, I saw what happened on 'A' Street and I called the police, but I also called you a cab so you can get out of here. I know the other guy started it, but I don't want to get into it with the cops." The cab pulled up to the Village dining room door and they got in. The girl told her rescuer, "I've got money for a motel." He/she said to the driver, "Take us to Old Town please, Front and I Streets." They whispered to the girl, "I have access to a safe house in Old Town."

"What's your name?" asked the girl who pulled a tissue from her pocket and dabbed at the blood on her lips. "My name is TommyLynn. Are you okay?" "Thank you TommyLynn. I'm Dani, with an "I," and I've been better. I've noticed you working the same spot a couple times. Do you have a pimp?"

"No, I work for myself, but I take it that was your pimp I just knocked out?"

"Yeah, his name is Markus, and he has a gun. I'm sorry to get you mixed up in my shit. I'm worried for both of us, now."

"Hey, as you witnessed, I can take care of myself. My place in Old Town is funky, but we'll be out of harms way. It wasn't your fault either. That asshole has threatened me a couple of times before, so it was only a matter of time before I had to deal with him. Here's our stop."

Dani insisted on paying the taxi after pulling cash from her shoe. "I got a big tip earlier. I'm glad I brought the rest of my money with me tonight."

Old Town was in party mode, with bars still open. People laughed and strolled in groups on the wood-planked walkways. TommyLynn walked with Dani and explained, "I had him drop us a couple blocks from my place in case Markus finds the taxi driver." TommyLynn led her down an alley and asked her to wait while they entered the back service door of a bar. They came out a minute later with a small bag of ice and a couple of bottles of water. "I've got a friend who works here and I do clean up for them sometimes."

She looked at her rescuer in the light as they came back outside, tall and wiry with beautiful brown skin and long shimmering dark hair. They smiled, with perfect white teeth and a guileless face. She smiled back, but it was disconcerting, with the dress and blouse and the makeup on their eyes.

Farther down the alley they came to an three-story building with a bronze plaque, the year 1850 engraved in large numbers. TommyLynn pulled out a key and unlocked a gate on the side of the building that opened to a downward staircase. Dani followed TommyLynn down the stairs where they keyed a heavy metal door that opened to a pitch black space, and Dani thought, I hope I can trust this guy.

TommyLynn took a couple of flashlights from clips on the wall and, handing her one, turned on the other. "Welcome to my historic basement safe house."

Dani saw the spacious, windowless room and asked her rescuer, "So, are you a man or a woman? You're like so andro..., what's that word?"

"Androgynous?"

"Yeah, even your voice sometimes sounds like a man and sometimes like a woman."

"Okay, you get right down to it. I like that. I'm intersex, or what they used to call a hermaphrodite." TommyLynn had offered this without shame or embarrassment. They looked closely at Dani to gauge her response and noted Dani's interest and absence of judgment, so continued, gesturing to a folding chair for her to sit.

"I got boy parts and girl parts. My xx/yy chromosomes are mixed up and about one in every two thousand babies are born with it. Lucky me. I'm one of the rare ones that have a vagina and a penis. My vagina works better than my penis as far as sex goes and I don't have balls - at least that you can see. So, I prefer to be a her, but I'm attracted to men and women."

She smiled at Dani and thought she saw the slightest blush. They both sat down in the matching folding chairs.

"I'm going to leave the door open to freshen the air for a while." He started to roll a joint.

Dani smiled crookedly, despite her damaged face. "I was just about to ask if you had any weed. I meet a lot of different people doing sex work, but I've never met anyone who is intersex. I read once, in an old medical book when I was maybe thirteen, about hermaphrodites and there was a picture."

"When I was born, the doctors told my mom and dad that they needed to decide right away whether they would raise me as a boy or as a girl. They told my folks they weren't sure whether I'd become a man or a woman. My folks decided to raise me as a boy, but gave me a name that could go either way."

Dani interjected, "Oh my god, that must have been so hard for your parents - and for you growing up?"

"My parents are smart people and they love me." Her voice caught in her throat, but she didn't cry. "I've got my dad's physique, He was a college football star. I've got my mom's dark hair and complexion. Her folks came from Mexico and we have some Yaqui Indian blood. 'Sangre de Indio's,' as my grandmother would say. She also told me that our family has a long history of what they call "mug Xj and xe." Basically, gay and intersex people; and some of them were tribal shamans."

Dani reached over and pointed to a tattoo on her forearm, of a mountain lion crouching. "The Puma is my spirit guide," TommyLynn said as Dani held her hand to let her know she didn't care about her sex or color. TommyLynn had been kind to her and risked her life for her and they had barely known each other. She offered, "It must have been hell, growing up. I know how cruel kids can be."

"I liked to do boy things as a kid. I was big and physical, so I fit in okay until I got to high school. Then all hell broke loose. I got this body like a linebacker, but I wanted to be a girl. I wanted to play boys' sports, but I wanted to wear girls' clothes. The boys wanted to know why I wouldn't use the boys showers, and some tried to bully me. The girls were scared shitless of me, so I didn't exactly fit in.

"After I beat the crap out of a couple of the biggest asshole football players, nobody fucked with me anymore. Not to my face, anyway. But there were endless looks and sniggers, and people talking about me behind my back." He took a hit on the joint and a sip of water.

"I dropped out my junior year when I started wearing makeup with girls' clothes and everyone freaked when I used the girls' bathroom. My parents were so disappointed that I dropped out of school. I couldn't stand to be around them anymore. That's when I hit the streets. What's your story?"

Dani took a deep breath. "Wow, I thought I had it bad, but your life must have been constant torture." Tommy-Lynn just nodded and said, "Pretty much, yeah, but it made me a damn good street fighter. You're a good listener, but I want to hear about you."

Dani was just over five feet, but solid. Her dirty blonde

hair was only an inch long except for her bangs, with purple highlights hanging down to her nose like a parade pony. She pushed the bangs out of her eyes as she frequently did, trying to make them catch on her multi-studded ear, and looked in TommyLynn's copper eyes.

"I'm better at asking the questions than telling my story. Well…" She took a deep hit of the weed. "My dad left me and my mom when I was four years old. I kind of remember him, but he never came back. My mom said he started doing meth, and when he began to beat on her, she kicked him out. My mom never finished high school because my dad got her pregnant at sixteen. Her folks were disabled, so she was always poor, but she loved me and did her best. When my dad left, my mom got by on welfare until I was six or seven and she got a job. It barely paid more than welfare, so we never had money to do anything but pay the rent and utilities on our tiny, crappy apartment. We had to get grocery handouts just to eat, at the end of the month.

"I had an okay childhood. I liked school, but the cool girls had money and looked down on me. I was embarrassed to bring friends over, but I had a few. When I was fifteen, my mother found a boyfriend who made a little more than we did and he'd buy us things and take us out to dinner once in a while.

"I didn't really like him. He was always staring at me and flirting when my mom wasn't looking, but she was happier with him around, and he eventually moved in with us. When I was sixteen my mother got really sick. She had cancer of the brain and she only lived about four months."

Dani saw TommyLynn was watching her closely and really paying attention. She said, "I feel like I can really open up to you. I really don't talk about myself much. I'm usually the one asking the questions."

TommyLynn replied, "Thanks for trusting me. I'm sorry you lost your mom so young. You look like you're sixteen now. How old are you?"

"I'm eighteen." Tears welled and ran down her cheeks as she continued. "Before Mom was even dead her asshole boyfriend started hitting on me for real. He would buy me things and give me rides, and it started with him feeling me up in the car. I was okay with that. My only real parent was dying, and I was lost without my mom. Then, in my mom's last days, he forced himself on me and I didn't do anything about it. I was just sixteen and he was nice to me afterward. He even left me forty bucks before he went to work."

"What a fuckhead!" TommyLynn blurted, shaking his head.

"I never told my mom. She was barely conscious at the end, on morphine, and I couldn't lay that on her. I let him fuck me a few more times and I tried to like the sex, but I felt, like, dirty. He disgusted me. My mom was gone, and I told him it was over and the sick fuck offered me more money to let him screw me. I told him if he didn't leave me alone, I'd tell the police. I was done with him and my old life. I didn't have any family to go to - my grandma was dead and Grandpa was in a home - so I just left him in the apartment and I walked away from school and my small group of "friends," who never even tried to help me."

TommyLynn said, "Shit, at least I've got some family who care about me. What did you do when you left?"

"My teacher and a social worker helped get me into a group home for teenage girls. I was lucky to get in, but I met these girls who were into drugs and tricks, so I started running with them. When I turned seventeen, three of us became emancipated minors and shared an apartment. They were secretly sex workers and showed me the ropes. I was making decent money, for once, until I got busted. Almost went to jail, but the judge gave me probation.

"That's when Trixie found me. She actually came to my court hearing and followed me out to recruit me to be one of her girls, even though I was on probation and not quite eighteen. Markus, that guy you beat up tonight, is her muscle. She considers me her property even though I've only been with her a few months. I'm worried for you now. She says she never forgives or forgets and there are rumors that a couple girls tried to leave and she sold them to someone in Mexico."

They were sitting on two folding beach chairs on either side of a low table beside a small lamp that was missing a bulb. The only other furnishings were musty sleeping bags atop cheap air mattresses, inside a tent. The underground fifteen by fifteen foot cell was dark as a cave. Only their two flashlights lit the dingy space. A fan plugged into an extension cord moved the still air around. TommyLynn saw her looking around and said, "I have the tent because bugs freak me out."

Dani's left eye and bottom lip were red and swollen, with bleeding cuts. TommyLynn handed her the small bag of ice. "You should keep this on as long as you can stand it. I know it must hurt."

"Yeah, it hurts, but not as bad as that fucker Markus is going to hurt when he wakes up. Man, you really cold-cocked him. Two punches and he was down and out."

"I'd usually give the guy a fighting chance, but I knew he had a weapon because he's threatened me before - once with a knife and once with a gun - out there, when we were working the same spot."

"Oh yeah, he's got a gun he likes to flash around to show how bad he is. Didn't do him no good tonight."

"Well, he won't find us here. I bring mostly gay or trans runaway homeless kids here to get them off the streets and out of trouble when their families kick them out. I don't always stay here. I can stay with my folks, too."

Dani looked up at TommyLynn with big green eyes. "I'm not sure what to do now."

"Don't sweat it, we're safe here. We'll figure something out after we sleep." TommyLynn pulled off a thick hair tie and let her long shiny dark hair out of its ponytail. They laid down on top of the bedrolls with their clothes still on and TommyLynn rolled on his side. Dani spooned him from behind.

After a few minutes, TommyLynn said, "We should lay low tomorrow and let things cool off. I'll take you to the homeless teen center at the Village in a day or two. It's safe, and they're cool there. I'm working on my GED (high school equivalent), and you could, too, if you want."

"I've heard of the Village and the Teen Center, but Trixie and her asshole Markus scare the shit out of me. I'm not sure if I should stay in town or how I'll work here anymore."

"Shush. I'll be with you if you want me to, and I'll make sure no one hurts you. I promise! I'm not afraid of those assholes." TommyLynn patted her hand, she hugged his back, and said, Thank you TommyLynn! They were soon fast asleep.

In the early morning, Dani's dreams were invaded by the pimp Markus.

She ran away from him, looked back over her shoulder, and saw him gaining on her. He punched a fist into his open hand, showing her that he would hurt her. His face was twisted into a hateful rage that horrified her. She ran right into the arms of Trixie, who clutched her and would not let her go. At first, she thought, Trixie will protect me from him, but Markus punched her in the ribs so hard that she fainted.

She opened her eyes in a very dark place like a coffin, walls close and confining, her hands and feet tied together and something in her mouth that made it hard to breath, much less scream for help. She felt her panic rise as she moaned her utter aloneness.

Dani woke up shaking and struggling to escape TommyLynn's embrace. TommyLynn repeated, "It's just a dream, it's just a dream" in her most soothing tone. "You're okay, you're safe here, I'm with you." Dani snapped out of the panic sobbing and hugged TommyLynn tight.

Later that morning, they were seated at an Old Town coffee shop and Dani insisted on buying. "By the way, my name is Dani Blue. What's your full name?"

She extended her hand. "I'm TommyLynn Watson-Arce. Pleased to meet you." They shook hands and giggled.

"So how did you find that basement space?"

"You do ask a lot of questions. Just kidding. The guy who owns that old building is a lover of mine. I do him "favors" when he's in town, and he lets me use the space as long as there's no problems and I keep an eye on things. He likes that I help homeless kids."

"Nice arrangement. Hey what should we do today? I don't think I can stand being in that dark space except to sleep. Don't get me wrong - I mean, like, I feel safe there, and I'm really happy to be with you and not in Trixie's clutches."

"We could walk along the river and have a picnic. I've got a little pot and we could get some beer and food to bring. I think it'll be safe as long as we aren't near any of our usual spots."

They brought a blanket and bought some sandwiches at the coffee shop and some beer at the gas station on Jiboom Street. Then TommyLynn showed her one of his favorite Sacramento River spots that was relatively isolated. They laid out the blanket they had brought and snuggled in. The river was low in September and summer was officially over, so river traffic had slowed considerably.

"Wow, this is so nice. I never get to do this. Just spending a day at the river is like...va-ca-tion." Dani drew out the word like it was a holy prayer and TommyLynn laughed.

"Yeah, I've camped here a few times, in a pinch. Being close to the river is so soothing - the smells and sounds, the way it changes every second, the light and colors.

I'm really lucky I'm a free agent and not beholden to anyone. It must be terrible to have to deal with pimps and other sex workers all the time?"

"I was just thinking about how, in only three months, I've gotten numb to it. It's close to slavery. I mean, its not, because I get paid, but I have to go where they say and do what they say, and Markus is always cutting in on my tips and threatening all of us. The house I share with the other girls is drug city and most are into crystal. I hate that shit. It makes me sick, and the others are total bitches when they're high."

"Sounds like hell to me. I mean, I sell my shit too, but I can stop if I want to. I want to move on to doing something that means more. Maybe helping people like me, or trying to change the conditions for sex workers. A lot of us end up on the streets with nothing and no one. Have you thought about doing something else?"

"Sure. I had a dream once, of being a teacher. I had some good ones, and they tried to help me. But, shit, I didn't even finish high school, and it seems like so far out of reach, I can't even imagine it any more."

Dani looked sadly at TommyLynn and he reached for her hand, squeezed it gently, and looked into her eyes. They kissed very softly at first, then with passion, but she flinched at the pain from her damaged face.

"I'm sorry, I forgot about your cuts and bruises." They embraced, but didn't take it any farther. They just enjoyed the moment and hugged each other for a long time. When they looked in each other's eyes again, Dani was wiping tears, and TommyLynn teared up. They were soon laughing together. Dani sniffled, "What a couple of crybabies, eh?"

After a while, they stripped to their underwear and dipped into the edge of the flowing river. Even in September, the water felt cold but refreshing. For the first time, Dani understood the concept of baptism: how the water felt like it washed away her pain and sins and gave her a new beginning. They relished the warm sun on their skin as they napped and dried, cuddled, and gently kissed. Dani thought about how happy she felt and couldn't remember feeling this way since before her mother got sick. I don't want this day to end. It feels so hopeful to have a friend, and it's not just about sex. Maybe I can dream a little, of something different.

TommyLynn couldn't stop smiling and couldn't remember when she'd smiled and laughed so much. Sure, they were a little high from the beer and weed, but it felt much deeper than that - an unfamiliar, warm happiness and calm as they cuddled, watching the colorful sunset across the river turning thin clouds to flaming gold and crimson.

Thursday, September 22, 2005

SAM White, the fifty-year-old director of St. Frances Village approached the Reverend Don Hood and his assistant director Jake Winters at the Dignity Park service center. Sam was over six feet tall, 230 pounds, with a white/blond mustache and goatee and dirty blond hair. He was wearing jeans, a collared, blue, short-sleeved shirt that matched his eyes, and comfortable shoes. He passed a line of homeless people with dusty hair and clothes waiting for help, and apologized. "Sorry I'm late."

"No problem," said Don as he opened the door to his office in Dignity Park, and the three men stepped inside the cramped space with crates of water bottles and clothing donations piled high against the walls. Outside, hundreds of homeless men were lining up for coffee and day-old pastries. A man with wild hair and a bushy beard at the coffee counter blurted loudly, "Blah, blah, bummer bitch." An older volunteer across the counter just smiled sympathetically to the mentally ill man and said "Good morning, Jeff."

Sam turned to Jake. "How's the family, Jake?"

"Billy turns eleven next month and things are better than I could have hoped with Sarah. I'm a lucky man."

"I'm so glad to hear that." Sam remembered back to when Jake was an alcoholic homeless camper and came to him to ask for help, a few years back. His young daughter had died in a drowning accident, and he'd been separated from his wife and son. His guilt and despair had driven him to drink.

"They must be proud of you, Jake. By all accounts, you're doing a great job here in the park." Reverend Don nodded and added, "He's so well respected by the campers and staff that I think we should make him co-director soon and drop the 'assistant.'" Jake smiled and took it in.

"Sounds good. Can you tell me the latest on the patient dumping?" Sam asked.

Jake jumped in, "Well, we've had several incidents this week. Two were elderly women, and one of them was eighty years old. One seventy-year-old was released by the mental health center, given a bus token, and told to come here. She's been working with the Open Door staff and is not doing well. The eighty-year-old was sent here all the way from a Reno hospital, if you can believe that. They actually paid a taxi to bring her here and she says she told them she didn't want to leave, but they pushed her into the taxi.

"She is a very difficult person, but shit," Jake finished, shaking his head.

Sam felt his anger rising. "This is B.S. We can't let them get away with this. Can you give me all the info you have on these folks and I'll follow up with the staff where they were discharged. If I don't get an instant response, I'm going to go to the media."

Jake added, "There were several guys of various ages discharged from the local hospitals, too. One guy in his fifties, named Buchanan, was dropped at the Salvation Army with a note that said he should stay off his feet, which were heavily bandaged.

"Of course, the shelter was full that night, and their staff tried to call the hospital, but couldn't get through to anyone who would help them. He spent the night on the street and somehow limped over here the next morning. When Nurse Janet saw how bad his one foot was she raised hell and got him readmitted. We gave him a ride back to the hospital. Here's all the info I have with names, dates and facilities."

Don said, "There has always been a certain amount of hospitals dumping people here, but this has become epidemic."

"Yeah" said Sam, "I've talked to the Gospel Mission and some of the other shelters, and everyone is reporting the same thing. We've got to bring some pressure on this soon.

"Thanks for these details, and if you hear about other egregious dumping incidents, please let me know right away." Sam stood up, and Jake said, "Will do. I've alerted the staff to be on the lookout."

Sam went into his office and sat at his desk. He thought for a moment, looking up at the framed saying on his bulletin board that his wife Sheila had given him after reading a book by Angeles Arrien called "The Four-Fold Way." In big black letters, it read:

SHOW UP!
PAY ATTENTION!
TELL THE TRUTH WITHOUT
BLAME OR JUDGEMENT!
BE OPEN TO OUTCOME,
DON'T BE ATTACHED TO OUTCOME.

Sam called the hospital in Reno which had dumped the eighty-year-old woman over one hundred miles away to a different state. He asked for the Discharge Coordinator, who said she was just doing what the doctor ordered. He eventually talked to the doctor who had given the order and he claimed the woman had family in Sacramento. When pressed by Sam, he couldn't come up with what relative the patient had in Sacramento, and Sam said, "If you don't arrange to pick up your patient right now and return her to Reno, the next call you get will be from a newspaper or TV reporter."

The doctor quickly acquiesced and Sam gave him the number to the Village's new mental health clinic, The Open Door, to arrange transport with his staff, and he made a note to check with staff later to make sure it happened.

At ten a.m. Sam walked to his meeting at the Teen Center, which was a separate non-profit agency housed for free on the north end of the Village's sprawling property. He was meeting with the Center's new Director, who had made some derogatory comments about the Village guests in a newspaper interview, saying he was trying to move the Teen Center because "it was too close to the dangerous criminal element of older adults in the Village."

Sam seethed when he had read this quote because most of their guests were extremely impoverished, homeless, and disabled and their only criminal acts were camping illegally because the shelters were full or using alcohol and drugs that they were addicted to.

The Director apologized after Sam pointed out the ten-year collaboration between their programs and the fact that the Village provided free rent and free security staff to the Teen Center. He still encouraged them to move, admitting it wasn't the best location for a teen center, but he admonished that it wasn't necessary to insult their adult guests in the process.

After his meeting, Sam saw Cat, a young black woman and a former homeless guest at the Village who had worked for him at Dignity Park, gotten off the streets, and now was a staff person at the Teen Center.

She smiled as he approached and they hugged. "Hi, Cat. Good to see you! How are you?"

"I'm great! I love this job. It feels like I was meant to do this, so things couldn't be better."

"I'm glad to hear that. How is Moreno?" Moreno was Cat's partner and had once been Jake Winter's camping mate when they were homeless together.

"He's good, too. We're still playing music as the Sling Shots, and have some regular gigs. We got scheduled into a couple of music festivals this summer, which pay better and give us more visibility. It's hard to make it as musicians, though, so this job really helps and Moreno's been working at a guitar repair shop that's pretty regular.

We've kept our apartment for two years, now. Life is good. Its amazing what finding twenty-five pounds of gold will do for you," she joked.

It was a reference to a situation three years earlier, when a homeless friend had been killed after finding a stash of hidden gold from the gold rush era. Cat and her partner Moreno had lead a group of campers, The Odd Squad, to defend the gold hidden in a tree when gangsters tried to take it. Sam had also been instrumental in finding the gold and a chunk of the proceeds had paid for a new men's washhouse at The Village. But that was another story.

"Hey, I'm leading a group that starts any minute. Would you like to meet some of the kids?" Cat nodded at a big round table, where about ten teens were waiting and looking in their direction. "There's one person named

TommyLynn, I want you to meet. They go by she/her and she helps other LGBT kids who are on the street. I don't have to tell you how many of these kids are homeless after their families kick them out and they stay in the shadows."

"Sure, I'd love to meet the group," said Sam, and they walked to the table. Cat introduced Sam as the Villages' Director, and invited him to address the group, which was about finding resources to get off the street. He asked the teens to go around the circle and give him their names and what they were interested in talking about.

As they went around the circle, a couple of the "kids" could barely give their names, and appeared to be distracted by serious mental illnesses. Sam was a licensed social worker who had worked at and managed mental health programs in the county. He was very familiar with serious mental illness and resources, so he asked if anyone was a client of mental health services, and only one kid admitted involvement. He invited a couple of the most distracted group members to walk over to "The Open Door" after the meeting and one nodded, indicating interest.

Sam was struck by the appearance of a muscular brown-skinned woman taller than Sam, who had beautiful long black hair. She introduced herself as TommyLynn and confidently asked about job training programs. Sam went over the few programs that he thought might be accessible to them. Then TommyLynn assertively told Sam, "Did you know that it is very difficult and even dangerous to be an intersex person at your facilities? Some of the men here jeer at me and even threaten me on the street or when I've tried to go into the Park for services."

"I'm very sorry to hear that," said Sam. "Have you had problems with our staff?"

"No! The staff here have always been kind and respectful, but some of the guys here are Neanderthals. I can't really use the women's center, either, because the women say hateful things too."

"I'm disappointed to hear this, and I can't control everything that goes on in the streets, but I'd like to set up a meeting with you and Sister Julie, the Dorothy Day Center director, to work out some accommodations for you there, so you will feel more comfortable. Are you available after lunch today - say, two o'clock?"

TommyLynn had a look of surprise on her face, but said, "Sure, I could come by if I can bring my friend Dani, here." She put her large hand on the shoulder of a small blond woman with a punk hair style, a black eye, bruised face, and a plethora of nose and ear rings.

Cat interjected, "Sam, TommyLynn helps recruit underage kids on the street to come here to the Teen Center and even houses some in emergencies at a safe house he operates, off the radar." Sam looked impressed and added, "Its not well known, but the Village operated the first hospice home for HIV/AIDS patients in the mid eighties and I really want to talk to you more about your work and what is needed for the homeless teen population Tommy-Lynn."

TommyLynn smiled and sat up straight. Dani looked at him with admiration and said, "I've been staying at her safe house and she rescued me from a violent pimp, risking her own life."

Dani then asked, "Are there any safe shelters or programs for sex workers who are escaping violence?"

It was Sam's turn to look surprised, because he thought Dani was only about fifteen, and her face was badly cut and bruised. "There are shelters for women escaping domestic violence, but they rarely take homeless women. I have heard of a program assisting sex workers in Oak Park. Sister Julie, the director of Day Center can give you more information this afternoon, when we meet." Dani nodded.

Sam said he needed to go, but coaxed the sick young man who constantly mumbled to himself to come with him to The Open Door. Cat thanked Sam and whispered to him, as he made his exit, "Hey, we've worked up a couple of new blues songs, including the one you collaborated with us on, and we wanted to invite you to sit in with us and play harmonica at the Old Ironsides tomorrow night."

"Cool, I'd love to."

After connecting the young man to the Open Door for mental health services, Sam stopped by the Day House Woman's Center, in the same building as his office, to make sure Sister Julie could meet with them at two.

"Hey, the Open Door staff told me a Reno discharge coordinator arranged pickup for the eighty-year-old woman they dumped here yesterday. You must have scared them to come to Jesus," Julie joked.

"I just threatened to bring in the media, which I probably should have done anyway. I might need your help tracking some of these hospital dumping cases and planning some advocacy. It's totally out of hand."

"I agree, and am glad to help." Julie said. "We end up dealing with these hospitals every week, and rarely get them to do much."

At two o'clock, Sam walked down to the Day Center and waited by the front door until he saw the two teens approaching. "Hi, thanks for coming. It's TommyLynn and Dani right?" Sam checked.

"Yeah, good memory," said Tommy Lynn. "Look we need to jam pretty soon, and I'm not sure how this meeting is going to help."

Sam said, "This won't take long, and I want you to meet Julie and tell her about your work and your difficulties here at the Village. She may also have some ideas for the kind of programs you asked about, Dani. Let's go in." They followed, albeit reluctantly.

Inside the Day Center were women of all ages and colors, wearing several layers of clothing on this hot day and sitting in all of the fifteen or so chairs along the walls. A fifty-something white woman was talking loudly to herself, while the woman next to her was crying. A young Latina was angry, trying to get the staff's attention. Sister Julie walked out of the staff office to meet them, introductions were made to his guests, and Julie took them upstairs where clothes, toiletries, diapers and other necessities were distributed.

Julie said, "Most of the moms have picked up their kids from our HomeSchool classes and have gone to try to get in shelters for the night. These are mostly single women here, now."

Dani asked, "All these women are homeless tonight?"

"Yeah and there are another ten or so in the shower/bathroom area." Dani was shocked. "There's no shelter they can go to?" "No, the shelters are all full, and we've spent the day trying to get these folks in somewhere, but if they're still here, it means they'll probably be on the street tonight."

Julie shifted gears. "How can I help you folks?" Sam encouraged TommyLynn to talk about his difficulties at the Village, which he did, and Dani asked about programs for sex workers. Julie gave Dani information on the Oak Park sex worker program, which didn't offer a safe house, but did offer health and referral services. Dani explained she had been beaten by a pimp who is armed, and would have been beaten worse if TommyLynn hadn't come to her rescue. She described the call service she worked for, how they provided housing, but took most of their earnings and controlled their sex workers through threats and violence. "I'm afraid to go back."

Julie offered, "It looks like the pimp who hit you is dangerous and the call service is human trafficking. You could go to the cops and give them up." Dani shook her head and replied, "I don't want more trouble than I've already got. I finally feel free from them. There are even rumors that when workers resist or try to leave they disappear to Mexico." Sam said, "These are serious crimes and the police might offer you protection if you give them names and evidence." Dani looked very afraid, "I'll think about it okay." TommyLynn offered, "I'm keeping her close and protected until this blows over."

They had a discussion about what the Village could do to better welcome and protect LGBT guests, acknowledging the problem and offering TommyLynn the Day Center's services. Sam and Julie thanked them for coming in and raising the issue. Sam offered, "TommyLynn, we would like to support the work you are doing by supplying your safe house with food or furnishings or whatever you need and I'd like you to think about working with us here at The Village to better serve LGBT guests and developing programs to meet their needs. I respect the volunteer work you're doing and could potentially pay you to consult with us on a part time basis." "Wow! I don't have any training or anything, but I know the streets and I've wondered how I can do more to help the teens and sex workers I come in contact with out there. So, yeah, that sounds good."

Sam and Julie gave them cards and encouraged them to come back the next day after they'd had a chance to think about things. Dani and TommyLynn thanked the staff for their help and left with some clothes and toiletries in bags.

They walked up 16th Street, which was out of their way, but they wouldn't have to pass by the adult book store where they had met two nights before. TommyLynn said, "Stay close and keep a lookout for that asshole."

They were passing through the cement pedestrian tunnel that went under the railroad tracks and were greeted by the strong smell of urine. They picked their way through the broken bottles and Dani said, "I'm not sure I can stay in this town, but I don't know where else to go."

"I think if you lay low and stay away from the usual working girl spots, you should be okay and they'll probably forget about you in a week or so," TommyLynn offered.

"I don't know. Trixie thinks she owns people, and the one girl I heard of who ran away was brought back for a couple days, and then disappeared. There was a rumor she was sold to someone in Mexico. That's one way Trixie keeps us in line - she gets pissed and threatens to send you to Mexico."

"I know these streets and I think I can protect you," TommyLynn insisted.

"Do you still have family in Mexico?" asked Dani, changing the subject.

"Yeah, I got aunts and uncles and cousins who live down in Baja. I've only visited family in Tijuana and near a town called Loreto a few times while I was growing up, but they were really nice people who lived on a big ranch. They took me horseback riding and we milked goats and ate the cheese. They don't even have proper houses out on the ranch, but they seemed so happy, and things were so much simpler there. We slept on hay bales under amazing stars at night. I'll never forget it."

"Wow, maybe we can go there? It sounds really cool." Dani sounded hopeful.

"Well, it used to be really easy to go down there and back, but we need passports to get back into the U.S., now, and I don't know if my family can put us up. I haven't seen them for years. I could ask my parents about them, though.

"In fact, if you'd feel safer, my parents might be able to take you in for awhile." They walked past Jalisco's Tacos and an old motel.

After thinking about it for a minute, Dani said smiling up at her, "That's really nice of you to offer, but I think once they find out I sell my ass, they wouldn't be too interested." Her smile faded to a sad frown. They were turning down G Street towards Twelfth and hadn't noticed the 1968 brown Impala, which had pulled over to the curb quickly behind them.

TommyLynn tried to cheer up Dani. "Hey, I've got a friend on the next block who always has good weed and sometimes other shit. Let's drop in. He's cool with that."

"Sounds great!" replied Dani.

They climbed steps up to the entryway of a two-story, run-down Victorian turned into four apartments and pushed the chime to number four on the second floor. TommyLynn's dreadlocked friend appeared on the balcony above and said, "Yo, Tommy! Whasup!"

TommyLynn looked up and said "Hey, I've got a friend I want you to meet." The door buzzed and they pushed through and walked up the steps. They could smell pot as they approached the door to Number Four. A small young black man with long dreads opened the door and handed TommyLynn a fat reefer before she was even inside. "Thanks, bro. This is my new friend Dani. Dani, this is Jethro." Dani took the big joint from TommyLynn and said, "Thanks, I need the buzz right now."

Jethro looked at her face and said, "You do need a buzz, girl." He handed Dani a lighter and gestured them to an old couch covered in Mexican blankets. They sat down and Dani noticed the big bag of skunk buds open on the coffee table with rolling papers, a scale, and a small handgun, probably a twenty-two, alongside them. TommyLynn started to tell Jethro how they'd met two nights before at the adult book store and Dani gave him a frightened look. TommyLynn said, "Its alright Dani, you can trust Jethro. He's cool."

Jethro said, "Man, you guys in a dangerous business. I don't know how you do it."

"Yeah, Dani thinks her pimp's out looking for her, and because I cold cocked the fucker while he was beating on her, he probably wants a piece of me, too, so we're having to lay low."

"Shit, I'd offer you my gun, but the drug business ain't that safe either," said Jethro as he pulled an ornate brass box from under the table to his lap and opened it. Inside the top was a mirror, and he pulled out a small clear vial of fine white powder. Tapping the vial, he made three one-inch lines of the powder on the mirror, rolled a twenty dollar bill and snorted a line with the rolled-up bill in his nose. Then he wiped up the white dust left from his line with his index finger and rubbed it into his top gums.

He passed it to Dani, who snorted a line and wiped the residue on her gums. After snorting his line, TommyLynn nodded to Dani and said, "Homie, here, has the good shit, don't he?" They all chuckled and Dani pinched the end of her nose and drew in a quick breath to propel the powdered cocaine farther into her sinuses. She felt the numbness on her upper teeth already and said, "Wow, that is the good shit."

Dani and TommyLynn together had about eighty bucks left, and they offered to spend half of it on some of Jethro's tasty buds, but Jethro counter offered, "I know you need the money. How about I give you the buds for some head?" Dani looked at TommyLynn and shrugged, wondering how she'd take it. TommyLynn shrugged back, "Okay then, if you're sure. I'll walk over to the Roma Bakery to get some bread. I'll be back in about twenty minutes." TommyLynn seemed okay with it, Dani thought, but she wasn't sure how she felt about that.

TommyLynn walked out of the building and back to Sixteenth Street, turning left. He didn't notice the Impala, which was parked across from the building and was now pulling out to follow him. The Impala couldn't track him down 16th because it was a one way street, so it waited at the corner. "Where is the freak going?" the driver said to himself as he rubbed his bruised and swollen cheek and chin. Then he saw him cross Sixteenth heading east, so he went down a block and hung a left on Seventeenth Street.

He watched from the end of the block until he saw TommyLynn cross Seventeenth. Then he covered the block and turned the Impala slowly around the corner of F Street. It was an elm tree-lined residential neighborhood with old two-story Craftsman bungalows and Victorians, and there was no car or pedestrian traffic at that moment. Markus already had his pistol in his right hand and his passenger window rolled down. He saw an opening mid-block between two parked cars.

The Impala slowly pulled up even with TommyLynn and she looked over just in time to see a gun pointed at her. She heard two quick shots as she dove over a four-foot front wall onto the porch of a house, and the sharp pain in her left leg told her one of the bullets had found their mark. The pimp said to himself, "Damn he's quick." He saw the guy grab his leg and was glad he'd drawn blood.

The shooter didn't get as far from the scene as possible, which would have been the smart thing to do. Instead, he doubled back to the building where he'd watched them go up to the second floor apartment, where he was pretty sure Dani still waited.

Dani and Jethro had concluded their business, and she came out of the bathroom after cleaning up, smiled at him and said, "If you or your friends ever want to do some more business, I could use it." He had bagged her a generous amount of weed and handed it to her.

She said, "I think TommyLynn should have been back by now though." They heard several sirens close by, and Dani started to freak. "Shit, I better go see what that's about." Just then, the buzzer sounded and Jethro opened the lower door. "See, there's Tommy now."

The doorknob suddenly moved slightly, but stayed locked and then there was a knock. Dani stepped closer to the door and said loudly, "Tommy, is that you?" There was no immediate reply. Jethro grabbed his gun and whispered urgently, "Dani, get away from the door." She stepped to the side just as a shot was fired from the hallway outside and splintered the door near the knob. Jethro flipped out and started firing at the door, which suddenly swung inward, knocking Dani against the wall.

Jethro saw a man laying with his back to the floor and his feet just inside the doorway after having kicked open the door with both legs. The man had a pistol pointed at him. Before Jethro could squeeze off another shot, he was hit and thrown backward on top of his coffee table, buds flying everywhere. Dani saw Markus come through the door gun first and started to scream. He quickly hit her on the head with his gun and she crumpled to the floor, blood flowing from her wounded scalp. Markus looked down at the man he'd shot who was face down and still breathing.

He threw a blanket over her bloody head and carried

Dani down the steps like a rag doll, paused at the bottom, looked out to see if anyone was around, and, seeing no one, dragged her across the sidewalk to his car and threw her in the front seat. She was still unconscious, blood flowing down her face soaking into the blanket and neck of her t-shirt. He pulled away slowly as if nothing had happened.

When Markus got to Trixie's sprawling two-story mansion in Colonial Heights on two lots with a pool in back, he parked in her three-car garage next to her 1968 black Mustang. He told her what happened and was surprised when Trixie flipped out.

"Goddammit! I told you to get the girl back you stupid fucker, not shoot up half of midtown. Two people shot! That's going to bring the heat on us. Shit!"

"I didn't kill them. They're just wounded."

"That could be worse, you moron! They probably saw you and know that you kidnapped the girl, too. We are fucked. Put some pressure on her wound, change her bloody shirt, tie her up, and stick her in the closet upstairs. I need to make some calls to Mexico. You have to leave town soon, and take her with you to TJ. Get ready to go, you dumb fuck."

He looked bewildered. He thought she'd treat him like a hero for bringing Dani back, but it was sinking in that things could get hot for him, and it was smart to head to Mexico until things cooled off.

Chapter Two
HUMAN DUMPING

Friday, September 23, 2005

SAM HAD JUST finished his daily practice of yoga and meditation. He and his wife Sheila Bright were now sipping coffee in their Adirondack chairs on the back deck of their house in River Park. They were shaded from the rising sun by the canopy of large trees on their street, while their chocolate lab Kabu lay on the grass, enjoying her morning chew treat. Sheila was looking at a map of Baja California and said, "Three glorious weeks in Baja! I can't wait." Smiling, Sam sighed. "Kayaking, diving, fishing, eating fresh seafood - yeah, that's what I'm talking about. What are the exact dates in October, again? I need to check my work calendar."

Shiela looked at her phone. "October seventh through the twenty-eighth. Only two weeks away. Its been what, eight years since we've gotten this much time off? I need this vacation." Kabu heard the word 'vacation' and she walked over to Sam with her treat in her mouth. "That's right Bu girl, we're going to Baja." Kabu dropped her treat and licked his knee, her thick tail wagging. He whispered, "Now I feel bad she can't come with us." "Me too," Sheila added.

Sam rubbed Kabu's rabbit soft ears. "You're gonna stay with Jake!" Kabu whimpered at the sound of her best dog friend's name. He said to Sheila, "I got the new kayak racks and I'm getting the car tuned up before we go. In Loreto, I got us reservations for the first two weeks at a new boutique hotel, Las Cabanas. The third week we're at another small hotel that recently opened in the center of town called La Damiana." "Perfecto!" Sheila sighed, rolling her Rs in a good Spanish accent. "I know you're excited to see your friend Juice, too." He nodded. "Yeah its been too long."

He smiled, thinking back to his high school days, running with his best friend since the fourth grade, whose real name was Jesus (Spanish pronunciation). Growing up as a Chicano in east L.A., Jesus had been embarrassed by his given name, so had adopted the name Juice, made popular by the football star O.J. Simpson. They hadn't seen each other since Juice joined the Marines at nineteen, in the mid-seventies.

Sam picked up the Sacramento Bee newspaper and soon startled Sheila. "Son of a bitch, unbelievable! I just met these kids yesterday." He read the beginning of the article to Sheila, describing the double shooting and abduction that had taken place in Midtown the previous afternoon.

"I met with these two kids - well, young adults, really - yesterday, after meeting them at the Teen Center. There's a photo of the girl who was abducted, and its definitely her. She said she was a sex worker whose pimp had beaten her. Her friend was an "intersex" (her words: a teen who had a body like a man but called herself a woman and dressed like it). This says one of the shooting victims was nineteen and was shot in the leg, but is stable. It says there's a third victim who's not identified, and he's in critical condition."

"Sorry, Sam, tough way to start your day," Sheila sympathized.

TOMMYLYNN lay on his back in the hospital bed, but he could not rest. The bullet had passed through his thigh, but had nicked an artery, and his wound had spurted blood. Thankfully, the woman who came out of the house where he had been shot was a nurse, and her quick actions had kept him from bleeding to death before the ambulance arrived. He had been rushed into surgery after arriving at the hospital. His artery was repaired and his wound cauterized.

"Shit, I have to get out of here. My friend was kidnapped, don't you understand? She's all alone in this world," TommyLynn pleaded with the doctor. The doctor looked at his patient sternly and insisted, "You cannot leave here, and you cannot walk on your leg for at least a week. Your artery could burst and you would bleed to death in minutes. How does it help your friend if you die?"

TommyLynn was crying now. "I told her I'd protect her, but I didn't."

DANI, unsure if she was conscious or dreaming, remembered waking up earlier in a space that felt like a closet. Her head pounded. She heard Trixie and Markus arguing. Trixie had lifted her head and brought a glass of water to her lips. She tried to get up, but her limbs wouldn't move. She was very thirsty, so drank from the glass. She tried to concentrate on clearing her head to ask where she was, but she felt so tired.

Now, she became aware that she was in a moving vehicle, but it was very dark and she still could not budge her arms or legs. She thought she heard voices, but they were too faint to be sure. Her head still throbbed and she felt nauseous. The vehicle came to a stop and she heard someone talking, but couldn't make sense of the words. She then realized they were speaking Spanish, and it sounded like a radio news report. She tried to call out, but her mouth and throat were so dry, it was more of a croak and was muffled by the close walls of her coffin-like space. Then the vehicle started again and she felt herself drift back to sleep.

SAM had arrived early for work. He called Captain Ortega of the Sacramento Police Special Crimes Team (SCT), whom he had developed a relationship with a few years earlier when two homeless men he knew were shot while asleep in their camp. He had provided Ortega with information that eventually lead to the killers and the arrest of a dangerous local drug lord.

"Captain Ortega? This is Sam White at the Village. How are you doing?"

"I'm good Sam. How are you? I see you on the news every once in awhile. What can I do for you?"

"I read the article in the Bee this morning about the shootings in Midtown, and I know no one was murdered, but I might have some information about the victims and I still had your phone number."

"No problem Sam. We do have the case since it was an attempted murder and the apparent kidnapping may bring in the FBI, as well. What have you got for us?"

"I met with two young people here at the Village just yesterday and the young woman, Dani looked a lot like the photo of the kidnap victim. I'm wondering if one of the shooting victims might have been a young...well, he was built like a man, but was dressed like a woman...who was with the girl?"

"That fits the description of one of the guys...uh, shooting victims. He, I mean she, was the one who was shot in the leg and who identified the girl for us. The other guy's in critical condition, and we haven't been able to talk to him."

"Well, you may already have my info, then, but the girl had been beaten and said she had fled from her pimp and was trying to get into a shelter for protection. Unfortunately, there are no shelters for sex workers, and we couldn't help her much."

"Yeah, the other guy - uh, girl - told us the name of her pimp and said that's who shot him and probably took the girl. Is there anything else you can tell us about those two?"

"No. It sounds like you know more than I do, but I wanted to make sure. Good luck finding the girl and her pimp, and good talking to you again."

"Same here, Sam. We'll do our best and thanks for calling. Hey, if you hear anything else, don't hesitate to call. I learned last time about your street telegraph - I think that's what you called it - and how helpful it can be."

Sam put down the phone and saw Jake Winters and his staff person Dave, a street monitor, waiting for him in his office doorway. "Come on in."

Jake was a bit breathless and said, "We just had another dumping and I thought you might want to see this guy with your own eyes. He wouldn't come up here with us and might be walking off, so we have to hurry."

Sam jumped up and they hurried down the steps and into the street. Jake asked Dave to explain. "This guy's name is Walter. He's black, age about forty. He's almost blind, but can see a little out of one eye. He's pretty out of it, though. We tried to talk to him, but he wasn't tracking." They looked around, but didn't see him. They walked to the park and asked one of the staff if she'd seen where the guy went. "Yeah, we tried to get him to wait, but he just walked off up Twelfth Street."

"I've got to stay in the park, Don's out today," Jake said to Sam.

"Okay, I'll look for him. What's he wearing?"

"He's got on a white tee shirt and blue jeans," Dave said as Sam nodded and strode off.

Sam turned the corner and hurried up Twelfth Street. He sprinted across the B Street intersection when the light turned yellow. Then he continued up the pedestrian corridor through a river of impoverished humanity - disheveled people slouched and stumbled, older men limping with large bags slung over shoulders, women wearing many layers of clothing for protection from sexual assault, and the occasional drug dealer. He scanned the streets right, left, and ahead, but didn't see anyone matching the description.

Sam walked from C Street past the historic Granary Building and the 524 Mexican restaurant. When he approached H Street he saw a black man who fit the description up ahead, crossing I Street. The streets were crowded with office workers moving like ants through a maze. The man's head was swiveling in confusion and his back was against the wall of Tony's Deli on the corner of Twelfth and J when Sam finally caught up. Sam was thinking, for a blind man, he sure can navigate the streets quickly. Sam approached. "Walter? My name is Sam, and I'd like to help you find some food and a place to stay."

Walter seemed dazed and worn out, but nodded at Sam as if he understood. "Where are we?" He didn't exactly look at Sam. One eye looked clouded and blank and his other eye protruded like a fisheye looking crossways. Sam touched him gently on the elbow and again said, "My name is Sam. Are you Walter?" The man nodded. "We're in downtown Sacramento. Let me get you something to drink, here, then we can walk back and get you something to eat." He asked for a Coke, and once he'd had a few sips, they started walking together back to the village.

Sam asked, "Where did you come from?"

Walter mumbled something like, "Jesus took me. The father told me to come."

"Do you have family or friends here in Sacramento?"

Walter shook his head, but seemed to understand. His lips moved, but he wasn't really talking.

Once at the Village, Sam took him up to the front office and introduced him to Ruth, his office manager. "Please bring him a plate of food from the dining room. I think the crowds down there will be too much for him."

Ruth introduced herself and he smiled when her hand gently squeezed his shoulder. Sam stayed with him while Ruth went downstairs to the dining room. "Where do you live?" Sam inquired.

"At the right hand of the Lord Jesus," he answered. Sam tried again. "Do you have family we can contact?" Again, his mouth moved without sound and Sam gave up.

When Ruth arrived with a steaming plate of food, Walter grinned again. Sam whispered to her, "Once he's eaten, see if you can find out anything about his home, income, or family." She nodded, smiling as he devoured his food.

Sam called Jake, who sent his staff person Dave up to his office. Dave had been on the street when the Placer County vehicle brought Walter to the Village. Dave saw that Walter was eating contentedly under the kind and watchful eyes of Ruth.

Sam invited Dave into his office. "Hi, Dave, could you tell me what happened with Walter? Any and all details would be helpful."

Dave explained to Sam, "Yeah, I saw this Placer County car pull onto the street around nine this morning. It was clearly marked, and the driver got out to open the door for Walter, who was in the back. Walter wouldn't get out and the guy was yelling at him. Then he reached in and yanked Walter by the arm, pulling him out of the car into a pile on the street. He just dropped a folder of papers on top of him and quickly jumped back into the car.

"I was watching this from about fifty yards away, and it all happened pretty fast. I started running over when I saw him getting pulled out of the car, but by the time I got to the car, the driver was pulling away.

"I picked up Walter's papers and helped him up. I tried

to get him to come up to your office with me, but he was pretty freaked out - just mumbling and walking toward Twelfth Street. That's when I radioed Jake and told him what happened. Jake had told us you wanted to know right away if someone got dumped here."

Dave handed Sam the folder of papers. Sam said, "Great work, Dave, you handled this as well as can be expected. Did the driver of the car have a uniform?"

"No, he just looked like a regular county worker. What an asshole though."

"I agree, and I'm going to follow up on this. Can you believe the dipshit had a marked county car?" Dave chuckled. "Yeah, not the sharpest pencil in the cup."

Sam looked through the paperwork and saw that Walter had been discharged from the Placer County Mental Health Center, and that there was even a doctor's name and signature on the form. He got on the phone immediately and called Sacramento Bee reporter Monica Fuentes. He had known her for about five years and had sent a number of notable stories her way. He told her about Walter and a few other dumping cases that were the most egregious. She was very interested and got all the information he had on each case. She asked Sam to let her know what happened to Walter after he talked to staff at the hospital.

He next called Placer Mental Health, and eventually got the doctor who had signed Walter's discharge papers. "Hi Doctor Jones. My name is Sam White, and I'm Director of

St Frances Village in Sacramento. One of your staff actually forced your patient, Walter Moses, out of his county car this morning, here at our site, dumped him on the ground, and drove off. I've got Walter in my office right now. I've already spoken to a Sacramento Bee reporter who will be calling you."

The Doctor sputtered, "Ah...well...he isn't from our county. In fact we're not sure where he's from. I figured he'd have a better chance in Sacramento, finding the help he needs."

Sam fired back, "According to his paperwork, he was hospitalized in your center, so he is your responsibility; and if you think he's ready for discharge, someone should have made some referrals for housing and follow-up care, not just dump him on the street."

"Well, yes, but I was looking at the client's best interest. He doesn't have any family or anyone in our county."

"I'm pretty sure of whose best interest you had in mind. Look, I'm trying to give you a chance to do the right thing. He doesn't seem to have any family or contacts in our county, either, and I'd even question whether he's stable enough for discharge. My next call will be to your Mental Health Director who I used to work with and we'll see if she agrees with your treatment of the client." Sam hung up.

He did call the Placer County Mental Health Director next. "Hi, Susan, this is Sam White. How are you?"

"Hi Sam, I'm holding up. I read about your exploits at the Village from time to time. What can I do for you?"

"I'm sorry to be calling with a complaint." He described the incident and she was very apologetic and promised to investigate.

"I wanted to give you a heads up that I've already contacted a Bee reporter about this and other dumping cases. We're overwhelmed with all the hospital dumping, from as far away as Nevada, and I'm sorry to sic the press on you, but this was a particularly disturbing case."

"I understand, and I'm as upset about this as you are. I assure you we will do right by the client now."

Next Sam called his old friend Kalen Jones, who was a former Sacramento City Council member and had recently been elected to the State Assembly. Kalen was a well-loved Sacramento native and public servant who had played football for U.C Berkeley and had a short career with the San Francisco Forty-Niners.

"Hey, Sam, good to hear from you. What's up?"

Sam told him about the increase in hospitals, adjoining counties and even Nevada, dumping patients at the Village and other homeless programs in Sacramento.

"I'm glad you got Monica on the story. She'll do a good job." Kalen added, "I'll get Karly to help you on this, too. When the story comes out, we'll push for reform legislation. I'll contact the Director of the State Hospital Association. He's a good guy, and I think he'll work with us to hold his hospitals accountable."

"Thanks Kalen, I appreciate the help." Sam added, "Let's grab a beer at the Rubicon soon, or catch a Forty-Niners game. They're looking pretty good this year."

"I'll have my people call your people. Just kidding." After a pause, "Maybe Sunday, you and Sheila could come by to watch the game. Lets touch base."

Ruth came into Sam's office. His door was almost always open. "Placer County is sending someone to pick up Walter," Ruth said smiling.

"Thanks for taking care of him, Ruth. Did he say anything that made sense?"

"No, not much, but he's a nice man and enjoyed the lunch. I told him someone was coming to take him to a place to sleep, and he thanked me."

Sam's phone rang and he picked it up as he waved to Ruth. "Hi, this is Sam."

"Are you Sam at the Village?" asked a familiar and urgent voice.

"Yes, I'm Sam White. Who is this?"

"I'm TommyLynn. We met at the teen center and talked yesterday. I don't know if you heard, but Dani, the young girl with me, was kidnapped yesterday, and you've got to help me find her. The cops aren't going to do anything."

"I read in the paper that a couple of people were shot, too. Are you okay?"

"Yeah. Dani's pimp Markus shot me in the leg, but he was trying to kill me, so I guess I was lucky. I'm in the hospital, and they won't let me leave here for at least a week. That's why I'm asking you to help find her. Dani told me that when another of Trixie's girls tried to run away, they caught her and she disappeared."

"Wait, now - who is Trixie? And who was the other guy that got shot?"

"Trixie runs Dani's call service, and Markus is her muscle. She's got a bunch of girls working for her that she puts up in flophouses around town. The other guy that Markus shot was my friend Jethro, whose place we visited. I hear he's in bad shape.

"I guess Markus followed us, and I went out to run an errand nearby when Markus shot me. Then I guess he headed back to Jethro's, shot him, and grabbed Dani - at least, I think that's what happened."

"Have you told the police all of this?"

"Yeah, I told them everything I know, but they won't do shit. They don't care about a sex worker. I'm afraid Dani might disappear before they do anything."

"I spoke to a police captain this morning after I read the article in the paper and saw the picture of Dani. He is a good guy, and is doing his best to find Markus. He said the FBI may be taking up Dani's kidnapping, too, and they know what they're doing."

"Please help me find her. I told her I'd protect her, but I didn't, and now I'm stuck in the hospital. She doesn't have any family left. I don't know what else to do."

"I'm not sure how we can help, TommyLynn. If the FBI's on it, they have the resources to find her. Look, I'll get some of our staff together to see if there's anything we can do, but you need to take care of yourself and get well."

"Okay, thanks, Sam. I'm in Room 435 at the Med Center. Can you let me know if you find out anything?"

Sam sat thinking for a few minutes, then he called over to the teen center and got Cat on the line.

"Hi Cat. I'm guessing you've heard about TommyLynn and Dani?"

"Yeah, I was just talking to a couple of the guests here, and word on the street is that TommyLynn was shot and Dani was kidnapped."

"There was an article in the Bee this morning that I caught before coming in and I've spoken to Captain Ortega about it already. You remember him, right?"

"Sure I do, he was a good guy."

"Anyway, TommyLynn just called me from the hospital and asked me to help find Dani. I'm not sure what we can do, but can you come to my office for a meeting ASAP?"

"Sure. I'll be there in about fifteen minutes."

Sam then walked over to Day House to find Sister Julie. Lunch was winding down, and the last seating of about one hundred men and women were still enjoying the day's meal of hamburgers and fries with salad and fruit. The dishwashers were hard at it and the scores of volunteers were breaking down the big pots and pans. It was a hot day and the smells of unwashed pilgrims was stifling despite the swamp cooler and fans.

"Hi, Julie, did you hear about what happened to the kids we met with yesterday?"

"I heard about a shooting. They weren't involved, I hope."

"The girl, Dani, was kidnapped and the guy - I mean

TommyLynn - was shot by the pimp who had beaten her. You remember Captain Ortega from the City Police? I spoke with him this morning about meeting with them yesterday, and TommyLynn just called me from the hospital, asking me to help find Dani. He was shot in the leg and sounds okay, but will be in the hospital for at least a week. I wondered if you could ask around and meet with Cat and I in my office as soon as you can?"

"Sure. There are a couple of young women here I'd like to talk to first, then I'll be right up."

"Thanks, Julie. I'm not sure there's much we can do, but TommyLynn says Dani told him that when other call girls in their organization tried to run away, they were brought back and then disappeared. So he thinks there might be a short window in which to find her."

"Got it," Julie said, before hanging up and bounding upstairs.

Twenty minutes later, Cat and Julie were seated in Sam's office. He could see that Cat admired Julie, who was everyone's favorite person, radiating fearless love and acceptance.

"Thanks for getting together on short notice. I've briefed you all on what I know about the shootings and Dani's kidnapping, but I'm not sure where to go from here. I guess if we can find out anything about her pimp Markus or this Trixie woman, who seems to run the call girl operation, then we might be able to help the police find her."

Julie jumped in. "I spoke to a young guest of Day House

just now, who I remembered was a prostitute before she got sick. She says she used to work for a Trixie, but wasn't clear about how long ago - maybe just months - but she is very mentally ill, schizophrenic, and not on meds. She calls herself Moonshine and is erratic, but I think she's telling the truth.

"She says she lived in one of Trixie's houses with other sex workers for about six months, but then she started hearing voices and they eventually kicked her out."

"I know Moonshine," added Cat. "She used to come to the Center. I tried to get her connected to Open Doors for counseling, but she's a tough one."

"Yes, we've been trying to get her hooked up there, too," said Julie. "But she's drinking heavily and bounces around on the streets constantly, so we're glad she still comes into Day House sporadically."

"Can she remember where any of Trixie's houses are?" asked Sam excitedly. "That would be huge."

"She's pretty hard to track, and I tried to pin her down about where she lived when she worked for Trixie, but she only mentioned First Avenue and Alhambra. She doesn't remember the exact street or number, but she's still at Day House and might be willing to help more. We don't want to bring in the cops, though. She'll freak out."

"I know her well, and have a pretty good relationship with her," Cat offered. "I'm done with my groups for the day. I can take her in my car over to Oak Park and we can look for where she used to live. If we're lucky, this Trixie might still be using the house."

Julie and Sam nodded and Sam said, "Thanks for offering to do this, Cat, but please be careful. If you do find the house, just let me know and we'll let the cops deal with it."

Cat nodded and Julie said, "We better get over to Day House and catch her before she leaves. I hope she'll cooperate. I told her one of Trixie's girls was kidnapped, and she seemed to be concerned."

SAM sat at his desk composing the next month's fundraising letter for the Village, and looked at the time on his computer. Four o'clock. He sighed, thinking about the weekend. He was beat from a long week and looked forward to meeting Sheila and his friend Mike at the Rubicon for a Red Bud (a strong seasonal ale they brewed to honor Jerry Garcia) and waffle fries. His phone rang and he picked it up.

"Hi, Sam. Monica, here. I wanted to let you know that this story is taking off. I just found out that Buchanan, the fifty-something guy with the bad feet you told me about, had his right foot amputated this morning."

"Shit, the poor guy. They really fucked up, then."

"Oh yeah. I've got an estimate from a friend at the hospital that this kind of procedure and rehab probably costs a quarter of a million dollars, and the guy didn't have insurance, which is probably why they dumped him in the first place. If they would have just discharged him to a motel or intermediate care facility and covered the cost, he might have recovered without losing his foot. Hey, but now he'll qualify for Medicaid, which will cover some of it.

"That isn't all, Sam. I have a contact at the State Attorney General's office who I called about the Nevada hospitals dumping patients in California cities, and they are already following up on other complaints around the state. They are seeking subpoenas for various hospitals' discharge records."

"When do you think the story will run?"

"It looks like it might be a front page Sunday story, but I can't promise anything."

"Thanks, Monica. Are you going to interview this poor Buchanan guy?"

"Yeah, I plan to as soon as possible; and thank you for sending this story my way."

Fifteen minutes later, Sam's phone rang again.

"Hi, Sam, my name is Steve Buchard of the State Hospital Association. I got calls from Assemblyman Jones and a Sacramento Bee reporter this afternoon. I understand they were contacted by you about the so-called dumping of hospital patients at homeless programs."

"Hi, Steve, thanks for calling. I didn't expect to hear from you so fast, but yes. I got fed up with what I would call an epidemic of patient dumping, not just at our programs, but throughout the homeless system and from as far away as Nevada. I had a particularly heinous case come up today and it put me over the edge, so I started making calls."

"I'm sorry to hear that, but I thought the reporter told me that Placer County had already picked up the patient and he was placed into a motel this afternoon."

"Oh, yeah? I'm glad to hear that, but it's too bad it took me calling a Bee reporter to make this happen. Look, this is not about one case. This is about hospitals inappropriately dumping patients here almost every day, including our local hospitals. We need to address this issue immediately, and I was hoping you were calling to help make that happen. The Bee story will probably come out this weekend, and it won't be pretty."

"How about if I set up a meeting with all four local hospitals and County Public Health for next week? You can describe the problems you're having and we can brainstorm some solutions."

"That sounds great, Steve, but warn them that they will need to bring their checkbooks if anything meaningful is going to happen quickly."

"I'll get back to you on Monday."

At a quarter to five, Sam's phone rang again. It was Cat, calling from a pay phone in Midtown.

"Hi, Sam?"

"Yeah, its me, Cat. How did it go with Moonshine?"

"Well, its been difficult, even though she has tried her best to help. We went to Alhambra and Second Avenue, which was a place she used to stroll when she was selling it, and she remembered that when she got sick, this woman Trixie threatened that she'd send her to Mexico if she didn't straighten up.

She said other girls talked about rumors that they'd be sold to the Mexican Mafia in Tijuana if they tried to leave. I didn't like it, but I had to buy her some beer to keep her cooperative after she told me this, because she got pretty agitated and paranoid about being sold to Mexico."

"Dani might be in deep shit, then. Did Moonshine remember anyplace she lived under Trixie?"

"I drove her all through the surrounding neighborhoods for like an hour, and she got a little tipsy, but we got to this funky four-plex set way back in a lot behind a bunch of distressed trees and jungle on Fourth Avenue, near Alhambra and the freeway, and she thought that might be the place she had lived. It was weird. There wasn't an address anywhere, but it was between 3241 and 3249 Fourth Avenue"

"Great work, Cat. I'll pass this on to Captain Ortega right away and let's hope they can do something fast. Do you still have Moonshine with you? They may want to question her themselves, at some point."

"I don't think she'd be open to that at all. She hates the cops, and I've already dropped her where she wanted to go here in Midtown. She's got some old guy who lets her stay in his apartment sometimes, though I'm sure she pays for it one way or the other."

Sam called Captain Ortega with the information and he promised they would follow up right away, adding, "We might need to question this Moonshine to get a warrant, though."

"Sorry, Captain. I don't know her, but my staff says she is very mentally ill and will not cooperate with authorities."

"Well, we can do a welfare check at the house and see if they'll let us in and talk to us. We don't have much else to go on, yet, but our sex crimes unit says this Trixie has been on their radar this past year. They have arrested girls who they think work for her, but they're afraid to give her up."

"Thanks, Captain. I'll let you know if we get anything else."

Next, Sam tried to call TommyLynn to let her know what they'd learned, but no one answered.

DANI awoke, and her head pounded. This time, she was in an actual bed. She could see a little daylight out of a grungy window and tried to focus her blurred vision. She moved her arms and heard someone say, "Careful, you have an I.V. in your left arm." Her vision cleared slightly and she saw a man smiling down at her. In English with a Spanish accent, he said, "You are awake, very good. I was beginning to worry. You've had a bad head injury and I need to examine you. Let me introduce myself. I am Doctor Luis."

"Where am I? How did I get here?" She tried to remember, but everything was foggy.

"You are in my care, and I will answer your questions

in good time, but you were hit on the head and have at the very least a bad concussion. I had to clean and stitch your wound, and now that you are awake, I need to finish my examination." He asked her to open each eye as wide as she could and he shone a light into them from several angles. He then asked her a series of questions, starting with "What is your name?"

On the top floor of the same building, Markus was ushered into a plush suite by an armed and unsmiling tough named Ricardo, who was five-foot-nine and two hundred fifty pounds of muscle. He had taken Markus' pistol and refused to respond to any of Markus' questions.

Markus was impressed with the suite, which was what you would expect from a cartel Jefe (chief). He looked around at the red and gold velvet furniture and wallpaper until his eyes came to rest on a very handsome man sitting at a computer behind an elaborately carved antique desk. The man was elegantly coifed and dressed in an expensive suit and tie.

The man eventually looked up at Markus and said, "Please sit, sit." His English was without an accent and he appraised Markus as he waited for him to sit.

"So, you brought us damaged goods. My doctor says the girl may not be able to work for several weeks because you hit her too hard on the head. Our other problem is that you apparently kidnapped this girl in public, and the FBI could become involved."

Markus began to squirm in his seat and started to respond, but El Jefe cut him off simply by raising his hand. "You have brought us trouble, my friend. Trixie has sent quality girls to us before and they have worked out well, but now we have a problem."

Markus offered, "I can work for you. I know how to handle whores, and I'm good with a gun. I can't go back to the States, so please give me a chance to show you what I can do."

El Jefe nodded and, turning to Ricardo, he said, "Perhaps. We can always use another gun. Now Ricardo will show you to your room." Ricardo nodded his understanding. Markus said, "Thank you. You won't regret it."

Ricardo and Markus walked down two floors of stairs, opened a side door, and passed into a long, dimly lit hallway. Markus asked, "What do I get paid?"

Ricardo suddenly opened a door and held it, gesturing for Markus to go inside.

"I will show you," he said as he quickly closed the door behind them.

The room was dark and Markus felt a plastic sheet rumple under his feet while he waited for his eyes to adjust. Ricardo said, "Let me find your light and I will pay you." He had already reached into his coat and pulled out a foot long, thick wire with knobs at both ends, which he expertly slipped over Markus head from behind and pulled tightly.

Markus hands went to his throat, but it was too late, as his breath and blood were cut off. He attempted to struggle and kicked back with one leg, but Ricardo was like the proverbial fire hydrant, solid and unmoving. He simply pushed Marcus down face first onto the floor with a knee on his back and held him down, squirming, for one minute then for another one until he lay very still. He could have squeezed harder and ripped Markus head off, but he didn't want to deal with all that blood.

Ricardo wrapped Markus in the large sheet of plastic, folded the ends, and stuffed the body into two big heavy-duty trash bags. He duct taped his package, dragged it across the room, and lifted an end over the edge of a three-by-three-foot chute that dropped straight down three floors into a dumpster in the basement. He heard the loud thud at the bottom, like so much trash.

SARGENT Diane Diaz and her partner, Detective Patrick O'Toole, approached the deep, overgrown lot on Fourth Avenue in Sacramento's Oak Park neighborhood. She made note that it was 6:35 p.m. A chain link fence leaned back awkwardly on one side of the property, with weeds and bushes poking through. The sidewalk was cracked and slightly tilted in front of the rusted metal gate. The gate was unlocked, so they passed through it and followed a narrow path through overgrown hedges under half-dead trees. The path wound back to a group of four tiny cottages barely visible from the street. The cottages were in disrepair, with peeling green paint and wooden shutters slightly askew. Behind the cottages loomed a two-story cement block wall which was the back of an ugly cement gray commercial building covered in graffiti.

As the officers approached, they smelled the strong and unmistakable scent of burning marijuana. Then they heard at least two women laughing. The smell and sounds were coming from the end cottage, and the front door was wide open. They split up and quietly approached each side of the front porch. Diaz pulled her gun and nodded to O'Toole, who unholstered his weapon and nodded his readiness. Diaz yelled, "Police! Come outside with your hands above your head!"

From inside, they heard two startled shrieks, then, "Shit! Don't shoot, we're coming out." A tall black woman with a tilted blonde wig, short tight cutoff jeans and an orange tube top stuck first her hands, then her head, out the door. She moved out on the porch, followed by a small Asian woman, hands raised very high, with purple hair, a blue bikini top, and a red miniskirt. The black woman sighed, "You scared the living shit out of us. What do you want?"

Diaz moved toward them and motioned them to turn around so she could see they weren't hiding a weapon. O'Toole, gun pointed down with two hands, came in behind them and looked into the cottage. It was a one-room cell with a toilet in the back, a disheveled queen bed, one chair, and a TV on a small table.

He spotted a blue plastic platter on the bed, with green buds and rolling papers and a thin film of white powder. He moved inside and touched a tip of his finger on the powder and touched it to his tongue. Nasty, definitely meth.

The black woman said, "Hey, the weed is medical and we got cards." O'Toole responded, "There ain't no such thing as medicinal meth, though, is there?"

"Let me see your warrant. You got no right to just walk into our place."

Sargent Diaz stepped in and ordered, "Sit down on the porch step." Both women did as she asked.

"We came here to ask you some questions about a shooting and kidnapping, and your door was open. We witnessed you using drugs, so we can arrest you, but that depends on your cooperation."

"You see us cooperating, don't you? So, ask your questions."

"Do you know this woman?" Diaz held out the photo of Dani and both women looked at it, then looked at each other. The Asian woman said, "Yeah. Her name is Dani, and she stayed here for a few weeks."

"So, do you know where we can find her?" They both shook their heads. "We know you work for Trixie and we need you to tell us her last name and where we can find her. Think hard about this, because if you answer no again, we will cuff you, take you into custody and charge you with aiding and abetting an attempted murder and kidnapping."

The black woman said,"We don't know no Trixie and we don't know nothing about no kidnapping."

Diaz nodded to O'Toole, who whipped out his cuffs, pulled the Asian woman's arms behind her back, and quickly cuffed her. Diaz did the same to the other woman and began to read them their rights.

"Wait, wait! Okay, we work for Trixie, but we don't know her last name, and if she finds out we talked to you, we are dead," the Asian woman said as tears rolled down her cheeks.

Diaz, in her nice cop voice said, "If you tell us where to find her and its not bullshit, we walk away right now and leave you alone. If you lie to us, we will shut this place down and find you, and you will be locked up for the fore-seeable future."

The black woman offered, "Okay, you didn't hear this from us, but we heard a rumor that Trixie's man Markus has Dani, and that he may be taking her to Mexico. I swear, we don't know where Trixie stays. We only see her when she comes by one of the houses."

"Okay, but we need you to tell us where the other houses are."

"Okay, okay, we can tell you, but you can't tell Trixie."

"If we find out you warned Trixie we were here, we will make sure she knows it was you who gave her up," Diaz threatened.

CHAPTER THREE
STRANGE BEDFELLOWS

Monday, September 26, 2005

SAM WALKED UP the stairs to his office in the old brick warehouse, smelling the bacon and eggs being cooked by volunteers downstairs in the Day Center kitchen for the women and families with kids.

"Hi Ruth," he said to his office manager as he passed the Administration office. "Good morning, Sam. I left some phone messages for you in your box that sounded urgent."

"Thanks, I've got 'em." He opened his office door with messages in hand and sat at his desk. He saw that Captain Ortega and Steve Buchard of the State Hospital Association had called. He called Ortega first and got his secretary, who said, "He's just getting out of staff meeting, can you hold for a couple minutes?"

"Sure, no problem."

Ortega soon picked up. "Hi, Sam, thanks for getting back to me. The info you gave me on Trixie's house was golden. We confirmed that she had girls there, and they showed us where Trixie keeps girls at three other houses."

"That's great," Sam answered.

"They also told us Dani used to stay there, and that they heard a rumor that Markus the pimp might have taken Dani to Mexico. So the FBI got involved and they found video of a car they believe was Marcus, probably driving Dani across the border into Tijuana early Friday morning."

"Shit! That's what we were afraid might happen. They sure got her there fast."

"Yeah, I know this is bad news. We haven't been able to find Trixie, either, but it's just a matter of time. We were able to get descriptions of the cars she and her pimps use, and that led to the FBI finding the car on their video of the border crossing."

"What now, Captain? Can the FBI look for her in Mexico?"

"Yes, they claim to have good relations with the Mexican Police and Federales. Criminals flee across the border all the time and they have a decent record of finding them, though not always alive, I'm afraid."

"Wow. I guess we've done what we can do, and now its up to them."

"Yeah, Sam, you've already helped a lot, and I appreciate it. If we can get our hands on Trixie we might be able to track her contacts in Mexico and find the girl, so we're still hopeful."

"Thanks, Captain and please touch base if anything develops."

"Glad to, Sam, thanks again."

Sam then called Steve Buchard and found out that a meeting had been hastily arranged for five o'clock that day, where he would have a chance to address representatives from all the Sacramento hospitals and the County Health Department. He was asked to invite the Salvation Army and Volunteers of America, so they could be represented.

Monica's story on the patient dumping had run on the front page of the Bee on Sunday morning with a photo of Buchanan, who had lost his foot. All the other TV and radio stations picked up the story, so the hospitals were made to look bad, and they were anxious to claim they were doing something to fix the problem.

Late that afternoon, Assemblyperson Kalen Jones called. "Hi, Sam, sorry we couldn't get together to watch the game yesterday."

"No sweat, the Niners were terrible and Sheila had to go to Oakland to see her sister anyway."

"Hey, I called to let you know that I have support from the leadership to push legislation to fine hospitals for egregious patient dumping. In fact, I'd like you to testify at the first hearing on my bill, on Thursday of next week. The State Hospital Association will oppose the bill, but they are voluntarily organizing mandatory trainings for their members, and Steve Buchard assures me that they will make things better in Sacramento. That Bee front page story really took them to task. Nice work!"

"Thank you, Kalen, for jumping on this issue. I'll definitely testify at the hearing, and Buchard has already organized a meeting with all the hospitals for later today, so I'm hopeful we can help them set up some interim care for homeless folks. Any chance of your bill passing?"

"Well, it's got a slim chance, to be honest, but it gets all the hospitals focused on the issue."

"I get that. Maybe we can grab that beer after the hearing."

"I'd love that. Good luck at your meeting later."

After they hung up Sam called TommyLynn at the hospital, and this time she answered. "Hi, TommyLynn, this is Sam White. How are you doing?"

"Hi, Mr. White, thanks for calling. I'm going crazy laying here, not knowing how Dani is and not being able to do a fucking thing about it."

"Well, I wish I had better news for you, but I just found out that Markus has Dani and the FBI is pretty sure that he took her to Tijuana."

"Oh, fuck! That was my worst nightmare - and Dani's, too. She had heard rumors that Trixie sold girls to the Mexican mafia if they were a problem. Goddammit! Now she's a fucking slave, forced to do God knows what. I'm going to kill Markus when I find him."

"Hey, TommyLynn, take it easy. The FBI is involved and is working with the Mexican authorities to find her. The police are on Trixie's trail and they think they will find her soon and get her to talk about where she sent Dani."

"I got family in Baja, and as soon as I can get out of here, I'm going to find her myself."

"Please promise me you will stay in the hospital until they think you are out of danger. Dani would want you to take care of yourself."

"I'm feeling better every day, and they're talking about sending me to a convalescent hospital later this week. Anyway, thanks for calling, Sam. At least I know what I need to do."

———

AT four o'clock, Sam was on the phone with Dr. Schwartz, the Medical Director of the County Health Department. They had worked together on a tuberculosis outbreak several years before that had killed a homeless woman and infected two of his staff. Sam considered her a friend. After pleasantries, Sam asked, "So, Gail are you going to the meeting this evening with the hospitals?"

"Yes, and I've got some great news about the Interim Care Program we've been talking about. My staff has gotten some program designs and budgets from other programs around the country, and I have a commitment from the Health Director to fund a half-time nurse position for the project."

"That's great, and good timing with the meeting today. I want to pin down the hospitals for financial commitments while we've got their feet to the fire."

"I know, and here's the best news. You were right that the Salvation Army has unused shelter space that was defunded, so I followed up with them and they are willing to reconfigure their space into twenty small rooms and provide staff for this program, if we can raise about eighty thousand per year. The beauty of it is that they already have a permit for the space."

"Fantastic! So, twenty thousand per hospital. That seems real doable, but how soon could we ramp it up?"

"They think they can use room dividers and beds they already have in storage, so maybe three to four weeks."

"Wow, perfect! Thanks for your work on this. Anything else I can do?"

"I'll bring an outline of the program design and budget to the meeting, and I've invited the Salvation Army. You just have to push the hospitals to get their financial support."

"I"ll call Buchard and see if I can get him on board with the program plan. I think if we're both pushing, the hospitals will line up in support."

"Okay, I'll see you at the meeting.

Wednesday, September 28, 2005

FIVE hundred miles away, Dani's head pounded from another wave of migraine headaches, and she moaned. She had crawled out of bed for only the second time and was bent over the toilet, vomiting. Her balance was shaky, so she had to grip walls or furniture as she attempted to move around her room. The nausea also came in waves and worsened when she sat up or tried to walk. She mostly slept, but her sleep was troubled by nightmares.

The doctor had told her she could be like this for weeks, but he avoided answering other questions she asked. She was pretty sure she wasn't in an actual hospital. The doctor and a cleaning woman were the only people she had seen. The Doctor had told her they were in Tijuana and that she was safe. The cleaning woman didn't speak any English and only shook her head when she tried to talk to her.

Dani had attempted to search her plain beige room, but there was only her bed, a bedside table with water, an IV setup, and a tray which the cleaning woman used to bring her meals three times a day. There was a tiny square alcove with a sink and a toilet and a trash bin. The window was too high for her to see anything but a brick wall and a small patch of sky. She heard and felt the hum of a city with cars, buses, planes, and sirens blending into an urban cacophony.

The woman had twice washed her with a sponge and dried her off while she laid in bed and turned over. The woman was gentle with her, but never smiled. The woman only scolded her for not eating all her food, after every meal. The nausea and headache she experienced when she sat up to eat made it very difficult to force food down.

She stood up from the toilet, wiped her mouth and chin, and looked in the small chipped mirror. She was dressed only in a green hospital gown that tied in the back. The doctor had shaved her head, and she counted the twelve stitches at the top front of her scalp. Her black and blue eyes and cheek had turned to yellowish purple patches, fading each day. God, I look like a fucking Zombie. She almost laughed, but could only manage a sharp breath through her nose.

She sat on the toilet for awhile and cried. She thought she remembered Markus telling her that he had shot TommyLynn, who he called "the freak." God I hope she's okay. I know she cares about me. She's my only real friend. Mexico! My god how did I end up here.

She felt empty and alone, hundreds of miles from everyone and everything she had known. She staggered to the door. It was locked. I have to believe that you are okay. You may be the only one looking for me, TommyLynn. She crawled onto the bed and reached for a pain pill, which they brought her with each meal. Wrapping her arms around her chest, she cried herself to sleep.

SAM entered TommyLynn's hospital room and found her eating an early dinner. She looked up, smiled and wiped off her mouth and hands with a napkin, still chewing, she gestured Sam to the one chair. Sam sat. "You're looking pretty good for being shot a few days ago." TommyLynn swallowed, "Thanks for coming by. You could have just called. I know how busy you are having seen you at The Village. I'm a quick healer and can't wait to get out of here.

I think in a couple weeks, or less, I'll be heading to Baja."

Sam looked very concerned and said, "I came by because we never got to follow up on my offer to hire you to consult with my staff and I on LGBT issues and program development. That offer still stands and I'm worried about you going to Tijuana on your own into a very dangerous situation. I think you would be wise to let the FBI handle the search for Dani. I've been in touch with Captain Garcia and he is putting resources into busting Trixie and her operation and Dani could be key in her prosecution, so the police are motivated to find her."

"Look, I appreciate the offer of the job, but I can't just let this go. I told Dani I'd protect her and I meant it. I won't be on my own either. I have a lot of family in TJ and I know they will help me. It looks like I'll get out of here on Friday and once I'm close to normal I'm going south to find her."

Sam turned to see a man and woman standing in the doorway and the woman was crying. TommyLynn turned to Sam, "Sam this is my mom and dad. Mom and dad this is Sam White, the director of The Village who I told you about."

Wiping her eyes, his mother tried to smile and said, "So good to meet you Sam. TommyLynn told us you kind of offered him a job. I'm Victoria, call me Vicky and this is Jim." Sam and Jim shook hands, followed by an awkward moment of silence.

Sam jumped in, "It's great to meet you. I came by to follow up on my offer to TommyLynn and to wish her well.

I'm impressed by what she's been doing on her own to help LGBTQ kids, like he helped Dani who was kidnapped."

"We didn't get to meet Dani." Vicky replied, but she and TommyLynn really had a connection and we heard that you share our concern about going to find her."

Another tear streaked down her cheek.

Sam excused himself, "Sorry I have to go, but let's keep in touch." He handed his card to TommyLynn and his parents. "Please give yourself a chance to heal TommyLynn. I was young once and rushed a knee surgery recovery only to have it get worse and eventually get infected, which still causes me problems. Take Care!"

Friday, September 30, 2005

DETECTIVES Diaz and O'Toole had been managing the surveillance on Trixie's houses for four days, but she had been smart and stayed away. They didn't think she was aware of their operation. They hadn't approached her pimps, who were managing the girls, because they were afraid she'd be tipped off. They'd attempted to follow the pimps, hoping they'd lead back to her, but so far no luck.

Their team had researched the owners of the properties used by Trixie's operation and discovered a complicated web of L.L.C.s (limited partner corporations) that eventually lead to a common shareholder, Ms. Ginger Gold. They first assumed that Ginger Gold was Trixie, but they were able to identify her, and it turned out she had a clean record and did not fit the description they had put together for Trixie.

Trixie and Ginger had finished their afternoon delight, showered, and were ravenous. They were gulping Kombucha and chewing their lobster salad in their black granite countered, state-of-the-art kitchen.

"Well, no sign of cops this week. I think we dodged a bullet," Trixie said while chewing. "I'm going to the houses today to check on things. The boys have been depositing the money and it seems about right, but who knows what they've fucked up since I've been laying low."

"It's been nice having you all to myself this week." Ginger smiled at her and slugged down Kombucha. "You know, between the cash and properties, we're pretty well set. You could walk away and fuck the cops and the bullshit from the whores and asshole pimps."

"I know, we've been over this. I just wanted one more year and we could be set for life. We were having a great run until Markus fucked up. I'm so close, and I think I nipped it in the bud, by getting rid of them both. Marcus is history, so they can't tie it back to me." She wiped her mouth, leaned over, and kissed Ginger long and hard. Then Trixie smiled. "It has been nice just hanging out and not dealing with all the dumb fucks. Who knows what I'm going to find today. I better get going."

It was four in the afternoon when a vintage black Mustang pulled up in front of the Fourth Avenue lot and a woman fitting Trixie's description entered the crooked gate. The two male cops on surveillance were in an abandoned house across the street and on their radio with Detective Dias.

"We believe the subject has arrived in a black Mustang. What do want us to do? Over."

"We're on our way. Hang tight until we arrive, but don't let her back in her car whatever you do. Over."

"Roger that. We'll position ourselves on Fourth Street by the car. Over."

Twenty minutes later, Detectives Diaz and O'Toole, wearing casual clothes, sunglasses, and baseball caps, drove up in their unmarked car and parked on Alhambra Blvd. Diaz got out first and walked down Fourth Street, lips moving as she checked with her surveillance team. O'Toole climbed out and crossed to the other side of Fourth, head swiveling, looking for their officers. He saw the Mustang and the big cop standing behind a tree in the front yard of the lot next door.

Trixie suddenly emerged from the unkempt lot through the crooked gate, walking briskly. She was almost to the corner of the lot when she spotted the big cop, who pulled his weapon and yelled, "Police, on the ground now!" Trixie had already turned and was running in the opposite direction. The big cop began to lumber after her, but Diaz sprinted past him and was gaining on Trixie, who was pretty fast herself.

Diaz had been a college soccer player and still played in city leagues. Trixie was in good shape, but she was no match for Diaz, who came up behind her before she could make the next street and kicked her feet, sending her sprawling onto the cement sidewalk. Before Trixie could gather herself, Diaz was on top of her, twisting her arms behind her back and clicking handcuffs onto her wrists. If it had been calf roping at the rodeo, Diaz would have taken home the champion belt buckle.

Trixie was howling, "Police brutality, get off me, you fucking pig." Trixie's knees were badly scraped and blood flowed down her shins as Diaz yanked her up on her feet. The other two cops arrived, breathing hard, as Diaz began to read Trixie her rights. O'Toole pulled up in the unmarked car and opened the back door. Diaz with a hand on Trixie's neck, shoved the howling madam into the back seat, and shut the door, muffling her cries of protest.

Trixie carried no identification, refused to answer questions, and lawyered up as soon as she could make her call. They had impounded and searched her car, which turned up only a cell phone, but they found it was registered to an address in Colonial Heights. Diaz and O'Toole requested search warrants and held a task force meeting, which included a local FBI agent, and laid plans for simultaneous raids that night on the five houses of prostitution and the residence in Colonial Heights.

TOMMYLYNN squirmed in her bed. She was being discharged from the hospital that afternoon. Her parents had offered to take her in while she recovered. The staff had referred her to a convalescent facility, but she had refused. The doctor had just cut the thin cast off her leg, so she could start physical therapy and begin some very limited walking. She was anxious to leave the hospital and her confinement to a bed or wheelchair.

TommyLynn was still stricken with guilt and worry for not protecting Dani after she had promised her she'd be safe. There had been no more news about Dani or the efforts to find her. I'll be back on my feet in a few days and will go find Dani myself, if I have to. Her parents knocked and entered her room. She was already moving onto the wheelchair and said, "Get me out of here, please."

SAM drove away from the Village at 5:30 and passed scores of homeless people on the sidewalks sitting on cardboard or dirty tarps and blankets, some with small tents. He could smell pot and waved at a few familiar faces, who smiled or waved back. On the corner of B Street, a thin mixed-race woman of about forty was raving at nobody in particular, her fists in the air. "Fuck you! Fuck you!" She screamed and was crying, all in a few seconds. He thought about stopping to ask if she needed help, but could see she was either very high or having a breakdown. Not to mention it was Friday night and he was feeling burned out, so he drove past, feeling a little guilty and helpless.

He had worked the streets as a mental health counselor for the County Mental Health Department in the mid-eighties when homelessness grew exponentially and hundreds of mental health clients ended up on the streets. He and the homeless team had been able to help many clients get stable and find housing, but he'd also learned that he couldn't help everyone.

He thought, At least the interim care program is going to happen, and twenty beds at the Salvation Army for homeless discharged hospital patients was going to be an improvement. One small step. He headed home, turning his thoughts to playing harmonica later that night with Cat and Mota and their band, The Slingshots. He was really looking forward to it.

DANI reached for her pain pill on the small stand next to her bed. Her head throbbed and the nausea took hold. She could barely move, but managed to grab the vessel on the stand and vomited her breakfast into it. She took the pill and managed to fall into sleep, her only escape from the pain and loneliness.

On the top floor of the same building, El Jefe sat at his ornate desk, looking at the doctor whom he'd hired to treat his "employees." "This girl, she cost me a lot. I need her to get to work to earn her keep. When can I expect her to start work?"

The doctor fidgeted in his chair. "She has a very bad head injury and her symptoms have not decreased, yet. She barely keeps any food down and sleeps about sixteen hours a day. This will take at least a couple weeks to monitor, and these kinds of injuries sometimes take months."

"I'll give her two more weeks. Not only is she not earning her keep, but she needs a lot of care that costs me. I'll sell her, if I have to, and the people that I would sell her to will not be as patient as I am."

"I'll do my best." The doctor stood up to go.

"Make sure your best is good enough, Doctor."

SAM ordered a Rubicon Brewery "Monkey Knife Fight" pale ale at the Old Ironside bar on Tenth and S Streets in downtown Sacramento. His friends Mota and Cat had set up the band's gear and finished the soundcheck. His wife Sheila was coming with friends Mike and Gloria, and Assemblyman Kalen Jones had said he'd stop by. The bar was filling up, and it was clear that The Slingshots had a growing fanbase.

Mota was always happiest playing music, and he beamed as Cat trash talked with the drummer and keyboardist at their table. "You wouldn't know an arpeggio if it set up camp in your eardrum." Sam laughed and recalled the night that Mota and Cat had led a band of homeless campers, armed only with slingshots, to take on an armed gang down by the American river at Paradise Beach. It was a battle over gold hidden in a tree, and the campers had won. It had proven to be a turning point for Mota and Cat and Sam had become a friend.

The band took the small stage and Sam joined them for a blues song that he and Cat had written. Mota played a smooth guitar intro, then was joined by Cat on the bass, and the drummer. Sam played a harmonica riff and then he and Cat took turns singing.

> *"I got the Blues this morning, Cause I ain't got a dime.*
>
> *I got the Blues this morning, Cause I ain't got a line.*
>
> *I asked someone to help me, but they ain't got the time.*
>
> *I got the Blues this morning, I got no place to call my own.*
>
> *I got the Blues this morning, I got no place that I call home.*
>
> *You know I asked the lord to help me, I guess the lord wants me to roam."*

The crowd really wound up when Cat belted her lines and Sam's harmonica solo got some applause. It was kind of an easy warmup song for the band, but it set the mood for the heartfelt blues and rock that followed. Mota spoke into the mic, "Only original songs, no covers!"

Sam saw that Sheila and friends had showed up and were sitting at the band's table. He bowed out of the next few songs and sat with them. He and Sheila talked excitedly about their upcoming Baja vacation. His buddy Mike asked, "So, are you going to see your old friend in Baja?"

"Yeah, we were best friends from the fourth grade into our first year in college. We grew up together in east L.A. through some crazy times."

"Sounds like an overdue reunion."

Sam nodded.

Kalen told Sam, "Your testimony to the Assembly Healthcare Committee will be Thursday at 3:00 p.m." Sam responded, "I appreciate you getting Buchard involved in the local hospital response to the dumpings. The hospitals are going to fund a 20-bed interim care program at the Salvation Army shelter, and County Health will provide a nurse."

Kalen offered, "Oh, yeah. Buchard called me yesterday to tell me what was planned and said you had a nice package ready to go that was a slam dunk with the hospitals. Good work! He's also putting together mandatory statewide trainings for all their member hospitals on homeless discharge policies and practices. Of course, he won't be supporting my bill, but that's no surprise."

"I'm looking forward to Thursday's testimony at the

Capitol. I'll send you my draft comments early next week, so let me know what you think. It's my last duty before I leave for vacation."

Sam smiled. "Enjoy, my friend. Have a cold one on the beach for me." Kalen and Sam chinked beers and tuned back into the music.

Chapter Four
THE TRANSITION

Tuesday, October 4, 2005

TOMMYLYNN WAS COMFORTABLE at home on her parents' couch and she was recovering quickly. She had told her folks about Dani and the situation with the pimp. She insisted on going to Baja to look for Dani, and this made her mom and dad very uncomfortable, bordering on panicky. They had tried to talk her out of the idea, but knew how stubborn she could be when her mind was set. She had asked her mom to put her in touch with their Mexican relatives, but Mom had to try to talk her out of it one last time.

"Tommy, you barely know this girl. I know you promised her you'd protect her, but you may not be able to protect yourself from these criminals. Look what they've done to you. The doctor said if the bullet that hit you was a fraction of an inch lower, you'd be dead."

She began to cry. "You're my only child and you still have so much of life to live. Please don't do this."

TommyLynn got up from the couch, her limp now

barely noticeable, and gave her mom a hug. They held each other close and her mom continued to sob. When the sobbing ended, she looked her mom in the eyes and said, "I have to do this, Mom. I'll be careful. I know how serious these guys are now, but I can't give up on Dani. I felt really close to her, and she has no one else who cares about her. Please help me connect with family there so I have some help. You know my Spanish isn't that great, and you told me some of my cousins are in TJ."

"Okay, I know how you are when your mind is made up. I'll call my sister, but promise me you'll be careful."

"I promise you I will be careful. I hope to leave in a couple days. And, Mom, I may need to borrow from my college fund. Did I tell you I'm close to getting my GED finally?"

"You better come back to me and finish it, mijo." Another tear streaked his mom's face, and they hugged again.

He whispered in her ear, "I'm going to see my friend Jethro in the hospital tomorrow and then I'll leave on Thursday. Can you get me a thousand bucks, by then?" She nodded, her wet cheeks dampening his shirt.

LATER that evening, Sam called. "Hi, TommyLynn. I'm glad you made it home, how are you doing?"

"I'm feeling about ninety percent. I told you I heal fast. In fact, I'm planning to go to Tijuana in a couple days.

Have you heard anything new about Dani from the cops or FBI?"

"Yeah, that's why I'm calling. I heard from Police Captain Ortega today that the FBI have the body of Markus Jones, the guy that shot you and your friend. His body washed up on the beach at the mouth of the Tijuana river. They say it has all the marks of a gang killing."

"Wow, that was fast. I'm not surprised. He was a hothead and an asshole. He's lucky I didn't get to him first, but what about Dani? Have they heard anything?"

"No, but they are getting closer to who and where Trixie sent her in Tijuana. Trixie and her partner are in jail and the FBI confiscated her phones and other records. They think they can track her calls, though it may not be clear who was at the other end."

"That's good news! At least they have something to go on. I'm not going to wait, though. My family in Tijuana will help me, so I'm going to find her."

"No offense Tommy, but that's a little crazy! They've already killed Markus, and it sounds dangerous as hell. The FBI won't be happy about you going on your own, either. I counsel you to give it another week to see what happens and to give yourself more time to heal."

"Thanks, Sam. I appreciate you helping out and keeping me informed, but I've made up my mind about going. Dani needs all the help she can get!"

"Okay, then let me ask you how you're getting to TJ?"

"I'm going by bus and I can stay with family, so I'll be okay. Why?"

"I probably shouldn't do this, but I can offer you a ride as far as TJ. My wife and I are driving down on Friday to start a three-week vacation in Baja. I think we can make room for you."

Thursday, October 6, 2005

SAM was early to work at the Village putting together his list of things that would need attention while he was gone. He could smell the bacon and eggs cooking in the kitchen downstairs that served homeless families breakfast each weekday. He walked through the bustle of staff and volunteers setting up the dining room as women and children with tousled hair and wrinkled clothes took their seats, hungry anticipation etched on their faces. Teachers from the Village's "Home School" program were talking to the guests to recruit kids who were no longer attending regular school. He stopped to say hello to staff and familiar volunteers, then passed through the door to the Dorothy Day Women's Crisis Center.

This would be Sam's last day at the Village for over three weeks, his longest vacation in eight years, and he needed to coordinate with Sister Julie, who would be in charge in his absence. Sister Julie, the director of the Day Center, was a Catholic Sacred Heart Sister and a force to be reckoned with. Sister Julie was an island of calm and unconditional love in a chaotic sea of despair, mental illness, and impoverishment that was the Dorothy Day Center on an average day. She saw Sam and her eyes, one green and one purple, smiled up at him.

"Hi, Sam, your last day, eh? Good for you, to get a break from all this fun for a bit."

A forty-something black woman was at the counter, yelling at staff, "I want my children back from the murder, satan, drug cult! Can anyone help me? I'm a good mother! " Julia glanced at her staff, who knew the woman and her recurring delusion and quietly calmed her down with an offer of breakfast and understanding.

"Yeah, I'm almost ready," answered Sam. "Thank you for covering for me, Sister. I know you'd rather be here with the guests, but managing the Village should be a nice change of pace." He handed her his long list of things she'd need to cover. "I've got some good news on the Interim Care Program. It should be opening with twenty beds at the Salvation Army while I'm gone. I've told them you'll represent us at the grand opening. The hospitals will need their strokes of 'attaboy'. I'm giving testimony at the Capitol this afternoon on Kalen's bill, so wish me luck. I know I'm leaving the place in your wise and able hands, so I can relax on my trip."

"I have to admit I'm jealous of you going to Mexico. Well, you enjoy a well-deserved break."

DANI awoke after her best night's sleep since she was with

TommyLynn. Her head wasn't pounding and it felt a bit clearer, too. She got up to use the bathroom and didn't have to grab the walls with every step, nor did she throw up. While sitting on the toilet, she realized that the woman might come in with her breakfast any minute and that she should continue to act as sick as she had been. If Trixie had sold her to this place, she could guess how they would use her when she recovered.

She heard the key in the door. She stuck her finger down her throat and dry heaved as loud as she could, then, moaning, she flushed the toilet. The woman set her tray next to the bed and then rushed to Dani who was curled up on the floor of the bathroom. The woman was strong. She lifted and dragged Dani to the bed. When Dani was covered up, the woman grabbed a spoon from the tray and put it to her lips, repeating, "Coma! Coma! Coma!" Dani spoke very little Spanish, but knew she was being directed to eat, eat, eat!

The woman spoke again in Spanish. "El Doctor dice El Jefe le gusta usted estar listo para trabajar in dos semanas o." She made a slashing motion with her hand across her throat. It was the most she had spoken to Dani. Dani understood the words Doctor and dos and the dramatic consequence. She wondered if it meant two days, two weeks, or two months.

Dani just turned on her side away from the woman and pretended to go to sleep. The woman said "stupido!" and left the room, locking the door from the outside as usual.

When she heard the door close, Dani quickly sat up and grabbed the tray to her lap. She was as hungry as a bear waking up from hibernation as she devoured everything on her plate.

The doctor arrived later and woke her up. "Sorry to wake you, but we have to talk. The man I work for and who runs everything here has given me an ultimatum. If you aren't ready to work in his brothels in less than two weeks he will sell you to really bad people who will treat you like a dog."

I know you are very sick, and sometimes these head injuries can take months to heal, but your time is almost up." He looked at her tray and noticed all the food was gone. "I see you're eating better. That is good. You must keep it down to build your strength."

Dani nodded her understanding. Her headache had returned and she exaggerated a wince, as if it hurt much worse. She asked, in her weakest voice, "Once I get stronger and can walk better, is it possible to walk around outside this room? I'm feeling closed in and need to move around more to get healthier. The woman could walk with me."

"We will see, but first you must eat. You are skin and bones. If you can keep food down for a few days, we will go from there. Now, continue to rest and sleep and eat."

IT was 3:30 p.m. at the State Capitol Building, and Sam was dressed in a rare suit and tie, sitting behind a large ornate wooden table and dais in Assembly Room 236. Kalen had introduced his bill and Sam as his first speaker. Sam nodded and looked out over scores of lawmakers and lobbyists seated at equally large and ornate desks, most looking up at him.

"Thank you, Assemblymember Jones and Health Committee members. I am a licensed Clinical Social Worker and the Director of St. Francis Village, which serves hundreds of homeless and hungry people everyday at our multi-service compound only ten blocks up Twelfth Street from here.

"I am here today to relate to you our daily experience of newly discharged hospital patients being dumped at our Village and other homeless programs without proper referral or adequate resources.

"You may have read the recent Sacramento Bee articles about specific patients being dumped from hospitals as far away as Reno and Las Vegas, Nevada.

"Two weeks ago, I was alerted by one of my staff that a man had been pushed out onto the ground from a car bearing a Placer County insignia by a Placer County Mental Health Center employee. The patient was black, totally blind in one eye, and had only 10 percent sight in his other eye. He was still suffering from delusions and other symptoms of schizophrenia, which made communication very difficult.

"He at first wandered off, but we were able to find him, feed him, and eventually return him to Placer County. He had no family or other social contacts in Sacramento, and I was told by his psychiatrist that he was sent because Sacramento had shelters and other resources that Placer County doesn't. If they had bothered to check, they would know that St. Francis Village has no overnight shelter and the other shelters are generally full with waiting lists."

Sam looked up from his notes at the people in attendance and most seemed to be paying attention.

"A week before this incident, an eighty-year-old female patient with a mental health condition was sent by taxi to our Village from a hospital in Reno Nevada. She was returned to Reno by the hospital only because I threatened to report them to the press.

"Lastly, two weeks ago, as reported in the Bee, a white male patient in his mid-fifties was dropped off at the Salvation Army shelter a block from the Village by a local hospital which had not called the shelter to make sure a bed was available. This man had both feet heavily bandaged and should not have been walking. When he discovered that there was no bed for him, he limped to our closed facility and slept outdoors. Our nurse was shocked at his condition when she saw him the next morning, and had him returned to the hospital, where his right foot was soon amputated.

"These incidents of hospital dumping have become daily occurrences and have worsened in severity. There are no checks on these hospital practices, which cry out for regulation and additional resources. I know how difficult it is to find adequate shelter and followup care for these patients, but they don't deserve to suffer life-threatening complications because of our lack of attention. I have been working with our state hospital association and local hospitals to fund an interim care program locally, but I hope you will consider Assembly Bill 437 as a first step towards humane care and discharge planning for indigent patients on a statewide basis.

"Thank you for your time and attention."

There was a spattering of applause lead by Kalen as Sam stood. He leaned into Kalen and whispered, "I'm out of here on my way to Baja tomorrow. I need the break."

"Thank you Sam."

"Thanks again, Kalen! See you in three weeks."

They shook hands, and Kalen introduced his next speaker.

TOMMYLYNN sat close to her friend Jethro's hospital bed in intensive care. Jethro's dreads were parted and spread over his shoulders and IV tubing ran to his left wrist. His breathing was labored and he was in obvious pain. His voice was faint. "Good to see you, Tommy. They told me you got shot, too, but it looks like you're okay."

"Yeah, I took one in the leg, but I'm most of the way

back. I've been at my folks' place, but I'm going to Mexico tomorrow to look for Dani. I'm really sorry I brought my trouble to your place bro. I'm glad you're getting better."

"It only hurts when I breathe, you know." He chuckled which made him wince even more. TommyLynn laughed. "You are a tough hombre, homey! I hope the cops aren't hassling you about your stash."

"I don't think so. I haven't heard back from them since the FBI was here. I gave them a description of the asshole who shot us, and I had taken a picture of Dani, which they got off my camera. So I'm hoping that because I cooperated, they will leave me be. They told me that Dani was probably taken to Tijuana. I'm sorry, I tried to shoot the motherfucker, but he got me first. Glad my gun was legal"

"I wondered where they got Dani's photo." She reached into her shirt pocket and pulled out Dani's image that she'd cut from the newspaper. "The latest is that Markus, the dude that shot us. is dead. They found his body in the Tijuana River. I got family in TJ, so I think I have a chance of finding her."

"Are you sure you want to do that, bro? If they killed Markus they must be serious, and going to their turf sounds crazy, man."

"I know, people keep telling me that, but I'm all she's got, and its partly my fault she fell into all this in the first place. Hey, man, do you need anything before I go?"

"I wish I could smoke a fat one, bra, but my one rib got splintered and punctured my lung. Coughing could fuck me up good. They say I should be okay, but it will be awhile before I can light up again. I wish you luck Tommy. Hey do you need some cash?"

"No, I'm good. My parents are letting me tap my college fund. I'll see you on the rebound, brother. You take it easy and get well and we'll toke a fatty when I get back."

SAM was at home in River Park, drinking a Rubicon "Rose Bud" and packing his bag for Baja. Sheila put together the food and filled their big ice chest. Together, they had loaded their sea kayaks onto the racks of their Subaru Forester. They called Ru. They had earlier dropped off their chocolate lab Kabu at their friend Mike's house nearby, which was sad until they saw how happy she was to be with Mike's dog Jake.

"I'm sorry I didn't talk to you first about inviting TommyLynn to ride with us. It felt like the right thing to do, after what he's - I mean she's - been through. I respect her courage to go look for Dani, but I just don't know about her judgment. She has family there, so at least she won't be alone."

"I trust your instincts and we have room, so it won't be bad to have company for the first day. Hey, I didn't tell you that I found out about these mule ride trips that a Loreto tour company offers to what may be fourteen-thousand-year-old cave paintings in the mountains.

"I know you want to spend some quality time to catch up with your old friend Juice, so I'm thinking about doing a six-day mule ride that's scheduled for the first week we're there. I saw some pictures online of some of the paintings which were spectacular, really well preserved, and really isolated in the back country."

"Wow, that sounds cool, sweetie. Since Juice has his own diving business, we plan to go out for several days to the island to dive, fish, and camp, so we can do that while you're riding. I can't believe I've found Juice after all these years. We were nine years old when we met. His real name back then was Jesus, and we were inseparable all the way through high school."

"I know. I'm not sure how many times you've talked about him over the years, and its so great that he's at one of our favorite vacation spots. It is a small world."

"Its been almost thirty years since he joined the Marines and I lost track of him. I wonder what he looks like. We have a lot of catching up to do."

PART TWO

BAJA - THE TREASURE

CHAPTER FIVE

LORETO PUEBLO HISTORICO
(LORETO HISTORIC CITY)

Friday, October 7, 2005

AFTER PICKING UP TommyLynn, Sam and Sheila took turns driving south on the Five Freeway for the last nine hours. TommyLynn shared the back seat with their gear, which was piled to the ceiling. Sheila had taken a liking to TommyLynn, who was remarkably open, articulate, and proud of her sexuality.

They had talked at length about Dani, TommyLynn"s family, and her life in Sacramento. Likewise, TommyLynn was very interested in the social work and healthcare professions and asked a lot questions about college requirements and job prospects. At one point, Sheila turned to look at TommyLynn and noticed the beautiful tattoo on his forearm. "Is your tattoo a big cat?"

TommyLynn held it up for her to see better. "It's a puma, which is my spirit animal. According to my grandmother, I come from a long line of Yaqui shamans. She lives on the family ranch near Loreto at the foot of Puma Mountain, and when I visited as a kid, she called me her 'little puma.' The top of the mountain actually looks like a puma head with pointy ears, and it's the tallest mountain around. You might see it from the highway before you get to the city of Loreto."

They were approaching San Diego around dinner time. Sam asked, "It is dinner time, should we stop for a bite? I went to San Diego State in the seventies and still visit my old college friend here often, so I know some great places to eat. Too bad my friend John is out of town, or we'd be stopping for a visit."

"I'm sure that my family in Tijuana is expecting us for dinner. My aunt Juanita is an amazing chef, so I think it will be worth the wait," TommyLynn offered.

Sheila responded, looking at Sam, "We don't want to intrude on your reunion. You said you haven't seen them for seven years"

"No intrusion. I told my family that you were being generous in giving me a ride, and they offered dinner. I told them you were going to Loreto, and they were excited because the family ranch is there. My grandmother on my mom's side still works the huge ranch with one of my grand uncles. They have lots of goats and some cattle, its a beautiful canyon where they live; pretty isolated."

Sam accepted the offer. "We're headed to Ensenada for the night, so we can't stay long, but it would be great to meet your family. Not to mention, home cooked Mexican food is the best! You know we've vacationed in Loreto several times over fifteen years and love the place. The kaya-king and diving are amazing, with all the islands and sea life. Do you know about the three large lagoons on the Pacific Coast of Baja? Hundreds of gray whales migrate to them each winter to mate and calve babies."

"No I haven't heard about those."

"You can be taken out in pangas by the local captains, and the whales come up to the pangas and can even be touched."

TommyLynn blurted, "Wow! Have you guys touched whales? That would be amazing."

Sheila replied, "Yeah, we've had the baby whales and larger ones hang out with us so close, we can stroke them and they spray you with their blow hole. Too bad its Oc-tober and they don't usually make it until December or January."

"I would love to do that some day. I know Dani would, too." She looked very sad, remembering that Dani was in danger and she might never see her again.

Sam asked, "Did you know that Loreto has the oldest surviving Catholic Mission that was founded in 1697?"

"No, I thought the Mission system started on the U.S. side. In fact, I just saw a sign as we entered San Diego County that said "San Diego, where California started."

"Oh no, Loreto was where the "El Camino Real," the original road to all the missions, began, when California and Baja California were one. It was all a colony of Spain, and later, part of Mexico."

"Wow" TommyLynn was impressed. "I remember learning about the Missions in grade school, and our class had to build a small model of one. Now that I think about it, my mom did mention that the missions really started in Baja. Where our family lived."

About an hour later, after negotiating rush hour traffic, they came to San Ysidro and the border crossing into Mexico. Sam asked TommyLynn, "I never asked if you had a passport. It's pretty much required when you cross back into the US."

"Yeah, I know, but I didn't have time to get one, and I figured Dani doesn't have one, either, so we'll cross that bridge when we get to it. Seems like the least of our problems."

They got waved through by Mexican border patrol, so the whole crossing took only fifteen minutes. Sheila sighed. "I can't believe how much easier it is crossing into Mexico. If we were heading into the US it might be a three-hour wait."

TommyLynn had directions to the house of her aunt and uncle. It was in an outlying suburb of steep hills of dirt and rocks, with big houses next to shacks of found wood and cardboard. The neighborhood streets were unpaved and addresses were infrequent, but they eventually found it.

Sam and Sheila were roughly the age of TommyLynn's Aunt Marta and Uncle Luis, and her two cousins, Juanita and Rogelio, were close to TommyLynn's age. Each member of the Arce family sized up TommyLynn, who was a foot taller than when they'd last seen her at age thirteen, then gave her a big hug. No judgment or distaste registered on their faces as they beamed at their long lost cousin with her long hair and women's clothes. They all spoke some English and Marta, who had worked in San Diego as a chef, was bilingual, while Sam, Sheila, and TommyLynn spoke intermediate Spanish.

Beers and tequilas were offered and accepted while Marta served Caesar salads, pointing out that Caesar salads were invented in Tijuana. TommyLynn offered proudly, "Aunt Marta runs a catering business, and she's cooked for some of the best restaurants in San Diego and Tijuana." Tamales of cheese, chicken, and vegetables were the next course, served with red or green salsas. "Muchas gracias for this amazing meal," Sam and Sheila must have said three or four times.

"De nada" repeated Marta and smiled. "I'm so happy that you like it."

They talked about Loreto, how beautiful and tranquil the area was, and about their family ranch, which was divided up into two ranches and worked by their family over several generations. It covered six hundred hectares, a huge swath of mountain, canyon, and valley area below "Puma Mountain" in the Sierra Gigante range, about twenty-five miles north of Loreto.

After dinner, Sheila and Sam thanked their hosts again and apologized for having to get on the road to Ensenada, which was another hour and a half of night driving. They were thanked, in turn, for bringing their nephew, (er niece - they, too, struggled with the pronouns,) which made TommyLynn chuckle. The family also gave them a contact number for the Arce family in Loreto and encouraged them to visit the family ranch.

TommyLynn thanked them for the umpteenth time after Sam gave her their phone number and the number of Captain Ortega. "If you find Dani or get into a bad situation, don't hesitate to call. Ortega is a good guy, and will work with the FBI. Please be careful!"

TommyLynn hugged them goodbye while assuring them she was in good hands with her family, and wouldn't put them in jeopardy. They took the toll road to Ensenada, which was the closest they would come to a US-style highway for the remainder of their trip.

Baja Highway One was mostly one lane each way, narrow and treacherous driving even under the best conditions.

Saturday, October 8, 2005

ON Saturday morning they enjoyed a great breakfast at Reyes del Sol in the Ensenada tourist district, which is also where they stayed. "I feel like I've already gained five pounds," lamented Sheila. Sam laughed and teased her. "Poor baby, that sounds like a Cadillac problem. We'll stop in San Quentin and take a run on the beach to make up for it."

They drove south on winding, hilly Highway One out of Ensenada for about an hour and saw a sign for the San Tomas Winery, which proclaimed itself to be the oldest winery in Baja California. "A bit early for wine tasting, but we should try it on the way back," Sheila said, and Sam nodded, smiling. After miles of winding hills and vineyards, they came to Camalu where they could see the Pacific in the distance.

Sam pondered, "I remember seeing photos of Camalu in old-sixties surfing magazines. I might try some body surfing at Playa Santa Maria when we stop, if there are any waves."

"We should have lunch at Cielito Linda (Beautiful Sky). I hope it's still there," Sheila wished. Then they looked at each other and howled in unison like the singing dog they had seen in the bar there over ten years earlier. The howling ended in laughter. "Hell, yeah, we're on vacation!" Sam yelled as they passed the turnoff to San Pedro Martir, the highest mountain in Baja California at over nine thousand feet, where it sometimes snowed. There was an international Observatory at the top that Sam had once visited.

After a slow stretch of stop and go driving through the San Quentin Valley with miles of corporate farming hothouses and recent development sprawling along the highway, they came again to the Pacific Ocean and the turnoff to Santa Maria. The mile-long road, once like a cave, completely lined and shaded with old Ironwood trees, was now half-lined with the ubiquitous corporate hothouses. They turned in at the Santa Maria Hotel right on the beach, which began as one in the La Pinta Hotel chain that the government built for tourism along the newly paved Baja Highway in the seventies.

They took the dirt road and skirted the hotel to the wide sandy beach littered with uncountable sand dollars, clams, and other shells. The sun was warm, the tide was high, and the glistening three-foot waves rolled in at regular intervals. They put on their swimsuits and ran barefoot across the soft sand where the Pacific lapped and foamed. They passed two pangas resting in the sand, recently returned from fishing, and after about a mile, they turned around and jogged back.

Sam sprinted ahead the last hundred yards and bounded into the waves, then dove in, when it was deep enough. The break was smooth and peeled off to the left in a nice tube with a slight offshore breeze. His feet could still touch bottom, and he watched the rhythm of the swells where the best waves curled off. After a couple of failed attempts, he hit it right and kicked hard, his body rigid. Belly down, he dropped into one of the larger waves outside. He felt the mass of water pick him up and propel him across the face of the wave, his head and shoulders out of the water, left arm leading the way as he dropped and dove to the bottom, engulfed by the wave. He popped up and whooped, still feeling the rush of the timeless ride. He saw Sheila wave from the beach and he waved back, beaming.

That was all he needed. One good wave ride made the

day - no, the year. He was grateful he could still do this, and remembered being a young man living in Newport Beach in the seventies, when he went out almost every evening after work and after smoking a joint to run barefoot in the sand and body surf his favorite break regardless of the weather or temperature, and without a wetsuit. It wasn't that cold. It was Southern California after all.

After a seafood lunch down the road at Cielito Linda (no singing dog, this time), they hit the highway to El Rosario, known for Mama Espinoza's Cafe. They gassed up at the last petrol station they would see for over three hundred and fifty kilometers of mountains and desert and hoped they could make Guerrero Negro, back on the Pacific coast, by nightfall.

Narrow and scenic Highway One snaked slowly up rolling hills of brown grass until the Cirius cactus (Boojum) trees began to appear. Some over thirty feet tall, they were the shape of bizarre elongated Christmas trees and were only found in Baja. They were joined by yucca and giant Cardon cactus in a desert forest unlike any other on the planet.

After climbing for over an hour, this forest was interrupted by massive rounded granite boulders the size of cars and cabins forming hills and mountains as far as the eye could see. The arroyos between heaps of gray, gold and brown granite spheres were filled with forty-foot Cirius and Cardon cactus trunks over eight feet in circumference.

Sam and Sheila loved this part of the trip. After leaving San Quentin, there were only tiny settlements and ranches separated by miles and miles of desert, the Pacific Ocean out of sight. They were on the lookout for their favorite stop just before the oasis of Catavina, when they spotted their turnout and pulled off the highway. Nearby, at the top of a mound of massive rounded boulders they could see what they called the 'amphitheater'.

A perfectly round granite boulder the size of a barn was hollowed out by millions of years of wind, sun, and rain until it looked like an eggshell with a bottom portion of the shell broken off. They climbed up, sat inside and hummed a long om which echoed out of the rounded chamber over the mountains of boulders and forests of giant cactus.

Sam smoked some pot, Sheila meditated, and then they climbed down the rough granite orbs, picked their way through cactus and thorn bushes, ready for a beer at the La Pinta Hotel in Catavina where pickup trucks with large barrels of gasoline lined the road and charged double the price at their makeshift gas stations.

Their thirst quenched, they began the three hour ride to Guererro Negro. As landscape unfurled from mountains of boulders to Cardon-studded arroyos to flat expanses of yucca forest and the last of the Cirius cactus, the sun fell toward the Pacific and afternoon faded to evening. The closer they got to the ocean, the cooler it became, and after the hot desert drive, the cool night on the coast was welcome.

After checking into the venerable Mallarrimo Hotel and restaurant, they used the wifi to reconnect with their alternate reality in Sacramento and rested a bit. The hotel had become a bit funky, but the restaurant, with its specialty seafood menu, was as good as ever.

Sitting in the dining room, Sam splurged on lobster and Sheila was enjoying her garlic shrimp. "It seems that all is well at the clinic, though I'm not sure they'd tell me if there was a problem." Sheila had been the director of the Health for All Clinic in Midtown Sacramento for twenty years. "I don't think I've told you, but I've begun to have thoughts of retirement from the Clinic." Her green/gold eyes looked into Sam's light blue eyes, which were smiling.

"Wow, that's a big change, but I'm glad you're considering it. You've been there a long time. You must be proud of the work you've done, building the organization and expanding services. Have you thought about a succession plan?"

"Yeah. Deb is running things in my absence, and she's got the inside track with our Board of Directors." Deb was her best friend and the Director of Operations at the Clinic. "The fundraising would be a challenge for her, but I think she's up for it."

"Yeah she'd be great. I encourage you to keep thinking in that direction. I must admit, I've thought about when I'd leave the Village, now that its been five years at the helm. This will be the longest I've stayed at a job, and you know I've always felt that moving on is good for me and the organization. I still love what I'm doing more than any job before, but I need to return to the County, at some point, to build my retirement." Sheila nodded, smiled and said, "It's good we use this time away to talk about next steps."

Sam changed the subject. "So, we covered a lot of ground today. Tomorrow just five to six hours to Loreto. Let's stop at Santispac or Burro Beach on Bajia Concepcion for a beer and a swim in the afternoon."

"Sounds perfect!" Sheila said as her thoughts lingered on what retiring would be like.

Sunday, October 9th, 2005

DANI's head pounded and her nausea returned, so she laid back on her bed and tried to sleep. I pushed it too hard, she thought, after trying a series of exercises, from deep knee bends to toe touches to leg lifts. She had felt a glimmer of confidence returning after eating the past two days and keeping it down. She took medication and cried. I'm still sleeping like twelve hours a day, when will this hell end? She thought again of TommyLynn, as she did every day. Please don't give up on me, please save me from this nightmare.

TOMMYLYNN had been busy. Her cousins had helped her develop a list of all the higher-end strip club/brothels in

TJ and it was a pretty long list in this town of over one million residents. Some clubs were more high-end than others, and she started with those. She just showed up in the evening and asked for the manager, saying she was looking for work.

They either told her to hit the road, they don't hire Putos (gay or trans), or they gave her a quick description of hours, pay and expectations. She at least was able to look around in the backstage employee quarters in a few of the clubs to see if she could spot Dani, but so far, no luck. She was amazed at the diversity of sex workers in the clubs - many Asian women, some black, some white, and mixed races of all types.

After two long days, she began to feel overwhelmed by her task, but she was not a quitter, so she bucked up, thought about what Dani could be going through, and knew she was Dani's best hope, however slim.

She got back to her aunt's house at about two in the morning and her cousin Juanita was waiting up for her with possibly good news. They hugged hello. "Hey, Tomas, you know we've been putting out the word to friends and family and showing the picture of your friend." She nodded and her eyes lit up.

"Well, Papa's got a second cousin, Alberto, who lives across town in Barrio Vincente, whose next door neighbor seemed to recognize the girl, but then got all scared because she said she 'works for a bad man who is very dangerous.'"

"Wow, that is a good lead. Would she say anything about where Dani is?"

"No. Alberto tried to press her, but she would only say that if it is the same girl, she is alive, for now, but she's been very sick, with a head wound."

"That could be her. At least we have some hope!"

"Listen, she told Alberto to leave her alone, and that her boss would kill her if he found out she talked. She told him she won't say another word to anyone, so don't ask. She is friends with Alberto's wife, but his wife has heard about her boss for years, and she too is scared. They've warned us to stop looking for her, for our own safety."

"Still that's great news. I knew it wouldn't be easy, but to know she is alive and to have a lead already…that's amazing! Thanks so much to you and la familia. Yes, you guys should stop helping me, for now, at least as far as asking around and circulating Dani's photo. Can you give me Alberto's address if I promise not to bother him or his family?" Juanita nodded and gave her the address. "Please be careful, Tomasito, these guys don't fuck around." They hugged again and said goodnight.

TommyLynn couldn't sleep. She formulated a plan to rise early on Monday and try to follow the woman to her place of work.

SAM and Sheila were approaching Loreto after a lunch of fish tacos and snorkeling in the turquoise waters of El

Burro beach on Bajia Concepcion. It was late afternoon, so they planned to check into their room at Las Cabanas de Loreto and meet his old friend Juice and wife Bella for dinner at the Pacha Mama Argentinian restaurant.

The last time Sam had seen his childhood friend was in August of 1975. Juice had told him he'd joined the Marines, and they had hugged goodbye. Sam had been a bit shocked since the Vietnam War had just ended in disgrace. He hadn't seen much of Juice in the year since they graduated high school and he hadn't thought this would be the last time they would see each other until now, thirty years later.

They met, and after hugs and introductions of their wives, they were seated outside on the patio. Both Sam and Juice complemented each other on looking younger than expected, but they shared a laugh about the extra twenty pounds or so that showed in their paunches. Even at fifty years old, they both looked like they could hold their own in a fight, as they had many times growing up in East L.A. in the sixties and early seventies.

"So, catch me up on your time in the service. You know I've been a peace activist since college," Sam joked. Juice smiled, dimples appeared, and Sam was reminded of Juice the homecoming king their senior year of high school, as voted by the girls. Juice's almond brown skin was flawless except for a new pink and jagged scar above his left eye. His squared jawline and perfect teeth completed his handsome countenance.

"Well, after boot camp, I applied to Special Forces and was trained by the best. I did a few tours in Guantanamo spying on Castro. Then I got promoted and was based in North Carolina for twelve years, which is where I met Bella. I was lucky that after Vietnam, things were relatively quiet, and we had a nice life on the east coast. I did participate in some classified actions in Central America, and later, Croatia, I can tell you more about that when we're alone on the boat.

"I feel kind of bad that I lost touch with you and most of my family. I'm in contact now with my mom and brothers, but my dad died in prison and my Nina and Nino passed about five years ago."

Juice's father had been in prison since he was a child, so he'd gone to live with his childless godmother and godfather, who were also his aunt and uncle, while his five siblings stayed with his mom. Both Sam and Juice had been the oldest sons of large Catholic families, and Sam had spent a lot of time at Nina's house, enjoying her amazing Mexican food over the years.

Sam said, "I'm so sorry to hear that. Your Nina was a force of nature. Being a successful Latina businesswoman back then was not easy. I did go back to see them once, but they had moved. I ran into your cousin Narci once, and he told me you were in North Carolina."

"Yeah, I feel guilty, too, about visiting with Nina and Nino only a handful of times before they passed. My sisters got married and moved away and my brothers became cops. I've invited them to come down to visit here, but they haven't."

Sam shared, "My mom died five years ago, too, but my dad is still hanging in there. My sibs are all doing pretty well and are still in SoCal."

Juice added, "Your parents were always super nice to me. I remember your little house was always bustling with kids and your little sisters were always looking up at me doe-eyed." Juice smiled as the memories flooded over him.

They had finished their first drinks and dinner arrived, so they enjoyed the tasty Mexican/Argentinian fusion. Sheila and Bella were getting along famously and it looked like Bella might join Sheila on her mule ride into the rugged mountains to see the ancient cave paintings. Bella had done some shorter mule trips and knew Trudy, the tour operator, so was game for the six-day adventure. Sam and Juice had no idea what adventure awaited them, but they would soon find out.

Monday, October 10th, 2005

TOMMYLYNN woke at about five, dressed in jeans and teeshirt, and put her hair in a bun under a brown plaid porkpie hat, so she wouldn't stand out. She got a ride to Alberto's place from Cousin Juanita, who pointed out the house next door where she was pretty sure the woman lived. The sun rose bright and hot over the eastern hills of Tijuana as TommyLynn stood at an outdoor taco stand, watching the house and drinking coffee. Her cousin had told him the woman would probably take the bus to work.

At seven o'clock, TommyLynn saw a woman carrying a lunch box leave the home she'd been watching. The middle-aged Mexican woman walked toward her and passed, heading for the bus stop. She watched her waiting and talking to neighbors for about ten minutes before the bus arrived. TommyLynn saw it approaching and walked slowly, arriving in time to stand at the end of the line of boarders.

They rode downtown and stopped at the crowded intersection of Calle Benito Juarez and Avenida Ninos Heroes, where the woman exited. Waiting until the last moment, TommyLynn quickly scooted out the back door. She recognized this block because there were two large strip club/brothels there, which she'd visited a couple days before. The woman walked past these to another corner where an ornate, nicely restored, four-story historic building stood. There was a large guy in nice civilian clothes, who looked like the bouncers at the sex clubs, guarding the door. The woman approached, and he nodded without smiling and opened the door. She walked in.

DANI woke earlier, this morning and walked around her room ten times. Unlike the last two mornings, she didn't fall back to sleep exhausted, so she decided to try to get up to the window in her room to see how high she was and what it looked like down below. She'd been thinking about how to do this for awhile.

Her caretaker wouldn't be in until about eight thirty, so she quietly pushed her single bed three feet until it butted against the wall under the window. It still wasn't high enough for her to get her eyes over the sill, so she went to the bathroom, grabbed the metal trash can, and dumped the trash in the sink. She placed the can upside down on the bed near the wall and took some deep breaths.

She was starting to get nauseous just thinking about climbing up, but her clock was ticking, so she had to try. She climbed on the bed, then up on her knees, and with her hands balancing on the wall, she slowly stood up and put a foot on the can. Her hands could reach the sill, now, so she pulled up with her hands and stood with both feet on the can.

Her balance was shaky at best, but she looked out the grimy window to see iron bars on the outside. Her heart began to sink. She stood on her toes to look down and saw that she may be on only the second floor. Suddenly, the bed started to slide away from the wall until she was left hanging by her fingers from the sill. Her hands had become weak from lack of use, so she fell, bouncing off the bed, sending the trash can flying, then sliding to the floor in a heap.

TommyLynn watched the doorman at the building for an hour while several more workers who looked like white-collar types went inside. Then a man who was dressed in a suit that barely contained his muscular body approached and the doorman straightened up, smiled, and opened the door as the strongman entered without breaking stride. He wasn't very tall, but he looked like a world class weight lifter with huge thighs and arms, a bull dog face and very imposing muscle.

Next, Tommy Lynn attempted to case the building going around to the backside, where she found an alley with another big bouncer/guard in civilian clothes at the garage entrance. The guard looked at her as she walked by, so she kept moving and walked around the block again. She saw an adult bookstore at the other end of the alley, so she went inside and pretended to browse some magazines where she could see out the window.

After about ten minutes, the proprietor approached her to say that if she bought something, she could use one of the back rooms. She didn't understand at first and looked confused until the guy made a hand signal for masturbation. She laughed and bought the magazine, but stayed at the window, where she was rewarded when a black Hummer with heavily tinted windows pulled into the alley just as the garage door lifted and bull dog man stepped outside next to the guard to wave it inside. TommyLynn noticed there was a camera pointed into the alley, by the door.

TommyLynn now sat at a cafe and ate breakfast where she could see the building entrance and considered her options. Her first thought was to call the police captain and try to get the FBI involved, but she realized she had no proof that Dani was there and if the Mexican police got involved, they might tip off the guys inside, whoever they were. She could try to sneak inside, but that seemed like a suicide mission. While she was eating, she saw a city trash truck picking up trash dumpsters from alleys between the businesses, and watched as it worked its way around the block and eventually headed toward the alley in back of the building.

She jumped up, laid fifty pesos on the table, and bounded out of the cafe. Careful not to run, she strode around the corner, arrived at the alley, and peaked around the corner of the building just as the truck pulled up to the garage door. The door was open and the guard was inside as two trash workers walked into it and came out pushing a large blue, heavy metal trash bin on wheels. Once in the alley, the trash truck used its back forklift to raise and dump the container, and the two workers returned it inside the garage.

Juice and Bella took Sam and Sheila kayaking, the morning after their dinner. They'd driven both cars with kayaks about five miles south of town on a dirt road and launched from a beach near La Picazon Restaurant which was directly across from Coronado Island. They had once before paddled the two miles to the island's picturesque beach, a unique lavender-hued sand with sparkling turquoise water. Several pangas were beached there, with tourists lounging under palapas (thatched roof shelters).

A hot, windless ninety degrees made it a sweaty but easy crossing. They saw jumping manta rays and a small group of dolphins. The eighty degree water felt refreshing and comfortable. After eating a snack and hiking around a bit, they headed back to La Picazon. Sam and Sheila had been to the island several times by panga, as it was a main tourist activity, but they hadn't been to the new, beautiful, isolated La Picazon restaurant which Bella raved about having "the best margaritas in town." Juice and Bella introduced them to the proprietors, Alejandro and Imelda, as they entered. Imelda was in the kitchen while Alejandro served them and concocted the drinks.

"These margaritas are amazing," Sam confirmed, holding up the huge glass.

"And I love these jalapeno slices in soy sauce," Sheila gushed as she dipped another corn chip. "Wait till you taste the main dishes," Juice added "You ain't seen nothin' yet."

They sat under the shady cement roof that was open all along the south side. The proprietors lived upstairs. Their table was at the edge of the beach, looking across at the island bay they had kayaked to earlier and Carmen Island to the south. "Wow! This is the place to be." Sam stated the obvious as their ample plates of seafood arrived. His was half a pineapple hollowed out and filled with soft little Catarina scallops in a red pineapple sauce. Sheila had the seafood salad with shrimp, scallops, fish, and clams, divided by slices of mango and avocado.

They ordered a second round of margaritas, still reeling a bit from the first one. Everybody was laughing, enjoying the view and the company. Sam and Juice had slid right into the comfortable camaraderie and brotherhood they had begun forty years ago.

After they had eaten, Sam and Juice played Frisbee on the beach to sober up while the women walked along the beach planning their mule ride the next day. "So, you ready for some diving and fishing, homey?" Juice asked, and Sam beamed.

"I'm ready for anything brother. I mean, Capitan. I can't wait to see your boat and dive together. I've got about 100 dives, but you must be a master diver, right?"

"Oh yeah, over a thousand dives. I first came here on leave from San Diego about ten years ago and fell in love with this place and the diving here. Its especially good this time of year."

"Sheila and I first drove here after a kayak trip out of La Paz about fifteen years ago, and we fell in love with it, too. It is kayak heaven!"

They said their goodbyes and profusely thanked the warm and efficient husband and wife team for an amazing meal and all around special day.

DANI was pinched between the wall and the bed as she dry heaved in a wave of nausea. She seemed to have weathered the fall without any serious injuries, but now she felt exhausted and her back was sore. She forced herself to push the bed back in place and to return the trash to the can before she laid down and fell asleep, only to be shaken awake by the woman an hour later. The woman spoke to her in broken English and Spanish, but all she understood was that the doctor would be coming later and someone she called El Jefe might also drop in.

That afternoon the doctor removed the stitches from her scalp, applied bandages and tape, and told her she seemed to finally be improving. "You are eating well. Now, let me see you walk around the room." She got up and walked slowly and feebly. She was sore, but exaggerated her vulnerability and asked if he could take her out of the room.

"I'm so tired of these walls. Can we please just walk down the hall for a minute?" He took her arm and opened the door. "Just to the end of the hall and back, then you must rest." She made note of the other closed doors in the hallway, and it seemed that the one at the end of the hall might be a stairway.

He returned her to the bed. "Thank you for your help. I do feel a little better. Does that mean I'll be released for work soon? What day is this, anyway?"

"Its Monday. Lets give it two more days, and if you continue to improve until Thursday, I'll release you for work and my boss will be happy, also.

"The boss might visit you later this afternoon. Be on your best behavior. You realize the kind of work my boss offers will be physically and sexually demanding? He sometimes likes to 'sample the talent' as he says, so you better do as he says. He is your boss too, now. He can send you to a nice club with good tips, or he can sell you to evil people."

"Given that I've been a prisoner here, and where I came from, I can guess what the work will be. I hope I have some freedom soon."

The doctor shrugged. "I hope so too."

TOMMYLYNN asked around to find out that the trash was collected Monday, Wednesday, and Friday, downtown. She formulated a plan to enter the building on Wednesday, hoping to find Dani and get her out without being caught or killed. She later told only her cousin Juanita about the building and her plan and asked her not to tell anyone, but she was very concerned, and thought TommyLynn was crazy to even think about it.

She posed an important question. "What do you do if you get her out? They'll look for you at all the border crossings, and you don't even have a car."

"I know. I've been thinking that they'll expect us to head for the border, but what if we go south to the family ranch in Loreto and wait until things cool off? They'll never find us in the mountains.

"I hate to ask you to get involved, but if you could pick us up downtown and get us to Ensenada, we could take the bus to Loreto and be there by the next morning. Look, think about it, and I understand if you can't. I'll think of something else."

Juanita looked at her cousin and thought for a moment. "The family catering business does have a van that goes to Ensenada once or twice a week to pick up large orders of fresh seafood. I guess I could make the trip on Wednesday, but what if you get caught and don't show up? I don't know what I'd do if you disappeared. Maybe we should ask the police for help?"

"This is something I have to do. I can't let Dani fall into some kind of slave labor - who knows what they'll do to her? But I also don't want to endanger you or the family. I don't think the police can be trusted. I can take care of myself. I've been living on the streets and in the shadows for the last three years. Please trust that I'll be there. I just hope she's there, but if I don't show up, just go about your business. I'll make it some other way and will get a hold of you as soon as I can."

TommyLynn asked Juanita if she could get access to a gun or other weapon, but Juanita didn't think a gun was possible to obtain in the short time frame. She told him about a store downtown that sold knives and other hand weapons, so he planned to visit it the next day.

Tuesday, October 11th, 2005

DANI dreamed, She and TommyLynn were riding horses on a bright sunny day in a beautiful desert canyon. She was so happy that she giddily galloped ahead, but when she looked back, TommyLynn was gone and a big puma sat in the road where he should have been. She startled awake in the middle of the night and was unsure of the time. She had awoken before when it was dark, and heard what was probably custodians in the hallway, but tonight she heard nothing but the reduced, omnipresent traffic and noises of a downtown that never slept.

The day before, when the doctor had taken out her stitches, she had grabbed a strip of used tape, and when he'd helped her walk in the hallway, she had feigned a stumble and smoothly placed the tape over the door latch as she reentered the room. The doctor hadn't seemed to notice when he closed the door that locked automatically, so she was hopeful for an escape, at least from her room.

She was still barefoot, her feet cold on the cement floor, but she could walk quietly. She stepped to the door, hoping that her tape had held. The door opened easily, so she looked out to the spare, darkened hallway and saw no one.

She passed two other doors, heading slowly to the end of the hallway where the only light came through two glass doors. She hoped there was a stairway on the other side.

There was no hardware on the door, so she pushed it lightly and it budged. Listening intently, she slowly opened it wider and stepped onto the stairs, still holding the door open. She was afraid it might lock from this side if she closed it. She looked down over the banner and saw two floors of stairs ending in a basement, which was partially lit. She examined the door and saw no lock, so she closed it quietly and stepped downstairs.

She made it to the lower floor without hearing or seeing anyone and saw that this was the first floor, but the doors off the stairway were heavy metal and triple-locked. She continued down to the basement, but at the halfway point she heard someone moving around and stopped. Next, she heard gears turn and a large garage door began to open, backlit by lights outside. She saw the legs of a man on the inside and the legs of two people waiting outside as the door slowly wound upward.

She figured it was a guard and probably the cleaning crew, and she quickly reversed course and ascended the stairs. When back in her hallway, she thought she would have time to try the other doors, which was risky because she had no idea who or what were inside. The first door she tried opened, so she peaked inside to see a room much like her room, with a bed and half bathroom, but apparently empty. The next was the same, so she crossed the hallway to try the last one. She could hear the cleaning people running vacuums below.

The door opened, but it was pitch black inside, with no windows, so she opened it wider and stepped in. She heard the crinkling of plastic underfoot and saw a light switch, so she closed the door and flicked the switch. The floor was covered in thick sheets of opaque plastic and the only other feature was a large garbage chute that stuck up from the floor about two feet. She walked over to the three-by-three foot opening and looked down to see that it dropped vertically two floors into a large open dumpster full of garbage bags of shredded paper and other odds and ends, in the basement.

Looking around the room, she noticed a wheeled cart with rolls of duct tape, rope, rubber gloves, and large plastic sheets and garbage bags. Then she noticed what looked like sprays of blood on the walls near the chute and cart. She shuddered as she realized the room was like a butchering station, and hoped it was only animals and not humans being butchered. She turned and quickly backtracked to the door, listening for anyone in the hall. Hearing no-one she opened the door and returned to her room, head spinning, heart beating like a drum inside her chest.

Sheila and Bella met Trudy at her home in Loreto at seven

as the sun rose over the Gulf of California. They loaded camping gear for the mule expedition and drove north together through Mulege and Santa Rosalia, then west toward the turnoff to Rancho Santa Marta, at the foot of the San Gregorio Mountains. They ate quesadillas with fresh goat cheese and frijoles and met their Mexican guides, Chema and Julio, and their mules. Sheila's tall mule, Betabel (beet), was named for his light red coat, and Bella's mule Gris was stout and gray. A young man named Diego showed up with five pack burros that were his responsibility and everyone loaded their gear, tack, and supplies and saddled up while getting pointers from Trudy and the guides.

There was another couple that had signed on to the expedition, but Trudy said they had canceled last night, so it was just the two of them with three guides. Sheila and Bella looked, with apprehension, up a very steep hill rising above the ranch after being told it was the first leg of the trip. Their expedition of six people and ten animals began the climb, and Sheila was impressed with the strong and sure-footed mules. They all leaned forward in their saddles and were soon enjoying the views and the warm morning.

When Sheila and Bella reached the top of the ridge for their first climb, they felt exhilarated, but then looked at the steep downhill ahead of them and cringed. The guides adjusted their saddles and belly straps. Downhill required leaning back in the saddle while their weight pressed down on their knees and calves in the stirrups, making their legs shake from exertion.

They had to have complete trust in the mules, who sometimes slid a foot or two on the scree of the steep hill with little or no trails. Finally, they dropped into a beautiful deep canyon with occasional water holes, desert trees (Palo Blanco, Palo Verde and Palo Roja), Cardon cactus, and many other plants replete with spines and thorns, like the dreaded jumping cholla.

They shuffled along the verdant, rocky canyon, marveling at spectacular, smooth granite faces, craggy outcrops, green water holes, caves, and grottos until they reached the famous cave painting site of Serpiente (serpent), in a huge granite grotto. Sheila had seen this site in photographs, but the enormous and elaborate paintings of a massive serpent, life size elk, deer, birds, fish, and shamans in red, black, and yellow paints were stunning, especially when you considered they might be fourteen thousand years old. They took photos without flashes and ate lunch, looking forward to several other amazing archeological sites ahead.

Sheila asked Bella, "It must have been difficult for you when Juice was gone on assignments, knowing he might not return?"

"Oh yeah! I knew what I was signing up for when I married him in eighty-five, but it was so hard when he left and couldn't even tell me what he was doing. Especially when he was assigned to go to Croatia where I knew there was a war. He said he was only going to be in an advisory role, but it turned into much more than that. After he was wounded, thankfully not too badly, he decided it was time to retire after more than twenty years, and I was so glad when that day arrived."

Sheila responded, "Sam and I got together in 1985 too, though we had known each other for a few years before that. We got married in eighty-eight and are just starting to think about retirement. I might be close, but I'm five years older than Sam, so he may have longer to wait."

Sam and Juice met for breakfast at the Oasis Hotel, situated on the beach at the south end of Loreto's malecon (beachfront esplanade). Juice had already loaded three days' worth of supplies, including healthy stores of beer and tequila, onto his thirty-two-foot diving boat, named La Aventura. After Taladega coffees and a generous breakfast buffet, their hangovers were manageable. It was a warm October day with a high of ninety-two degrees Fahrenheit predicted, and the cooler northern winds that blew during the winter hadn't developed yet.

Juice remarked, "I'm so glad Sheila and Bella hit it off and are doing the mule ride. Bella's talked about wanting to do a longer ride to the cave paintings, and she tried to get me to go, but I've been busy with work and getting our house fixed up. Those rides aren't pleasure cruises, you know. They are challenging, but Trudy has been leading mule trips since the seventies with the best local guides, and she knows all the ranchers and sites really well."

"Yeah, it sounds like quite an adventure, and the photos I saw of the cave paintings were amazing. Are they really fourteen thousand years old?"

"Well, there is some debate about that, because its difficult to carbon date the paint, which is made of fish oils, ocher, charcoal and other natural dyes; but some may be at least over ten thousand years old. Well, are you ready to launch?"

They climbed into Juice's truck, which pulled his boat and trailer. "Sure am! What a beautiful boat! I'm so looking forward to diving and hanging out with you, brother. I still can't believe we found each other after all these years." Juice nodded, smiled, and started the truck.

The local fishing pangas were twenty-one to twenty-nine foot, open fiberglass boats with canvas roofs and outboard engines, and lined the squarish marina framed by massive gray boulders. The Aventura was a thirty-two-foot split level with a small sleeping cabin and kitchen in the bow below a raised pilot cabin and twin inboard five hundred horsepower Volvo engines. From mid-boat to the stern was a lower deck, with rows of oxygen tanks in the middle and an open area around the tanks, with bench seats that were also gear and supply storage, and two step ladders that were lowered for climbing back onto the boat from the water.

They lowered the boat down the marina ramp and Juice powered it alongside a wooden dock with pelicans diving all around while Sam parked the truck and trailer on a dirt side street. Finally, they were cruising across the bay, heading due east to the northern end of Carmen Island. They brought some fishing poles, but were more interested in spear fishing while diving.

The silver-blue water was calm and flat and the endless blue sky almost cloudless, so they made good time on the eight-mile crossing that took them to the back side of Isla Carmen. As they rounded the northeast point, they spotted hundreds of dolphin, which were coming their way. Sam hooted when their paths intersected. Dolphins jumped all around them and surfed in the boat's wake. Juice experienced this all the time, and Sam had too, but he never got over the rush of these beautiful mammals cavorting en mass.

They headed south along the east side of Isla Carmen, passing a few pangas with fishing lines in the water. When asked how the fishing was, they shrugged and called out "poca cabrilla, nada mas" (a little sea bass, nothing more), which was a mainstay at most restaurants in town. They eventually passed the mouth of the salt flats which had been a site of human salt gathering for millenia. In the past hundred years, it had been one of the largest commercial endeavors in the region, and many locals could trace back to family members who had worked there.

About halfway down the fourteen-mile-long island, there were stunning rock cliffs with Cardon cactus dotting the stark landscape. They came to a tall cliff of red shaded rock, and Juice pointed out what the locals called "Mono Rojo (Red Monkey Rock)

Sam blurted, "Wow, I can see the monkey, now that you point it out."

Juice responded, "There is local lore about some kind of treasure near this spot, which has been thoroughly searched, so it's probably myth, but I've dove here once before and liked the underwater geography and life, so I thought we'd hang here for two or three days, away from the crowds. You can see the little beach down a ways, so we can explore the island a bit too if you like. Let's drop anchor over there."

Sam marveled at the site with its southern views of Danzante, Monserat and Catalana Islands to the south. "Man this is idyllic. Lets get in the water, it's hot. I've been diving a couple times off Isla Coronado, but I've only snorkeled off Carmen. Its been about a year or two since I dove, so could you walk me through all the gear adjustment?"

"No sweat. We'll only be diving to sixty feet, at most, on this dive, so we'll take it slow so you can get comfortable. I've got a light wetsuit and BCD for you under that seat, over there. I'll bring my spear gun, but maybe you should just do a relaxed dive and follow me."

"Sounds great!"

They were soon suited up, weighted down to compensate for the buoyancy of the wetsuit, and rolling backwards off the boat into the eighty degree water. Visibility was about fifty feet, and conditions were perfect. Sam pushed the button on his BCD (Buoyancy Control Device) vest to let air out, pinched his nose through the scuba mask, and pressurized his ears, then followed Juice down the anchor line, his heart beating fast and his breathing too fast, as well.

Near the surface were schools of sergeant majors, yellow and white fish with black stripes no more than six by six inches. They and many larger fish were following schools of hundreds, no thousands, of small silvery fish that Sam thought were sardines. Sam looked at his depth gauge and saw they were at forty feet. Juice looked back and gave a thumbs up, which Sam returned, and they dropped another twenty feet to the tops of massive rocks covered with purple sea fans, large round scalloped shells, and golden coral heads. Large cabrilla and other rock fish dodged in and out of crevices and fissures in the rocks.

Juice turned towards the cliffs, which were about forty yards away and whenever they saw a large cabrilla, he would head that way to see if he could get close enough to spear some lunch. Closer to the rocks, Sam spotted rainbow wrasse and other small, brilliant, black, orange, or blue fish. Everywhere he turned there were schools of pink or gold cabrilla, green sierra. and skipjack following clouds of tiny fish that moved in unison. He spotted a large bat ray and, later, a sea turtle resting between huge rocks.

Sam watched Juice disappear behind a massive boulder and a few minutes later return with a two-foot cabrilla on a fish wire attached to his belt. He signaled his intention to surface and Sam gave a thumbs up, then they checked their air gauges. Sam's had started with his air gauge arrow pointed at 3,000 pounds per square inch, but was down to 1,000. They had been in the water for half an hour and he had used twice as much air as Juice. Oh well, its my first dive in a while, he thought. They put more air in their BCDs and rose to fifteen feet, where they stopped and hovered for several minutes before rising slowly to the sun-strobed surface and kicking to the boat.

DANI spent the rest of the night in a restless turmoil, her brain in overdrive, thinking about a possible escape. She kept going over the layout of the floor and basement and the butchering room across the hall. She couldn't think of any other way out. She'd seen the ornate double doors of the main building entrance and they were chained and padlocked on the inside. She wondered about somehow going down the chute to the trash bin and hiding until the trash was picked up.

She wished she had checked out the items on the cart by the trash chute more closely. Particularly the length of the rope which had been wound into a circle. It looked pretty thick and long, definitely more than twenty feet, but I need at least forty feet to make it to the basement dumpster. I don't know if I'm strong enough to lower myself down without falling. The chute looked about the right size for me to brace myself with my feet and back though. She pictured herself bracing her legs and back against the sides of the chute as she lowered herself down the rope. I can shift my wait from my arms to my feet and back as I go down.

She had loved to climb trees and ropes and playground equipment as a kid, and she hoped she could pull it off - except for having been bedridden and held captive for the last few weeks, not to mention her head injury. She was going back and forth in her mind about whether to try it when the woman caretaker opened her door without knocking. She brought in her breakfast and said, "Tomorrow maybe last day, you eat good." She almost smiled as she spoke broken English. Both were firsts, and Dani responded, "Thank you for taking care of me."

The woman had been feeling guilty ever since her neighbor had showed her the picture of Dani and said his family was looking for her. A tear came to her eye when Dani thanked her and she whispered, "De nada. Some people, they look to you, but dese men, dey bad, dey own girls, dey hurt peoples." Dani was so relieved and hopeful to hear someone was looking for her. She took a chance and asked the woman, "What day does trash get picked up here?" The woman looked confused and then frightened, but she said, "Manana in morning."

"Gracias" Dani said to her back as she hurried out without looking back.

Her door was opened again a few minutes after the woman left and a handsome, middle-aged, well-dressed man entered, looking her over carefully. He said, "I hear

you are finally feeling better and are ready to go to work?"
She nodded slightly.

"Tomorrow a woman like your Trixie, who runs one of
our clubs, will pick you up, and she will be your boss. It is
a nice club where many tourists and decent people go for
sex, so you are lucky." Looking at her shaven head he said,
"She will find a wig for you until your hair grows back. If
you behave and work hard, you will stay lucky. If not, well
- you don't want to know what could happen to you."

He stepped closer to her and unzipped his fly, putting
his hands on her breasts, then ripping open her hospital
gown. He pulled her head toward him with both hands
and she cooperated reluctantly. He was rough, making her
gag and holding her tight so it was very hard to breathe,
but it was over fairly quickly. Without another word, he
zipped up and smiled as he turned and left the room.

Later that afternoon, the doctor came in with a cart
piled high with food. She was sitting up, and feigned a
headache by rubbing her temples. He said, "I've brought
you much food for your lunch and dinner. Still having
headaches, eh? I wish I could buy you more time to get
better, but the jefe - er boss - says you leave tomorrow. A
Madame, your new boss, will come get you in the morning and take you to where you'll be working, but I don't
know where that will be. Sometimes it is in nearby clubs,
but they have many all over Baja and northern Mexico."

Dani tried to look weak and pained, but said, "At least
I'll be out of here. Hey, could you help me take one more

walk out into the hallway before you go?" He nodded and took her arm, but only walked her out the door and said, "You must walk on your own, now." She tried to look more unsteady than she felt, but she had duct tape in her hand that she had grabbed from the butcher room and she managed to place it over the door lock, on her return. He had gone into the room to grab a bag from his cart.

"I forgot to give you these clothes to wear when you leave." He handed her the bag. "The care woman put them together for you. I wish you luck."

"Thanks for your help, but can I ask - how can you do this - work for a slave owner? You're a doctor, you could get work anywhere right?"

He looked at her, startled and guilty. "I'm sorry, but I too am not free, but we are not technically slaves because El Jefe does pay us." He turned and left without another word.

"Wow! That was so beautiful, what a great spot," Sam gushed while shrugging out of his wet suit. "It took me a while to relax, but that feeling of floating weightlessly is always amazing and surreal."

Juice had already shed his gear and pulled off his wet suit. It was getting quite hot, and he headed into the galley as his golden cabrilla wriggled, dangling from its wire. "I'm usually diving with customers, these days, so its nice to just pleasure dive. You want to dive again before lunch, or wait and dive after? We need to stay up here for at least a forty-five minute interval."

"I can help you get lunch together and change out the tanks." Sam stood in the galley doorway watching Juice quickly fillet the cabrilla. "Man, you've done this before, I see."

"Yeah, this is a one-man galley, but the fan in here is nice. Why don't you change tanks while I get lunch started. Bella already cut up a bunch of vegetables for us, so there's not much for you to do in here."

Sam did as asked and then took his time rolling a joint from some buds he'd brought. "Damn, its smelling mighty fine in there." He handed the joint to Juice, who looked mildly surprised, but he took the smoking spliff and had a small hit, holding it in for awhile. He coughed a little and exhaled. "This fish is as fresh as it gets and wow, that's some fine bud, too."

"Yeah, a little dab will do you. This is some of Humboldt county's finest."

"I rarely smoke anymore. Hey, remember when we toked our first joint in my backyard? We must have been fourteen, and we barely felt anything from the crappy leaves and stems that I had."

Juice uncovered the skillet to reveal steaming white fish chunks with tomatoes, olives, orange slices, onions, and peppers, and handed Sam two plates and forks. "This is my version of Cabrilla de la Vera Cruz. Man, I got high off that one hit."

Mouth watering, Sam said, "Damn, after diving and getting high. I'm starving." They both laughed, but were soon devouring the dish with gusto. In between bites, Juice recalled, "Remember when we were juniors in high school and those two guys from Chino High showed up at our dance in their letterman jackets? The one guy was huge and we kind of got up close and personal and he pushed you."

"Of course I remember. He had about fifty pounds on me, and was like one giant muscle. I was lucky he started it by pushing me, because he gave me space to escape his grasp. If he had gotten ahold of me, I'd be dead now." They both chuckled.

Juice was picturing the chaotic moments in his mind. "Everything happened so fast. The other guy swung at me and I ducked and lost it. All I remember is punching him until he went down, and then I thought, I'm going to have to get a chair to hit the big guy before he kills you, but when I looked over, you were dancing around him on your toes and tagging him in the head."

Sam reminisced after finishing another bite of the delicious dish. "Yeah, all that boxing we practiced, all those playground fights, helped me survive that one." They had relived this legendary battle before, but it had been thirty-plus years and they still felt the adrenaline rush. Juice smiled and said, "I was glad when Father Peter came over to break it up and kicked those guys off the campus. We came out of it without a scratch, but if it had gone much longer, that big guy would have put a hurtin' on us."

"I'm happy to say that was almost the last real fight I ever had. When I quit playing football and got serious about getting my social work degree, I read Ghandi's autobiography. I switched to nonviolent civil disobedience and became a peace activist. I've been arrested for demonstrating over a dozen times, but never resorted to violence. Shit, you must be a badass, with all your special forces training. Anything you can tell me about?"

"Yeah, but I'll have to kill you," Juice joked, and they chuckled some more. "What did you get arrested for?"

"Mostly blocking the federal building in Sacramento, protesting Reagan's war in Central America in the early eighties. In fact, that's where Sheila and I met. We were both organizing opposition to the illegal war. We haven't talked politics much - I'm pretty left of center - but I've always respected veterans, and have helped more than my share of homeless vets. I still feel lucky that the Vietnam War ended right after we registered for the draft."

Juice looked more sober and said, "Good for you, brother! I can't say I'm proud of everything I did in the service, especially my short time in Central America. Its hard for me to talk about that. I'm proud of my involvement in Croatia in 1995, assisting with Operation Storm, when we were unofficially sent in to capture a racist, ethnic-cleansing war criminal who was holed up in a well-fortified compound.

"It was a serious firefight, the worst I was ever involved in. We had to blast our way in, but it took hours, and I know I killed a couple of guys, at least. We lost a couple friends, too, but we did bring the fucker to justice. I am proud of that one, and that's where I got this scar." He pointed to the rough red scar over his eye. "I got a couple of medals, too, but I'd trade them in a hot second to have my two friends back." He took a deep breath and teared up a little.

"Thank you for your service and sacrifice, my brother. I'm proud to know you, a fucking hero." Juice had that double-dimpled smile on his face, and shrugged.

Sam added, "I can't believe you were involved in Central America. That was a life changer for me."

Juice looked sadly into Sam's eyes. "I spent several years going back and forth to Cuba, defending Guantanamo Bay and doing surveillance on Castro, but was posted for a few months in El Salvador in the early eighties, and I fucking hated every minute of that.

"I went on "training missions" with Salvadoran forces. Once I was in a U. S.-made helicopter with a squad of Salvadoran soldiers, and the fuckers just started dropping hand grenades and shooting indiscriminately at small farms, women, and children.

"They looked like me and my family, bro. They were just trying to survive. I lost it, telling them to cease firing at noncombatants, but they just shrugged and some laughed, saying, 'Todos communistas!' (They're all communists). I immediately protested to my superior officers and they put me on desk duty until I could get out of there.

That's pretty much why Lieutenant was my highest rank after twenty-two years in the service. I still have nightmares about that day - even more than the battle in Croatia, when I was wounded"

Sam just shook his head. "I'm sorry you got put in that position, Juice, but you did the right thing, even though it probably cost you. A lot of guys would have turned a blind eye."

"Maybe. How did you get involved in Central America?"

Sam finished chewing. "I was in Nicaragua for a summer, studying Spanish in 1983 when I was in graduate school at Sacramento State. I lived with a family in Esteli near the Honduran border, sharing a bedroom with three brothers. The illegal Contra War organized by the CIA from Honduras against Nicaragua started that year.

"A few months after I left, one of the brothers of my Nicaraguan family, Arturo, seventeen years old, was killed by a Contra land mine while riding on a bus full of civil surveyors." Sadness washed over Sam's face.

"I also helped build a school for a community of Salvadoran refugees who were terribly traumatized by war crimes that, you know too well, our government assisted. That experience really changed me. I learned firsthand what the Vietnam War had taught many already - that we, the U.S., are not always on the side of freedom and justice."

"I hear you, man, its interesting how our paths have been so different. You know how it was in the day - I never felt fully accepted. I longed for acceptance. I wanted to be white in the worst way. I was kind of lucky that our working class neighborhoods in the Pomona Valley were not totally segregated, and our Catholic schools were sort of integrated - at least with brown and white kids.

"You know me well. Remember how I never used my Mexican name and made fun of the guys in the low-rider club in high school. You were a good friend, and kind of my door into the white world. You know how cliquish it was in high school. I was sort of accepted in the popular white clique partly because we were so tight. In the military, I felt like I'd finally earned respect, but by the end, I just got tired of trying to be accepted in the white man's world."

Sam said, "Shit, I remember in the fifth grade that handwriting teacher who slapped your hand with a ruler for writing Jesus, your fucking name, on your paper. Your Nina went off on that one, but racism was everywhere. I don't think I ever told you this, but I would go to family parties, and some of the adults would be making jokes about beaners and wetbacks, and I'd laugh to fit in and then felt guilty when I saw you. Its shitty how so many people feel like they need someone to look down on."

Juice nodded. "You know how it was…still is, sometimes. Man, I couldn't walk down the street as a brown kid without white teens driving by and yelling 'wetback' or 'beaner', or 'go back to Mexico.' I just flipped them off, but that kind of shit really got to my dad. He just lost it, eventually. That's how he ended up in prison."

"Yeah, I remember the time we visited him. It was some minimal security setup in Tehachapi, as I recall. He was such an intelligent and interesting guy. I'm sorry he died inside."

"He got cancer in his late fifties. I was lucky to have him in my life until I was eight, but my younger brothers and sisters barely knew him, growing up. Hey, but we turned out okay. Let's dive again."

"Fuck, yeah! Let's dive."

They did a bro handshake, but then hugged each other like they meant it. "Best friends for ten years. I've missed you, Juice!"

"I missed you, too, Sam." They started to suit up for the dive.

Juice put on his wetsuit. "I've thought about you often, Sam. Remember that first day we met in fourth grade, and the guys in class were divided into two cliques, so we were recruited to pick one of the two leaders and we chose to hang together and not join either one?"

"Oh, yeah." Sam slipped an arm into his vest. "We upset the balance of power. Pretty impressive for nine-year-olds, looking back. I remember all the playground fights. Some were knock-down, drag-out battles, and the nuns just let us settle things on our own."

They were ready for the second dive, and Juice explained that they were going to the bottom of the cliffs where there were some good sized fish, so Juice had his speargun and Sam brought a Hawaiian sling, which was a handheld spear about five feet long with a circular rubber band of surgical tubing and a three-pronged spearhead. Sam would have to get a lot closer to spear something, but would be less likely to accidentally spear his partner.

Again, they did their last adjustments and dropped backwards off the boat. They pressurized their ears and started kicking slowly down the anchor line. At the bottom, Juice looked back at Sam with a thumbs up and Sam gave the okay sign. Juice beelined towards the cliffs, kicking through clouds of fish, and Sam tried to keep up while controlling his breathing. The current was a bit tricky, this time and pushed them sideways, so they had to constantly correct their course, which Juice did expertly - but Sam struggled, at times.

They finally made it to the cliff face at about fifty feet of depth and began the hunt for dinner, working their way upward around giant boulders and outcroppings. Sam chased a big cabrilla into a narrow fissure, but couldn't quite get close enough before he lost it. He looked over to see how Juice was doing and spotted him thirty feet away, stalking a very big copper pargo that looked close to four feet long. He reminded himself that underwater, everything was magnified by over twenty percent (okay about three feet long).

The pargo dropped over a large jagged ledge and seemed to disappear in the shadows. Juice didn't hesitate - he followed it over the ledge, but it was gone, and a giant boulder confronted him. He quickly moved to the right side of the boulder and found a black hole just big enough to squeeze through with his spear and tank. He found his flashlight in his vest pocket, yanked it out, and turned it on. The scene took his breath away. There was a large, rounded cave mouth behind the boulder and his light glinted off the copper skin of the pargo, just inside the cave. He pulled a fluorescent yellow flag with a weight in the corner out of his vest and left it at the small opening. If something bad happened, he wanted Sam to find him.

Sam counted to ten, then twenty, but there was no sign of Juice, so he kicked to the ledge and dropped over it. Nothing but a huge boulder, and no Juice. He craned his neck and did a full roll, looking all around. No sign of his friend. Shit, where the fuck are you, buddy? He quickly searched the perimeter of the large boulder. He couldn't have gone far during this last minute. Then he spotted a yellow flag at the bottom of a small dark hole set back under an overhang, well hidden.

He didn't have a light, but he stuck his head through the opening. He saw a flash of light and a vague silhouette of the cave opening. A car could have driven through, except for the massive chunk of rock that served as a sentinel. The light strobed off and on, but he couldn't see Juice. He pulled his way through the narrow opening, scraping his tank. He had a second thought, Maybe I should just wait out here, but he was already most of the way inside.

The light continued to strobe off and on. That's weird - he must have his flashlight on blink mode. He could see that the cave narrowed and angled upward as it receded into the cliff. He positioned himself inside the cave mouth and saw a bright light flash off the walls about twenty feet inside of the narrower five-foot tube.

It was like an old fashioned black and white video flashing on and off. When on, he could see Juice in a struggle with the speared pargo in a cloud of blood, then total darkness. He watched as Juice fixed his light to stay on, wrapped his spear line around the gun, grabbed the spear with the pargo still wriggling on it, and kicked toward the entrance. He startled at the sight of Sam, but motioned him to go first, out the small exit.

Outside the cave, they checked their gauges. Juice's air gauge read 1,500 and Sam's read 1,000. Juice signaled Sam to follow and kicked hard toward the boat, pulling his catch. When they were about halfway back, Juice headed upward and checked that Sam was following. They again stopped at fifteen feet from the surface and floated for several minutes. Sam worried that he could run out of air any second, but he had enough to partially fill his vest, and they rose to the surface.

The north wind had come up while they were under, and the surface water was quite a bit choppier. It was hard work to kick their way to the boat. Sam had switched to a snorkel and swallowed some sea water and Juice dragged his wriggling pargo alongside, but they made it. Juice handed Sam his catch, slipped off his vest and let it float, then took off his fins and threw them over the bow, quickly climbed the ladder, pulled his fish and gear onto the boat and then helped Sam, who was coughing and sputtering. Once in the boat, they looked at each other, shaking their dripping heads. "Wow!" they both said at the same time.

"That is some kind of volcanic tube we found," Juice said excitedly. "It just kept going beyond where I speared the pargo, but it keeps narrowing and angling upward. I want to go back there tomorrow to check it out with some more lights and ropes."

Sam looked at Juice with incredulity. "You are batshit crazy, buddy. That was a dark and dangerous place. Why go back? It looked like you can't even turn around once you're deeper inside." Juice just shrugged. "I know you well enough that you're always up for some adventure. I bet you're as ready as I am for a beer and a shot. Then I'll cook us some pargo filets in a wine and garlic sauce." Sam smiled. "Man, this is really roughing it."

———

Captain Garcia had just hung up from a call with FBI Agent Don Needles of the Sacramento Regional FBI Office. He next called Sergeant Diaz. "Hi, Diane, this is Captain Ortega. I just heard from the FBI, and I wanted to share some good news. The FBI, in coordination with the Mexican Federales, has traced calls on Trixie's phone, the burner we found in her car, to a building in Tijuana that is owned by a cartel-connected boss of strip clubs and brothels all over Baja and northern Mexico. There is a good chance our kidnap victim is there, if she's alive."

Sergeant Diaz responded, "Will the FBI or Federales search the building in Tijuana?"

"The FBI is making a request to do just that, but given that its cartel-connected, they could pull strings or get tipped off. We'll have to wait and see. You did good work on breaking up Trixie's outfit, so I will keep you in the loop. If we can prove Trixie sold Dani to someone in Mexico, the human trafficking charges can be added to kidnapping, and we could put Trixie away for a long time."

"That should wipe that smug look off her face. I hope it works out for the victim, too."

After his call to Sergeant Diaz, the Captain thought about calling Sam, but remembered that Sam had told him he was going on vacation to Mexico. Oh well, *I can't really tell him much at this point, anyway, but he'd probably like to know we got a big lead and that there's some hope of finding Dani.* He called Sam's number and left a message that was vague but hopeful.

━━━━━━━━━━━━━━━━━━

Wednesday, October 12, 2005

DANI lay in bed, debating when was the best time to execute her plan. She had no way of telling time, but the street sounds coming in her window hinted that it was after two in the morning, as the usual sirens and traffic noise had dropped a couple notches. She thought her best chance was when the cleaning crew showed up, which she estimated was four in the morning.

Her very rough plan was to make it down the chute to the dumpster and hide until the trash was picked up. She might have to hide for hours, but the dumpster had been half full, yesterday, of what seemed to be large plastic bags full of papers, and could provide both a soft landing and a place to hide. One of many things that could go wrong was that she might not have enough rope.

She thought, I better get to the butcher room to check things out and get ready. If I need a sheet to lengthen the rope, I could come back.

She was already fully dressed for the first time in weeks in a weird assortment of green jogging pants, a blue Micky Mouse t-shirt, and a black zippered sweatshirt. She even had shoes, which were the cheapest tennis shoes imaginable, but the rubber soles should help her negotiate the chute. She had eaten all the food she could handle. She was ready.

She found her door unlocked. The tape had held, and hearing no one outside, she was quickly out in the hall and down to the door of the butcher room. If the door is locked, I am fucked, she thought, but it opened as it had before, and she was inside. Music from the basement came up the chute and she smiled, because it would cover some of the noise she would make. She also saw that the dumpster was full of more large, clear plastic bags stuffed with shredded paper. Looks like a soft landing, but if there're any sharps, in there I'm screwed.

She immediately went to the rope and uncoiled it, lowering one end as quietly as possible down the chute. The end of the rope came to the end of the chute and she still had enough to tie off in the room. She breathed a sigh of relief and continued to her next obstacle - how to tie it off? The cart by the edge of the chute was her best hope, so she tied her end of the rope to the thick stainless steel handle of the cart. She couldn't remember the name of the knot she had learned from her mom, but it seemed like it could hold her.

She then took a thick roll of duct tape and wrapped it around the whole chute and the bottom of the cart. She barely did three wraps around before the roll ran out. She found another full roll and slowly wrapped it around the top of the chute and the cart, three times. There was only another half roll of duct tape left, which she wrapped around her knot and sweatshirt to fashion a thick belt under her armpits.

She now had to wrap the rope once around her belt for a kind of brake on the way down, so she lifted the rope again, wrapped it, tied a loop in the end, and let it back down. Next, she pulled all the rubber gloves out of a pack on the cart and found that she could only manage three layers, but, they should help her grip and protect her hands.

Unsure of the time, she thought, Now is probably as good a time as any. She lifted her legs over the edge of the chute, grabbed a large trash bag and stuck it in her back pocket, and played out the rope a little, which didn't go smoothly because the belt of adhesive tape grabbed the rope. She thought, its good for braking but I'll have to wedge my feet and back into the chute to release the weight to play out more rope, over and over.

She held her breath and pushed off the top of the chute, putting her weight on the rope, which stretched more than she expected, but everything held. She was able to get in a position to wedge herself, but was quickly confronted with pain. Her back felt knifed, her legs were weak and her head began to throb.

Concentrate! Step one: play out the rope as quickly as possible, switch weight to hands, and wrap legs around rope to rest, weight on the belt. Well, I just have to do this about forty more times. She proceeded down, switched weight to hands, moved legs to the side of the chute, wedged against the walls, stifled her moan, played out a foot of rope, switched weight to hands, moved legs to rope, hung on the belt, wedged, played out, rested, wedged, played out, rested, wedged, played out, rested.

She was sweating, and her legs trembled. Her back, shoulder, and hands soon joined her legs, sore and shaking. She found that her arms and the belt were what she relied on, and was glad for the grip the gloves gave her. She tried not to focus on the deep throb in her head. She'd made it down about halfway. There was no turning back.

The Mexican rancho music got louder as she went down, and she strained to hear any sign of the guard below. The basement was a fairly large space with room for about three big cars, and the dumpster was against a side wall, so she hoped he wouldn't be close to the dumpster when it came time to drop. She continued to wedge, play out, rest, wedge, play out, rest.

As she approached the bottom, she heard a door close, and stopped to listen intently. She heard water running. He's in the bathroom, this could be my chance.

She quickly wedged and played out rope for the last few feet, until she could go no further. I'm at the end of my rope for real. She was wedged at the bottom of the chute, which was a good eight feet above the top of the dumpster. She pulled the last of the rope from her belt, legs screaming. She heard a toilet flush and knew she had to let go. The next second, she was free falling, her feet leading the way into the dumpster, her right hand covering her mouth to stifle an involuntary scream.

Everything slowed outside of time, outside of her body, as she watched herself fall in slow motion from the chute. It feels so fucking good to let go; give it all up to gravity - aching muscles relax, tension release, life flashing - mom singing and rocking, dad angry/out of focus, laughing with friends in second grade, playing cards with Grandma, Mom dying, stepdad sweating and grunting, Trixie, TommyLynn!

Just before landing on the pile of plastic bags, her left

forearm clipped the side of the dumpster. The pain brought her back into reality, this moment, lying on her back in a trash dumpster in Tijuana, Mexico, trying to escape from slavery, pain, and possibly death.

She made it, but her arm screamed in pain.

I did it! I made it! I better cover up in case he heard something. With her good hand, she yanked the large trash bag from her pocket, pulled it over her head and down as far as she could manage, then pulled a couple more bags over her legs while wriggling deeper into the pile. Just after poking air holes and eye holes in the bag where her face was, she heard a door open. Her heart still pounding, she held her breath.

TommyLynn had risen early and put on the coveralls she had bought, which were the closest she could find to what she'd seen the garbage workers wearing. Rolling her long hair into a bun, she pinned it up and donned her porkpie hat. Her cousin Juanita gave her a ride and had promised to be available to pick her up later that morning, parked in the white, unmarked company catering van they would take to Ensenada.

Truth be told, Cousin Juanita thought she was crazy, and feared they may never see TommyLynn again. These people are evil and violence comes so easy to them, Juanita thought as she made the sign of the cross with the three middle fingertips of her right hand and drove to her assigned waiting spot about two blocks away.

TommyLynn wasn't sure if the garbage truck came at

the same time each pickup day. She hunkered down in the cafe she'd frequented before, so she could watch the streets bordering the building where she was pretty sure Dani was being held. She had a strong feeling she was on the right track, and she had come up with the only plan that seemed feasible. I just need some luck - well a lot of luck actually - but I need to do something, she thought, while sipping coffee and breathing deeply to remain calm.

At about eight-thirty that morning, TommyLynn saw the garbage truck a block from the building, working its way toward her. She thought, Wow, glad I came early. She jumped up and checked the cash she had stuck in her front pocket, left money for the bill, and walked toward the truck, which had a driver in the cab and two men in gray coveralls hanging on steps and handholds on the outside of the truck.

The truck stopped and the two men jumped to the ground, grabbed a dumpster from an alley, and rolled it to the back of the truck while TommyLynn approached the driver by climbing up to be face to face with him through the side window. In Spanish she said she needed a favor, and showed the driver two hundred-dollar bills. The driver smiled and held out his hand, asking what he needed to do, thinking it would be some special garbage pickup. TommyLynn held onto the bills and explained, pointing to the building, that she needed to sit in the cab with the driver until they got to the garbage pickup in the alley behind the building, and after the dumpster was emptied, she needed to jump into it without being seen by the guard.

The driver looked at her closely and said he'd heard rumors of that building being a dangerous place, with the dumpster often having bloody bandages or plastic bags. TommyLynn nodded to indicate she knew it was dangerous and the driver motioned her to get into the cab. Once up in the passenger seat, she handed the driver one hundred dollars and indicated the other one was his when they got to the building.

━━━━━━━━━━━━━━━

SHEILA, Bella, and the rest of the cave painting expedition had camped in tents on soft sand in the canyon and slept well. After a breakfast of rancho coffee, eggs, machaca, and tortillas, they were headed to Santa Theresa Canyon, where Trudy explained that no expedition had been for over fifteen years.

It was slow and rough going, as the guides rode in front with machetes to hack the spiny cactus and thorn trees enough to let the animals and riders scrape through the overgrown "trails." The guides wore leather chaps that were so wide, they covered their legs and the sides of the mule's belly, but the mules still had nasty two-inch spines sticking out of other parts of their hides including their legs, heads, and necks.

Sheila noticed that her mule had a cactus spine in his forehead two inches above the eyes. Without thinking, she quickly reached over and pulled it out. The mule stopped suddenly and turned its head, its huge eyes saying, "What the fuck are you doing!" She looked up to see that Chema had seen her do it, and he shook his head and said, "Muy peligroso (very dangerous)! The mule, he might throw you."

After a hearty breakfast of pargo and egg burritos, Sam tried to do his daily practice of stretches, yoga, and calisthenics on the boat deck while Juice collected equipment for the morning dive back to the cave. Sam started his daily practice with an affirmation he'd learned from the Vietnamese Buddhist monk Thich Nhat Hanh.

Breathing in, I am a flower; breathing out, I feel fresh. Breathing in, I am a mountain; breathing out, I feel solid. Breathing in, I am still water; breathing out, I reflect things as they are. Breathing in, I am endless space, breathing out, I feel free.

Juice was excited about exploring the hidden cave, and Sam had relented to go with him. The morning sky was ablaze with the eastern clouds lit by the rising sun. A dark, red sky turned the water to blood.

"I hope this isn't a bad omen. It's a sea of blood, for God's sake." Sam joked, and Juice chuckled. "Seriously, it is so beautiful, but doesn't the saying go, 'Red sky at morning, sailor take warning?'"

DANI tried to lay still, but her arm throbbed, along with

her head, and she felt nauseous. It took a great deal of effort not to moan or cry out or throw up. God, its hot in this plastic bag, but I've made it unnoticed; my luck is holding. I just need to wait. The cleaning crew had come soon after her drop and a couple more hours, which seemed like days, had passed. They had deposited several more trash bags in the dumpster before they left, so she felt well concealed. Then more hours passed, and she managed to nod off at times.

Dani heard the guard use the bathroom again, and came wide awake. I wish I'd brought some water, but then, I'd probably have to pee. Damn, I'm tired of this music. I just need to hang in here a while longer, then I'll be free. I hope I can climb out of this dumpster quickly, with this hand hurting so much. I'm not sure what to do when I get out, or what to expect, but I'll cross that bridge when I come to it.

TommyLynn waited in the cab of the garbage truck with the driver while they emptied dumpsters for another two blocks before they came to the building. The driver had asked her if she planned to rob or hurt anyone, which seemed like a fair question, but she was adamant that she only planned to rescue her friend. The driver believed her, took the other hundred, told the other workers what was up, and wished her good luck.

TommyLynn was out the door and around the side of the truck to the back, where the dumpster would be forklifted and he could climb into it. The real trash men had rung a bell on the outside by the garage door and were waiting for it to open. The door was slowly raising up and she saw the guard, who was taller than her and more muscled, holding a metal rod and poking it through the trash in the dumpster.

She heard a scream and then the big guard was leaning the top half of his body into the dumpster and came up pulling out a garbage bag that was yelling and had legs sticking out of it that were kicking. He pulled the bag off the kicking person's head, and Tommy could see it was Dani, with very short hair, screaming, "You're hurting me! Let me go!" The two real garbage men were frozen in the doorway, watching the scene, not knowing what to do.

TommyLynn was instantly in motion. Reaching into her overalls pocket, she hurtled through the doorway past the workers, whipped out the small, thick leather sack filled with lead shot, and swung it above her head as she bounded through the garage. The guard was raising his left fist to knock out the screaming, struggling woman he had found, but before he had a chance, he felt someone coming at him and began to turn just as TommyLynn brought her load of lead down above the guard's temple.

Dani was instantly released from the big man's grasp as he crumpled to the floor. She couldn't believe her eyes, which streamed tears, looking at TommyLynn, who was checking that the guard was out. Then they were holding each other tightly. Dani was still shocked and confused and her arm screamed in pain from the guard poking it with the metal rod, grabbing her roughly, and lifting her from the dumpster. Tommy Lynn whispered in her ear, "I was coming in to get you through the trash pickup, but you must have had the same idea. Let's get the fuck out of here."

Dani was stiff from lack of motion and the climb down the chute, and stumbled when she tried to run. Tommy-Lynn quickly told her to put her arms around her neck from behind and to hold on as she bent down and grabbed the back of Dani's knees with her arms and lifted her onto her back. Dani whimpered as her damaged arm tried to hold on, but couldn't. "I think my arm is broken."

"Okay, just use the good one to hang on to my neck. I've got you. I've got a plan"

The workers decided to get the hell out of there, and were waving and whistling for the driver to take off as they lunged for the side of the truck. TommyLynn jogged past them with Dani on her back and turned the corner at the end of the alley. She ran as fast as she could for the two blocks, and was relieved to see the catering van.

Juanita about jumped out of her skin when her cousin arrived at the window carrying a white girl who looked very pale and was obviously in pain, with very short hair and a nasty scar on her front hairline. Juanita gestured them into the side door where there was a beanbag chair (Juanita's idea) and rows of empty plastic produce containers.

TommyLynn carefully placed Dani on the beanbag and turned a container over to sit next to her. Juanita craned her neck, staring at them in disbelief. "Thanks, Juanita! This is Dani. Dani, this is my cousin Juanita. You better take off before they come after us."

Her cousin needed no further explanation and hit the gas, swerving into the lane and flooring it down the street. Dani put her good arm around TommyLynn's neck and kissed her on the cheek. "Thank you for finding me. I don't know how you did it, but you were there when I needed you, this time. Do you have any pain pills?"

Ten minutes after TommyLynn fled with Dani, Ricardo entered the basement to escort El Jefe into the garage, as he did most mornings. He found the door already open and his man splayed on the ground, unconscious. He tried to wake him, but couldn't. He could see the large lump on the side of his head and thought about calling an ambulance. The guard was breathing and alive and Ricardo knew El Jefe liked to handle things without outside involvement. He called the upstairs office and told them to send the doctor and another guard to the basement, pronto. He noticed there was a plastic bag with holes punched through it on the floor next to the guard and he looked up into the chute to see the rope dangling inside.

El Jefe's black Mercedes SUV pulled up to the door and Ricardo motioned them into the garage, but told them to stay in the car. El Jefe rolled down his window and asked "Que paso?" (What's happening?). Ricardo pointed to his man, laid out on the floor by the dumpster, and in English said, "We've had a breach. You should leave or wait until we've had a chance to search the building. We don't know if they're still here or what they're after, but the girl may have escaped."

"Interesting. I just got a tip that the FBI and Federales want to search our building. I think it might be about Trixie's girl. I also found out that Trixie is in jail. If she ratted us out, I'll fuck her over. Take me upstairs. I'll be secure there. Then go check on that girl, and if she's there, get her out of the building. If she's gone, put people on the border crossings, and you better fucking find her. I've got to supervise the removal of sensitive documents, computers, and phones. Let's go." Ricardo opened his door and they hurried into the building just as the doctor and backup guard arrived. "Secure this door and take care of Arturo."

A half hour later, they'd discovered no one else in the building and nothing else out of place, except that Dani was gone and appeared to have escaped down the rope. "Call in more help and canvas the area. Somebody must have seen something. Take a look at the camera footage of the alley. I've got more people coming to help us move things out of here. I can hold off the cops for twenty-four hours."

"Si Jefe, ahorita! (Yes, Boss, right away!)."

JUICE and Sam were more weighted down with lengths of rope and lights instead of spearguns. "Now, your buoyancy control will be trickier, so leave a bit more air in your vest than yesterday. I've made our weight belts a tad lighter, so we should be okay. I've thought about how to handle the narrow tunnel. I don't think I'll be able to turn around, so when we're inside, you tie the rope to one of my ankles, and when I flash my light off and on three times, pull me out slowly. But if you can't see the light, I'll give the rope a good yank. Ready to go?"

"Ready as I'll ever be. We could just drink all day and leave the cave alone, but I know you won't let this go. I've never done a cave dive, but there's a first time for everything. Let's do it!"

They rolled backwards into the calm waters. Juice checked that their gear was secure and they kicked downward to about fifty feet. Juice gave the thumbs up, Sam returned it, and they were kicking to the cliff bottom. A lone bull sea lion crossed their path and checked them out before moving on. Clouds of small fish moved as one, and schools of green sierra and pink cabrilla moved in and out.

They had a little trouble finding the right ledge, but made it to the entrance marked by Juice's weighted flag. They turned their lights on and squeezed inside. Juice led the way into the gaping cave to where he had speared the pargo the day before. They were soon inside, where it was five feet in diameter and the depth gauges read sixty feet. Both Juice and Sam shone their lights, peering into the narrowing cave which angled upward as far as their lights would go.

They each unclipped the others' rope from their BCDs and Juice offered Sam his left leg. Sam tied a taut line hitch around Juice's ankle, then tied the ends of the two ropes together. The cave around them had clouded up, as they couldn't avoid stirring the sediment in the bottom. Sam added air to his vest so he stayed off the bottom of the tunnel and Juice gave the thumbs up. Sam realized he didn't have anywhere to gain purchase should he need to pull Juice out. He shook his head and backed up about ten feet to straddle a large rock on the cave floor. He gave Juice the thumbs up and Juice gave another okay sign.

Juice kicked very slowly into the cave as it narrowed to four feet, then three feet, about twenty feet in. His kicking stirred up sediment, so he now moved forward by pushing off the rough walls with his hands. He had a little trouble with his buoyancy, his tank bouncing off the top of the tunnel a couple times, but made his adjustments. Sam could still barely see Juice's light, but not Juice, after he'd risen slightly upward for about forty feet into the tube.

Juice moved forward, feeling more claustrophobic farther in. He breathed deeply and focused on each advance. He could see ahead that the cave was blocked by at least two big rocks, where it seemed to take a sharper angle upward, and he saw his depth gauge read forty feet. Sam peered into the tunnel, watching the rope continue to play out, but between the sediment and the deep darkness that seemed to swallow his light, he could only follow the rope into the murk and the now faint glow of Juice's light. He then turned his light off so he could see Juice's signal.

Juice thought, Well, this might be the end of the line as he approached the rocks blocking his way. The one in front was about half the size of the one in back, which seemed to fill up the whole cave. He startled when the big rock seemed to be moving. What the fuck? It took a second or two for his eyes to focus before he realized he was looking at the biggest octopus he'd ever seen. It covered a three-foot rock and part of the cave, its' skin copying the brown and gray colors perfectly. It moved slowly, seemingly bothered by the bright light and large visitor.

He had touched octopus before while snorkeling and diving, and always sensed that he was in the presence of a sentient being. This one was cornered, so he moved closer, pointed his light upward so as not to blind it, and reached out. At his touch, the octopus instantly turned a bright green. This was meant to shock and his hand retracted. He found himself looking into its green eyes. He reached out again, and at his touch, the octopus turned back to the color of the rocks. Then, using its beak, it blew a jet of water at his hand, which he quickly withdrew. He persisted in touching the creature again. A jet of black ink squirted and darkened the water around it while it moved away toward a crack that seemed impossibly small for it to fit through (but it did).

Curious, he shined his light into the three-inch-high by twelve-inch-wide crack at the top of the larger rock, and could see that there was another large rock behind and that the cave arched directly upward. A straight-edged corner that seemed an unnatural contrast next to the rounded rocks and tube was on top of the large rock behind. He could only see about six inches of it, but it could be a crate. He had disturbed sediment while playing with the octopus, so he waited for it to settle, and when he looked down, he saw two small, black rectangular rocks that also seemed unnatural. Puzzled, he reached down and rubbed sediment off one and tried to move it with his hand, but it was quite heavy and barely budged.

Hmm, that's odd. What the hell is that?

He reached with both hands, and was barely able to move the rock and get his fingers under it and lift it. My god, it feels heavy despite the lower gravity. He rubbed it with his rubber-gloved hand and guessed it was a little over a foot long, four inches wide, and an inch thick, definitely rectangular.

Is it a stone carving, or some kind of building tile or ballast? He pulled his knife from its sheath with one hand while holding the heavy block with his other, and tapped it. He was surprised by the sharp ting of metal on metal. Next, he scraped at its top. He saw the slightest glint of silver, like a hair through the black tarnish. Then he turned it over and saw what could be a large stamp pressed into the metal. This could be some kind of image. Hard to believe, but it almost looks like a silver bar.

His heart was beating fast, and he remembered to check his gauges. It didn't seem like he'd been in the tunnel long, but thirty minutes had gone by, and his air was down to

1,500. He quickly shoved the object into his vest pocket, put more air in his BCD, and turned his light backwards, flicking it off and on three times.

Sam had been trying to stay calm, conserving his air and peering into the inky darkness, looking for the sign. He was getting anxious about the time and his air supply, so was relieved when Juice finally blinked his light. He dumped air from his BCD, sat with his knees astride the rock, and began pulling the rope.

Juice had been trying to move backward on his own using his hands, but his big fins were awkward (great for going forward, terrible for backing up) and he wasn't getting very far. He, too, was relieved when he felt the rope tugging him back.

They were back on the boat and shedding equipment piece by piece. "Well, did you see anything cool?" Sam asked expectantly, because Juice had a wide smile and was acting dodgy. "Well, I encountered the biggest octopus I've ever seen in the wild. It must have been six feet long and totally covered the big rock I found blocking the end of the tunnel." Juice told of his octopus-touching experience. Sam looked impressed. "Wow, I wish I could have seen that. I've touched a couple snorkeling, and seen them change color, but all their various defenses are amazing."

"Yeah, octopus always feel to me like very intelligent, almost alien creatures. I understand that when they touch you, they can taste your chemical make up because their brains aren't centralized. They have brain cells in their extremities, too.

"It squeezed its big body through a crack that was about three by twelve inches. We looked into each others eyes and I was reminded of the times I've looked whales in the eyes. Some kind of deep knowledge and understanding passed between us."

They were both silent, reflecting on their experiences, and Sam said, "Sheila and I have made a few trips to Laguna San Ignacio during the annual gray whale migration, and we pet the baby whales."

"Yeah, I took Bella last year, and it was incredible. We should plan a trip, so we can commune with them again."

Sam nodded. "Absolutely!"

Juice looked Sam in the eye. "But this is the unbelievable part of the dive. I could see the tunnel turned upward, where I was blocked, and then I found this on the bottom, next to the rock."

He reached into his vest pocket for the coup de grace and held the rectangular black object. Sam could see that it was heavy, and when Juice handed it to him, it felt almost as heavy as lead. "Shit, this is too heavy to be a rock. What kind of metal do you think it is?" Juice took it back and tapped it again with his knife, watching Sam's face as it tinged again. Sam said, "What the hell!" Then Juice turned it over to show Sam the slight indentation that seemed manmade, and the silver scrape he'd made with his knife.

"Whoa, could this be a silver bar or tile? That would be crazy."

"Yeah, I still can't believe where I found it, and it looked like there was another under it. I need to get the tarnish off it to see what this image is." Juice started looking for some wipes he used to keep rust off metal and electrical connections. The sea and salt air took a toll on any metal that wasn't stainless steel. He came back with a wipe and rubbed it on the indentation. It didn't work perfectly, but seemed to take some of the thick tarnish off.

They both looked at it closely. "Jesus!" Sam exclaimed, and Juice answered, "Yes?" It was an old joke that always got a laugh when people who knew Juice's real name figured it out. Sam chuckled and said incredulously, "Do you see what I see?"

"Yeah, looks like a partial stamp with some writing under it." Juice turned the wipe over and rubbed it some more. A few letters began to stand out, 'ARO', and they saw the dull metal underneath. "Unfortunately, I'm out of wipes now, but if I had to guess, this is an ingot of Spanish silver, and we may have found the treasure of Red Monkey Rock."

The possibility washed over them and Sam, who had helped rediscover a lost cache of 49er gold in a tree near the American River in Sacramento, three years earlier, felt both a familiar elation and dread at what they might be in for, if there was more silver. He replied, "Hell, if its silver, just this one bar is an historic find. You da man, brudda Juice!"

"Shit, we've got to go back down! I haven't told you the other strange thing I saw on top of the big rocks. The octopus lead me to the crack where I may have seen a wooden crate."

The mule expedition had finally hacked its way into Santa Theresa Canyon and the intrepid riders pulled a few cactus spears out of their shins and knees. It had been rugged going, but now they felt like they were in the movie "10,000 BC" or "The Lost World."

Three different arroyos converged into the canyon, where there was a big water hole around the corner from a sheer hundred foot cliff that sported bigger-than-life paintings of elk, deer, big-horned sheep, birds, turtles, and a shaman figure. Across from the cliff was a smaller shallow cave twenty feet above the canyon bottom with a puma painted on its roof and an ancient grinding rock and rock pestle on the flat bottom of the alcove.

Shiela and Bella were dumbfounded at this sacred place where the guides seemed more reverent. Trudy stated the obvious with a big smile. "Is this amazing, or what? Worth the difficult ride wouldn't you say? You're free to swim and explore, just be careful and don't drink the water." They were sweaty and grimy from the ride. Bella said, "I didn't think to bring my bathing suit." Shiela rejoined, "I'm getting in the water even if I have to wear these clothes!"

The guides gave them privacy as they set up camp, so the women swam in their underwear, and after a very refreshing dunk in the water, changed into fresh clothes and hung up the wet ones. They climbed up to a long flat rock ledge at the bottom of the steep, painted granite cliff and could see that the painters would have had to build massive ladders or scaffolding to paint their ancient masterpieces. They also discovered scores of hand-chipped obsidian arrowheads and small spear heads scattered along the ledge.

After lunch, Bella and Sheila climbed up into the puma cave and sat next to the large, thick, square-cut grinding rock and thick rock pestle with a view over two of the canyons. They sat as women had for thousands of years, silently meditating on what life might have been like grinding seeds for nourishment, and how these ancient ancestors had once thrived enough to create human art and ritual so sacred, they were reminded of the ancient natural monuments, temples, and churches where pilgrims across our planet traveled and congregated, over the millennia.

Bella and Sheila had already shared how they met their husbands. Juice had coached a little league team in Jacksonville, North Carolina outside Marine base Camp Lejeune, and Bella's nephew had been on the team. Bella asked Sheila, "I heard you talk about your younger sisters, but did you two have any kids?"

Sheila replied, "They're my half sisters and ten to twelve years younger than me. My mom died in a traffic accident before they were teens and their father wasn't in the picture, so I stepped in to take care of them. Sam never really wanted to have kids, being the oldest of seven, and my sisters are more like our daughters, so no, we never had our own kids, but we have a 'grandchild' on the way."

"That's exciting! How about you and Juice? You haven't mentioned any kids either." "I wanted kids more than Juice did, but we tried and tried until we found out that I can't get pregnant. We talked about adopting, but I come from a big Italian family and we have like, fifteen nieces and nephews on both coasts, so we have a lot of kids in our life. Moving here a few years ago has taken us farther away and I miss seeing them so much. Many of the kids have grown up now though and are scattered all over. I do volunteer work here with a local elementary school too, and its really fun and rewarding."

Sheila added, "Its so great to see Sam and Juice reunited. Sam has been so excited to see Juice and I'm really happy to make a new friend. Thanks for coming on this trip with me Bella."

They hugged and Bella smiling offered, "This excursion has been tougher then I realized, but Its been so good to do it with you and I'm feeling like we've bonded by the challenging conditions and amazing beauty." They held hands silently for a long time just appreciating this sacred spot.

Sheila went for a nap in her tent after lunch and fell into deep sleep. She dreamed of a box canyon in similar terrain, at the bottom of a tall mountain. Her eyes followed the mountain up to the peak which, at its highest point. looked like the head of a puma, with two pointed ears on each side of the summit. She was riding her mule up steep cliff trails until she came to a tree shaded spring. As she focused on the water pooling and shimmering, she saw the puma drinking. It raised its head, and their eyes met and held until she woke up.

———————————

SISTER Julie was in Sam's office at the Village in Sacramento, going through piles of mail, while in the dining room below, hundreds of homeless men, women, and children were eating or waiting to be seated for a nutritious lunch cooked and served by scores of volunteers. She longed to be back at Day House Women's Center, helping her guests, but knew it was in the capable hands of her co-director. She tallied donations, read through letters, and checked Sam's phone messages. She wrote down the message from Captain Ortega and thought, Maybe I should try to call Sam to let him know. I guess I can at least leave a message on his cell phone. She left him the Captain's message.

Her phone rang, and it was Steve of the State Hospital Assn. "Hi, Sister, I wanted to update you on the opening of the Respite Shelter at the Salvation Army's facility. It looks like we have to postpone the grand opening for a week or two. The Salvation Army is ready with the rooms and beds, but the County Health Department is still trying to hire a nurse to serve at the shelter, and its taking longer than they thought. We do have all the hospital funding in hand for the first year, so we're close."

"Can't say I'm surprised, but I appreciate the update,

and thank you for your efforts with the hospitals. This shelter is so badly needed, I hope it can open sooner than later. I haven't talked with Sam, but I know he'd love to be here for the grand opening, and maybe that can happen, now. Take care!"

A few minutes after the call, Cat knocked at the door and Julie welcomed her into Sam's office. "Hi Sister. I was just wondering if you've heard anything from Sam and Sheila in Mexico? The last I saw him, he said he was taking TommyLynn to Tijuana against his better judgment."

"Oh, he didn't mention that before he left. No, I haven't heard from him, but I expect he'll check in soon. By the way, Captain Ortega left a message for Sam that they had a lead and there's some hope that they could find Dani soon."

"Wow, that's great news. I wish I could tell that to TommyLynn, but I have no way of reaching him."

AFTER the white catering van stopped at a pharmacy in Rosarito Beach for pain meds, Dani said, "I might need to see a doctor in Ensenada. I know its risky, but I might need a bone set, or a cast, and I definitely need stronger drugs." TommyLynn and Juanita both looked at her and nodded without a word. Juanita took the free road to Ensenada, which would take longer, but she feared the toll road might have cameras where they could be tracked.

TommyLynn had changed into jeans and a t-shirt. Dani was tired and in pain, but so happy to be out of her confinement and with friends that she felt buoyant, even giddy. She kept smiling at TommyLynn and shaking her head. "You are crazy! You know that, right?"

Juanita chimed in, "Yeah, she's fucking crazy, alright!" TommyLynn chuckled deeply and felt a pride and happiness that warmed her heart and filled her chest. Juanita still feared for them all and hoped that the danger was over, but knew that the cartel had unlimited resources and very long tentacles.

Dani remembered something that had been bothering her. "TommyLynn, I've been wondering what happened to your friend, Jethro. I have a vague memory of him shooting at Markus and getting shot before Markus hit me with his gun, but I was hoping I had that wrong."

"You have it right. Jethro got shot in the ribs and a bone splinter punctured his lung, but I saw him in the hospital a couple times, and he was expected to recover, in time. He was bummed he couldn't smoke weed for awhile, but he's going to be okay." "Oh, good. I'm relieved to hear that."

"There's another thing or two. I don't know if you heard that Markus' body was found floating in the Tijuana River a few days after he drove you down, and it looked like a gang hit job."

"I wondered why I hadn't seen him while I was in that place. I expected him to come by and gloat about what a mess I had made of everything and what a badass he was. You know, he told me he shot you too."

"Yeah, that's the other thing I wasn't sure if you knew. He shot me in the leg as I was walking to the bakery, before he went back to Jethro's place for you. I was in the hospital for a week, but after several weeks, I'm almost as good as new."

"I'm so sorry I got you into this mess, TommyLynn, I can't believe this whole nightmare." Tears welled in her eyes and splashed down Dani's cheeks.

Ricardo had been busy for the last hour, and now reported to El Jefe. "We've got people at the border crossings from here to Mexicali, watching the pedestrian and car lanes. I looked at the camera footage and saw a big guy in overalls who looked like part of the garbage crew, charge into the garage. Arturo is conscious and said that when the garbage crew came, he searched the dumpster and found the girl hiding. He pulled her out and then this guy hit him with something. The camera caught the guy running down the alley with the girl on his back. So she had help, but how in the hell they could have coordinated this is beyond me." "Maybe we have a leak inside?" El Jefe wondered.

"We talked to a couple of people on the street who saw the guy run with the girl, but we don't know where they went, yet. I talked to the garbage crew myself, and they swear he just showed up dressed like a garbage man, hit the guard, and took the girl. They claimed to have told a cop on the street about it. This does seem like a coordinated escape, Patron, so I'm questioning our people in the building."

"We need to find this girl, Ricardo, and she needs to disappear completely. Keep canvassing the neighborhood. They can't have vanished without someone seeing something. I bet they had a vehicle waiting nearby. Get out of here and find them!" Ricardo just nodded and turned to go. "Wait, did we get a good shot of the guy on the camera?"

"Well, he had on a hat and rushed into the garage, never standing still for the camera, but I'll get the best image I can to you soon."

"Get it quickly, and we'll circulate it to the police and say he assaulted our guard and robbed us. We will post a reward of twenty-five thousand pesos. They'll help us find them."

———————

IT was now afternoon. Sam and Juice were diving again at a depth of fifty feet, kicking their way towards the cliff bottom. They had a similar complement of gear for the cave dive, but this time Juice had included a two-foot crowbar, which probably wouldn't be able to move the large rocks blocking the cave, but might help him explore the crack where he thought he saw the crate. They were diving with quite a load, so he had cut the weight in their belts again, but Sam was struggling a bit with his buoyancy and there was more of a current than earlier.

Given their limited air supply, they wasted no time in

finding the entrance to the cave and squeezing through, with lights on. They proceeded to the spot where Sam would wait, and he tied the rope to Juice's ankle. Juice had his crowbar in hand as he adjusted his buoyancy and moved into the cave. He again tried to breathe slowly and relax as his feeling of claustrophobia rose, heightened by the clouded water.

He made it to the end, where he waited, as still as possible, for sediment to settle, then looked to the ground where he'd found the alleged silver bar and used his crowbar to find and pry up the second bar, which he deposited in his buoyancy control vest. He poked around, trying not to stir things up too much, but found no other bars on the floor of the cave. He hadn't seen his octopus friend, so he shined his light into the crack again.

Juice again saw the straight section of what might be a thick crate. He poked his crowbar into the crack to try to widen it, but the rock was unyielding. He tried to lever it under the straight edge of what looked like wood. He didn't have enough room to get much leverage, but found that a piece of the wood broke off easily. He looked at the three-inch chunk and confirmed it was wood, by its look and feel.

He placed the piece of wood in his other vest pocket and again poked the sharp end of the bar into the wood and loosened another chunk. He kept at this until he'd made about a four-inch hole in the wood and cleaned out the crack. He shined his light at the hole he'd created and saw two black corners of what could be metal bars, side by side. When the point of his crowbar hit them, it made an unmistakable metal-on-metal ding that echoed through the cave. When he pulled it away and looked closely with his light, he saw a glint of silver where he'd scratched the tarnished metal.

Juice let his discovery sink in. "Shit! This is for real! More silver bars, and if these are Spanish, there's no telling how long they've been here or how many there are. I can't picture any scenario where the bars were brought in the way we've been entering the cave, unless they were put here in modern times. They must have dropped these big rocks into the tube from above, then lowered the crate. We'll have to search the surface of the island to see if we can find the other end of the tube. He took a compass reading and saw that the cave traveled due west before it turned upward.

He tried his new toy, also, and took a GPS reading. I guess I'm done here.

Juice turned his light around and flashed three times, then relaxed so Sam could reel him backwards. He was pulled to the bottom of the cave by the additional weight, so he used his crowbar under him to push off the bottom as he was pulled out to the larger section of the tube. He turned around and gave Sam the thumbs up, with a smile, and reached into his vest to show Sam the other bar. Sam smiled back and returned the thumbs up.

As they kicked to the mouth of the cave, they both saw

for the first time a deep trench, about a foot and a half in width, along the bottom of the massive rock that hid the cave entrance. It wasn't the fifteen-foot trench itself that drew their attention. It was the massive moving creature that rose slowly from the trench and began to materialize before them. In their light, it appeared to be a giant copper/brown wolf eel twelve feet in length and three feet in height, though its width was narrow enough to fit easily in the trench. Its huge head and mouth with spiked teeth could have easily wrapped its jaws around either of their heads.

They were perilously close to the large "sea serpent." Its eyes appraised them, its mouth in a dinosaur grin, beard-like appendages hanging from its chin and mouth. It's body slowly waved, snake-like, to keep it in place. They were at first frozen, in awe of this creature and mesmerized by its unflinching stare, but, slowly, Juice grabbed Sam's arm and pulled him back into the cave mouth. Sam thought, I'm not sure if we want to be trapped in the cave by this monster.

Juice raised his crowbar and Sam pulled his dive knife from its sheath while they stayed close together, shining their lights in its eyes. They both had the same thought: I'm so glad there are two of us.

Juice peeked at his air gauge and read 1,000 lbs. of pressure. Sam probably has less air, so we can't wait too much longer. We might have to take a chance and rush this thing. Sam read Juice's thoughts and nodded to him. Juice held out three fingers, then two. Then the massive creature wriggled back into its trench, but it continued to watch them, as they had to pass within ten feet of it to exit the little side hole.

Back on the boat, they shed gear. "Have you ever seen an eel that big? It could have bit my head off!" Sam said excitedly.

"Hell, no. I've seen wolf eels before, and I know they get big, but that was a fucking monster!" Juice wasn't smiling.

"Yeah, I know now how the sea serpent "myths" got started - they're not so mythical, after all. When you pulled me back, and I'm glad you did, I was, like, hypnotized by its eyes. I've looked into the eyes of gray whales and orcas, but I never felt they wanted to eat me, like that eel did. I was thinking it had us trapped and we were running out of air - a scary feeling!"

Juice looked Sam in the eyes. "First the big octopus, now the monster wolf eel. I'm starting to wonder if this treasure has some badass juju?"

"So, don't leave me hanging, I know you found something else down there besides the second silver bar."

"I was able to poke a hole into what looked like a wooden crate..." He showed Sam the piece of crate he'd kept. "... and sure enough, it held more silver bars. I couldn't get them out, but I'm guessing that the rocks blocking the lava tube were lowered into it from the top of the tube on the island and the crate was dropped down on top of them. The fact that there's no light getting through from the top means that the upper cave has been backfilled with rock, caved in or somehow covered up. I think our next move is to explore the island near where we've been diving."

"I'm game, as long as we don't have to go into that fucking cave again," Sam said, smiling. "What do you think we should do about the two bars you found?"

"Good question, let me think about it. After we've checked out the island, we can talk about next moves."

"Sounds good, but when are we going to celebrate your finding the Red Monkey treasure? I think this calls for a shot of tequila, don't you?"

JUANITA had found a doctor in Ensenada, and after a half hour wait, he had x-rayed Dani's arm and confirmed that the ulna bone in her arm was indeed cracked. It was good news that she just needed a cast, and after grabbing some food and water for the trip, they were on their way to the bus station after an hour and a half detour. TommyLynn asked Juanita to get word to his parents that they were okay. They said their thanks and goodbyes to Juanita, with hugs and promises they would see each other again soon.

TommyLynn and Dani had only a twenty minute wait for the bus south to Loreto, which was good, because the pain pills and exhaustion had hit Dani and she could barely keep her eyes open. She was fast asleep with her head on TommyLynn's shoulder as the bus pulled out of the station.

———————————————

Ricardo reported to El Jefe later that afternoon. "We did find out that the guy carried the girl to a white van a couple blocks away and they drove off, but we don't know where. The cops have the guy's photo and are on it, and our people at the border crossings are looking for a white van. They might wait until the middle of the night to cross the border, but we'll get them."

"Good, I hope so, Ricardo. We'll be moving out with everything and everyone in about two hours, and I've told everybody to stay away for the next few days until I give the word to come back, but we'll have to set up at our warehouse across town, and it could be for awhile, until things cool off. If the FBI gets the girl, we may be in for a long haul, so don't let that happen, Ricardo."

———————————————

Sheila and Bella, after restful naps, had a great dinner of chicken tacos with onions, chilies, rice and beans. Trudy had even cooked a cake in a Dutch oven buried in campfire coals, and after dinner, the guides took turns singing traditional rancho songs, with Trudy singing along. Sheila and Bella sang a folk song or two and Sheila made up a funny song about her mule Beet who had doble tracion (four-wheel-drive)" and the guides laughed. Later, they sat in silence and marveled at the Milky Way in a silky night sky of resplendent planets and faraway suns. They fell asleep to the hoots of owls and the croaks of desert frogs.

Sam and Juice took beers and crowbars and paddled an inflatable dinghy to Carmen island just before sundown. The wind had faded and the blue-green water had changed to silver glass. Juice and Sam were a bit tipsy after a couple shots of tequila, a joint, and beers, Sam burped and said, in an awe-filled tone, "This is God's alchemy, changing the sea to a silver sheet with the fading sun. How appropriate is that?"

Juice laughed. "Yeah, but what if the red monkey jumps off its cliff to come after us for finding the treasure?"

"Hell, we've already confronted a giant wolf eel and octopus. We can deal with the monkey." They both laughed heartily.

Once on the island's beach, they walked along a rocky ledge, and Juice got out his GPS. "These things are like magic. I got trained on them early on, when the first models came out for military use. I took a reading in the cave where the tube turned upward, and I think I can get fairly close to where the tube would surface here." He read his device and said, "We're on the right track toward this little canyon at the side of the cliffs."

They'd only walked about a hundred feet over the rocky ledge when Juice said, "This is real close." They looked around, and right at the bottom where the cliff rose steeply was a round hole, four feet in diameter and two feet deep. It was filled with large rocks and it looked like the water had receded, since it was low tide. Juice took another reading and saved it on the device.

"We're not going to get far trying to dig these rocks up with our crowbars, but I've got the GPS reading, so we can easily find it again. I think we'd need some kind of government-sanctioned permit to dig here, anyway. Let's walk a bit and move our sea legs around while we have some light. I think our next move is to head back into town in the morning. We can do some research on the silver by computer and I think we should consult with the President of our local college, who is a friend of mine."

"Sounds good. Capitan. Maybe we found some pirate loot. Aaaaarrrrrgggg Matie! Yo ho, Yo ho, its a pirate's life for me." Sam's beer sloshed as he raised it over his head, then he lit up another hooter.

"AAAARRRRGGGG!" bellowed Juice, after a hit on the joint. They both cracked up like they were kids in high school again as the sun sank behind the island and the sky turned the pink color of a puppy's belly.

Chapter Six
THINGS GET CRAZY

Thursday, October 12, 2005

TOMMYLYNN AND DANI spent the night on the Aguila (Eagle) bus, and after sixteen hours heading south on beautiful Highway One, stopping at many small towns, they pulled into Loreto. Dani had slept okay, with the help of exhaustion and strong painkillers, but TommyLynn had slept fitfully, maybe twenty or thirty minutes at a time. She'd always had trouble sleeping in cars and buses, but she also felt the need to be vigilant.

It had been a very long day and night for both of them, but they had made it to Loreto without incident, and TommyLynn tried to call her Loreto family on a pay phone at the bus station. She wasn't able to get through right away and considered with Dani whether to call the number Sam had given her for the Sacramento Police Captain. They decided against it. They shouldn't trust the Mexican Police, and weren't sure what the FBI could do, at this point, but they knew they remained in danger and would call if needed.

They walked down Hidalgo Blvd, the main entrance to central Loreto from the Highway, past taco stands, cheap motels, hardware stores, Tecate and Modelo beer stands, a gas station, a school, the Pescador market and the historic Spanish Mission, which they read was the longest surviving of all the California Missions dating back to 1697. While walking TommyLynn filled Dani in on Sam and Sheila giving him a ride to TJ and that they were vacationing in Loreto. "I'll try to call Sam on the number he gave me. He could help us with the police and FBI."

It felt really good to walk, especially for Dani, despite her stiffness. She just felt amazed to be free and outside in the cool of the early morning, and she was finally getting to experience Mexico. They had walked about fifteen minutes when they came to City Hall and the Zocalo (Town Square). Famished, they looked for a place to sit and eat and found the pleasant-looking Cafe Ole, which was crowded and appeared to fit the bill.

At that very moment, Sam and Juice were parking nearby, "I'm starving!" Juice asserted, "Let's get some breakfast." As Juice and Sam sat outside at an empty table, Sam looked into the cafe and blinked unbelieving when he saw TommyLynn and Dani without hair, sitting inside. TommyLynn's eyes met Sam's and a look of wonder lit his face. Sam turned to Juice, "I'll be damned if it isn't the kids from Sacramento I told you about, who were shot and kidnapped. How in the fuck did they make it here?" TommyLynn was now at their table and Sam stood up to hug him tightly,

They were soon seated together, after introductions, smiling, eating and shaking their heads at the unlikely meeting. Juice looked at them in wonder, "Loreto is such a small town I run into people I know everywhere I go, but this is a fucking miracle! Sam told me some of your story about the kidnapping and shooting. How in the hell did you find each other?"

Sam asked Tommylynn and Dani to tell their story, which took awhile. After the amazing tale sank in both Sam and Juice marveled at their bravery and luck, then got very concerned looks on their faces. They couldn't help but glance around furtively and Sam offered, "I think I should call Captain Ortega ASAP! These cartel thugs must be looking for you. Sheila is gone for a few days if you guys want to stay at our hotel room until the FBI arrives. I could find another room."

TommyLynn replied, "Thanks, but our plan is to stay at my family's rancho in the mountains and my Tijuana family has probably already told them to expect us. I need to call them again right away."

"We can take you there." Juice offered.

"The problem is, I don't remember how to get there." TommyLynn answered. "I need my uncle Gerardo to come get us and take us there. There's no way they can find us up there. I'm okay with you calling Captain Ortega Sam, but I worry about the Mexican authorities tipping them off."

Juice insisted on buying breakfast while TommyLynn called her rancho family again on Juices cell phone. This time her uncle answered to say he would pick them up in thirty minutes. Sam called Captain Ortega and had to leave a message about finding Dani and TommyLynn in Loreto that morning. Sam and Juice thought about following the uncle to see where the rancho was, but Juice had an appointment. Sam insisted on waiting with them until Uncle Gerardo arrived in a 1980 faded red Ford pickup and was introduced to everyone. Before he left, Juice got directions from the uncle to pass along the info and maybe visit them later at the rancho.

Seated three abreast in the front seat of the old truck, Dani and TommyLynn were feeling safer during the thirty-three kilometer ride south on the highway, then west, up a beautiful steep-sided arroyo on a dirt road that ran for about twenty minutes. Gerardo pointed out the Rancho on a short plateau in the back of a box canyon, where the road ended. The Sierra Gigante mountains, rising precipitously around it, were quite green, for desert, as the hurricane season had been active. Scores of brown and white goats gathered at a small pond fed by a waterfall, trickling down from above.

TommyLynn saw a gray-haired woman wearing a black skirt and a white blouse, with a goat over her shoulder, emerge from a clump of palo verde trees, and immediately recognized his grandmother. She turned to them and waved with a big smile, missing a couple front teeth.

"Wow! This is beautiful," Dani gushed, as the truck came to a stop. Gerardo looked at Dani, with her quarter-inch hair, studded ears and nose, and the two-inch pink scar at the front of her hairline, and said, "Welcome to Rancho Tranquilo."

"Tranquilo means tranquil, or peaceful," TommyLynn translated. "Back here, you only hear the wind, water, the goats, and the birds." After a warm hug and kiss from her abuela (grandmother), she introduced Dani to her grandmother Marta, who hugged and welcomed Dani.

Her grandmother didn't speak much English, but Gerardo did, so he translated. TommyLynn saw her grandmother sizing her up, smiling. "Mijo, mi grande hombre, que milagro! (My grandson, my grown man, its like a miracle.)" She smiled broadly, and TommyLynn thought she looked childlike with her missing teeth. Marta said something to her brother. Gerardo translated, "She says you look so much like our father when he was young, except for the long hair."

TommyLynn laughed, put her arm around Dani, and said, "My mom and dad send their love, as does the family in Tijuana." Gerardo translated while Marta asked for updates on all the family members.

They were invited into the small home, twenty feet above the pond, which had a palm frond roof with no windows or plumbing and the great outdoors for a bathroom. Grandma set about making coffee and tortillas, beans, and fresh goat cheese on her comal (a thin slab of metal balanced on rocks with a wood fire underneath) as TommyLynn, with Gerardo's help, explained what they had been through and the danger they still faced while they were in Mexico, leaving out the part about being sex workers.

Gerardo looked concerned. "I think it would be very hard for them to find you here, but the town is small, and all the ranchers and their families know everyone else. Most would never give you up, but the young people sometimes have problems with drugs, and could be bought."

TommyLynn replied, "I really don't want to put you in danger, but I couldn't think of anywhere else to go. As you can see, Dani has been through a lot. First a bad head injury, and she broke her arm escaping, so she needs some rest. We're sure the gangsters are watching the border, but I think in a few days or a week, at most, things should quiet down and we can head north." Dani nodded her agreement, and after Gerardo's translation, Grandma said, "Nuestro casa es su casa. No preoccupado mijo, su amiga es familia (Our home is your home. Don't worry yourself, your friend is family)."

They were shown to the back of the house where a three-sided overhang was attached, covering two twin beds. Grandma had the only room inside the house, and Gerardo had been using this side room, but he assured them he would be fine, as there was a small trailer with a bed by the horse stables and goat pens, which they could see a hundred yards away. TommyLynn, who looked exhausted, thanked his family again for their help and said, "Necesitamos una siesta" (We need a nap).

THE clock struck eight in the morning as a bilateral task force, including U.S. FBI agents Juan Morales and June Black and Mexican Federales lead by Capitan Moreno, wearing SWAT gear and masks, surrounded El Jefe's building in downtown Tijuana. They used special cutting tools on the alley garage door and eventually streamed inside with automatic rifles at the ready, but found no one and very little of anything useful.

The FBI agents weren't surprised, but the Federales were embarrassed that El Jefe had been tipped off, probably by one of their own.

Ricardo watched the drama unfold from another building close by, smugly smiling. He was on his phone with El Jefe giving him the play by play so he could also enjoy it. "Well, Ricardo, lucky for you, it seems that they haven't found La Puta (the whore), or they probably wouldn't have moved forward with the raid. Any news or clues of their whereabouts?"

"We're fairly certain they haven't tried to cross the border, or we would have seen them, and as you said, the raid wouldn't be happening. We think they're hiding out here in Tijuana, laying low until we relax, so they can try to cross.

"The police have pulled over many white vans, but they haven't turned up yet. I just got word of a possible sighting in Ensenada from a doctor's office who treated a girl that looked like La Puta for a broken arm, so I'll check this out personally. The police there sent photos to hospitals and doctors, and we got lucky. As you know, a lot of gringos go to Ensenada, but this one had short hair and a scar, so we might have something."

Jefe was silent for a few seconds. "Hmm. I wouldn't expect them to go south, but maybe they are playing it smart, going where we wouldn't expect. Take the helicopter to Ensenada, now, to see if this tip is plausible. This escape of an injured girl does not reflect well on your security measures, Ricardo. I'll have to cut my losses with her. I want the girl found and discharged from our employment."

"Of course Jefe, I promise you they will both be found, and you won't have to think about them again."

———

Sam and Juice were anxious to check their treasure and do some research. After Juice's appointment they met at Juice's office, near the zocalo and were now on his computer, researching Spanish silver ingots. They eventually found some for sale and looked at their photos and measurements, but they were mostly different shapes, weights, and with different stamps. The closest one they could find to the two ingots they had was dated 1521, from a sunken Spanish ship off the coast of Bermuda, which was much older than any of the others with photos listed.

This older ingot was a closer shape to theirs, and they had found some tarnish remover Bella used for her jewelry, so could now make out more of the stamp marks on their ingots. The 1521 ingot they were looking at had similar lettering to theirs, though only a few letters were readable. A footnote to the photo of the 1521 ingot explained that its letters added up to "'CAROLVS QVINTAVS IMPERATOR' - Charles V of the Holy Roman Empire (also known as Charles I of Spain), who ruled from 1521 to 1556. On the left side of the stamp on their ingot, they read the 'ARO' of CAROLVS. On the right side, they could see 'IMP' of IMPERATOR. They were able to make out part of a date on their ingot that read 155, but the last digit was worn off.

They looked at each other wide eyed, and Sam spoke first. "Wow, these might date to the fifteen hundreds!"

Juice offered, "Yeah, that's surprising, because the Loreto Mission wasn't founded by the Spanish until 1697. Why would an earlier expedition bury silver on Carmen island? Maybe they had to abandon ship or something. This is incredible."

Sam asked the question again. "What now, my brother?"

Both of their faces turned serious, and Juice was thinking hard. "I know there is a Mexican government agency that certifies and protects historic sites and artifacts because they're involved with the cave paintings and other ethnographic sites in Baja. I've seen their acronym, INAH, on signs. I'm thinking that we try to find the closest, highest-ranking agency rep and show them what we've found. I doubt we can have the bars cleaned up and analyzed by a lab here in Loreto."

They next looked up the Mexican agency INAH and found a number for La Paz (the capital of the state of Baja Sur, four hours south). They called and left a message about finding one Spanish silver bar near Loreto, and gave Juice's mobile phone number. Juice said, "I made an appointment with my friend, the president of our local university - what you'd call a community college, up north - whom I've heard speak about the history of Loreto. We've had beers a time or two. I trust him. Let's go meet with him and see what he thinks."

Sam checked his phone messages. "Okay, but I got a message from the police captain investigating the shooting and kidnapping, so I better call him."

After waiting for his call to transfer, Captain Ortega answered, "Hello, this is Ortega. Sam, is that you?"

"Yes, hi, Captain. I saw that you called, and I have some amazing news about TommyLynn and Dani. I know its hard to believe, but we met TommyLynn and Dani here in Loreto this morning and had breakfast together. They had just arrived by bus from Ensenada and were picked up by TommyLynn's uncle to be taken to the family ranch. Here is the phone number, though they warned that the cell coverage is spotty.

"Really! I had called you to let you know that we had a

lead as to where Dani was being held in downtown Tijuana. The FBI and Mexican Federal Police raided the building this morning, but found it abandoned. The FBI said the Cartel was surely tipped off about the raid. We thought we were back to square one, but this is great news. I wonder how TommyLynn pulled off a rescue and got Dani to Loreto? How far south is Loreto?"

"It's about seven hundred miles from the border. We just drove it. There is good bus service. I wonder why they didn't call you?"

"Yeah, they might have trust issues, but I'll have to inform the FBI immediately, and they'll be calling you. Thanks for calling Sam and call as soon as you hear anything else."

Sam called Sister Julie next, after getting her message that everything was going pretty well, but that the respite shelter was late in opening. She wasn't in, so he left her a message that their relaxing vacation had gotten pretty exciting, and that they had met with TommyLynn and Dani that morning in Loreto and they were, so far, safe and close by.

The mule expedition had left beautiful Santa Theresa Canyon after cups of ranch coffee with frijoles, huevos y quesa fresca (beans, eggs and fresh goat cheese) for breakfast. They climbed out of the canyon and kept climbing into the San Gregorio Mountains on mostly clearer trails. Later that morning, it became cloudy and misty when they came to a steep incline where the trail had been washed out and their mules had to jump three feet to gain a rocky overhang. Sheila and especially Bella weren't so sure about this part, but they followed the lead guide, and the mules performed perfectly.

They rode for another two hours through the mist, and with the higher elevation came a change of landscape - rolling treeless hills, rocky with sparse vegetation - until they came to a high point on the trail. Trudy explained that this was a sacred area, with smaller rocks and many petroglyphs (ancient images carved on the rocks). They had to spread out to find suitable flat tent spaces, and even these were rockier than they would have liked.

Once the camp was set, the guides put out sandwich materials for a late lunch while Bella and Sheila wandered around the site. There were ancient petroglyphs of beetles, butterflies, frogs, snakes, birds, rabbits, lizards, suns, moons, and star constellations on one to three-foot, low-lying rocks, almost everywhere they looked.

Again, they could picture the ancient pilgrims, through the millennia, at work and worshipping on this site. They were moved by the chain of human culture. "Where there are people, there is art!" exclaimed Bella.

RICARDO had arrived in Ensenada before noon, and had gone directly to the doctor's office and confirmed that the huera, (blond girl) Dani had been there, and was treated for a broken arm. The office assistant told him she'd been with someone tall and young who was described as a puto (gay or trans), with very long hair. This surprised Ricardo.

A fucking puta? he thought, as he'd expected a manly man who would be bold enough to attack their guard and building. He also confirmed that they'd arrived and left in a white van, but they didn't get a license number.

He next went to the police to see if they had any other leads, and after greasing some palms, he asked them to put out an all-points bulletin for a white van heading south, and the two young fugitives. His last stop was at the bus station, in case they had abandoned the van and left by bus. He spent half an hour talking to the security guards and staff at the large bus station and did find someone who had possibly seen the pair, but all they could tell him was that they thought the couple took a southbound bus, which wasn't super helpful, since there were over nine hundred miles of road south, with numerous large and small towns.

He called two of his men in Tijuana and ordered them to drive to Ensenada immediately with photos of the couple (the photos from the security camera in the alley weren't great, and TommyLynn had been wearing a hat, but they had a decent photo taken of Dani, which was recognizable). He ordered them to drive south, stopping at every bus stop and station to ask if anyone had seen them. He told them about the twenty-five thousand peso reward for finding them.

He knew this was a shaky proposition, and could take at least twenty-four hours if they had to go the length of the peninsula, even with a fast car, but he was running out of options.

———————————

JUICE drove Sam to the small college complex off Hidalgo Street and they entered his friend's office, labelled "Presidente." They had to wait about twenty minutes while he was meeting with someone, and Sam answered a call from FBI agent June Black.

"Is this Sam White? Captain Garcia of the Sacramento Police gave me this number." "Hi, this is Sam and I'm in Loreto, Baja Sur." "Yes, he said you're on vacation there. I'm calling from Tijuana, though I'm based in our San Diego office. We're working with the Mexican Federal Police to find alleged kidnap victim Dani Blue, who we think was being held in Tijuana, but Captain Garcia said you have information that she may have escaped and is in Loreto?"

"Yes, We happened to run into Dani and her friend, TommyLynn Watson-Arce in Loreto this morning and they explained that TommyLynn with help from her family had rescued Dani from the building where she was being held in Tijuana and were driven to Ensenada where they caught an overnight bus to Loreto. They're together and staying at TommyLynn's family ranch now, here in Loreto. Do you know who TommyLynn is?"

"He's the man who was shot the day Dani Blue was reportedly kidnapped in Sacramento, right? What's he doing in Mexico?"

"Well, TommyLynn refers to herself as she, and she describes herself as Intersex. My wife and I dropped her off at her family's house in Tijuana on our way here when she insisted she was going to TJ to find Dani, one way or another."

Sam explained how he met Dani and TommyLynn in Sacramento, the day before the shooting and how he and his staff had assisted the police in finding Trixie after the shooting and kidnapping. Agent Black asked, "Why do you think they went south after escaping instead of crossing the border right away?

Sam explained that TommyLynn and his family were afraid the cartel would be watching the border, and they may still be in danger.

"Okay, how long are you in Loreto?"

"We have over two weeks left on our vacation."

"Good. My partner Juan Morales and I will soon fly to Loreto. Can you be available to meet with us by tomorrow or the next day?"

"Sure, you have my number and I have yours, now, so just call when you get in. We're staying at the Las Cabanas Hotel in town." After hanging up, he turned to Juice. "The FBI is flying in tomorrow or the next day, as if we didn't have enough going on." Juice just chuckled. "Shit, Sam, does trouble always follow you like this?"

The college president came out, and Juice introduced Sam to his friend, Chucho Rodrigues. "Good to meet you." he said in perfect English. "Chucho is my nickname. My real name is Jesus, like your friend here, who tells me you grew up together."

"Yes, we've been friends since we were nine years old, but we hadn't seen each other for thirty years."

"I'm sorry I have only another fifteen minutes before I have to go, but what is this about finding Spanish silver?"

Juice explained how they had found the two bars, then reached into his bag to show him an ingot, while explaining what they had found out so far about its provenance.

"Oh my, I have seen these Spanish silver bars before, on display in museums, but here in Baja California, these are extremely rare, especially ones so old. You said they were found near the Red Monkey cliff on Isla Carmen? So the treasure myth might be true, and you say it dates to the sixteenth century?"

Juice nodded. "Well, the bars seem to date to the fifteen hundreds, the fifteen fifties to be more precise, but we don't know when they were buried. We think there is a whole crate of these, but as I said, they're in a narrow cave - what we think is a lava tube - forty feet deep, and protected by very large rocks. However, we may have found the surface entrance of the tube on the island, covered in rocks." He explained that they had a call into INAH and could use his help in getting their attention and figuring out next steps.

"Sorry, I have to go now, but I will follow up with INAH. This could be a very valuable discovery. Please don't tell anyone else about this until I have a chance to follow up. Trust no one else! Wait, may I take a photo of the silver bar before I go?" "Sure, go for it!" Juice laid the bar on a table.

TommyLynn and Dani had napped for over two hours, and though groggy, were much relaxed and re-vived. Grandma Arce was again at the comal hand roll-ing and patting tortillas, and filling them with goat meat, and cheese. They had eaten twice already, but were still hungry. Gerardo asked them if they would like to go for a horse ride and they saw that he had already saddled three horses and tied them up outside the ranch house. Dani looked at TommyLynn and back to Gerardo. "Really, I've never ridden a horse before. Is it hard?" TommyLynn said, "You'll do fine, but how is your arm?" "I can use my fin-gers to hold on, so I should be okay."

Gerardo was smiling at her excitement over riding. "When you finish eating, we'll go for a short ride to look for stray goats. These horses are older and very gentle, so I trust them. By the way, Juanita called from Tijuana while you were asleep and was relieved to hear that you made it safe."

"Oh yeah, I should have called her sooner. Thanks, Tio (uncle)."

They were soon in their saddles, wearing cowboy hats supplied by Gerardo, but their clothing made them the strangest-looking Caballeros (cowboys) around. Baja cowboys generally wore blue jeans, leather boots, and long-sleeved collared shirts, and were often covered in protective leather. It was a beautiful hot day, and they rode on a wide truck trail around the box canyon. Dani was so excited, and TommyLynn loved to ride, that their excitement kept Gerardo smiling.

After they had dismounted, Dani started to tear up. TommyLynn asked if she was okay. "I had a dream while I was locked up that we were riding horses together, and it was a lot like this. I wasn't even sure if you were still alive after that bastard Markus told me he shot you, but the dream gave me hope and the strength to try to escape. I was ready to die trying. I couldn't believe my eyes when you showed up to help me. Some Madam was coming to get me to take me to a bordello, god knows where. I can't believe this nightmare may be over."

"I couldn't believe my luck at being there when the guard pulled you out of that dumpster. I thought I'd have to break inside the building to find you. I wasn't sure you were still alive after Markus' body was found floating in the Tijuana River." TommyLynn was tearing up also and they embraced.

"We were meant to find each other again!" Dani said as she hugged her friend tightly. "Thanks again for not giving up on me." Dani whispered in her ear.

Sam walked back to Juice's office a few blocks away and found him on the phone with Presidente Rodrigues. Juice hung up and told his friend, "Good news and bad news,

Sam. Chucho talked to the INAH official in La Paz and our message got his attention, so he's driving here tonight and wants to meet with us. That's the good news. Chucho asked some of his friends about the official and his friends say he can't be trusted. Chucho is trying to go over his head to the Mexico City INAH staff, where he has some contacts, but so far, no answer. Chucho's going to have dinner with us and we can talk strategy later. What about the FBI agents you talked to? They were flying in soon, too, right? This is already getting crazy."

Sam nodded. "Well, hopefully the silver is a good kind of crazy, though my one experience with treasure taught me that greed makes people do crazy shit. I'm sorry I brought this other drama down with me, Juice. I really didn't expect it to get this far. I'm glad the young woman, Dani, is free and okay now, and that TommyLynn didn't get killed trying to help her, but I didn't think I'd be spending my vacation dealing with other people's problems. That's pretty much what I do for work."

"No worries Sam. I know you just want to relax and enjoy your vacation. I was just venting. I don't know how you do what you do with the homeless. It must take a toll. Hey, we can deal with what comes along, but I've gotten used to the simpler life here, and I've had my fill of people wanting to kill me, so I'm not anxious to complicate things."

"I hear you, brother. Thanks for taking me out on the boat. It was so beautiful and mostly tranquillo (peaceful), and it got pretty exciting, with the hidden cave, the silver and the giant fucking wolf eel. I'll never forget it. Just to be clear, though, you found the silver Juice. You insisted on exploring the narrow, pitch-black tube. You messed with the big octopus. I'm just here to witness that you are the certified, bonafide, justified silver treasure discoverer."

"Wait, now - we were…are…in this together, viejo amigo (old friend). If you hadn't come, I'd never have taken you out there and chased that pargo into the cave, and if you weren't there to pull me out of the tube, I couldn't have gone in there. Hell, the Spanish government will claim the silver if they find out about it, which INAH is probably bound by international law to tell them.

"At best, there'll be a finder's fee, but the one crate of silver (if that's what it is) ain't worth millions. We're talking tens of thousands in total value, at most, and maybe a ten percent finders fee, but hell, we've got a ways to go to get there."

Sam said, "I know you've got stuff to do, so I'm thinking of driving out to the Arce family ranch to visit our fugitives and make sure they're okay, so I can assure the FBI agents all is well. I need to let the kids know that help is on the way tomorrow. I think it will be a relief for them to finally hear that."

"Sounds good and I'll see you for dinner with Chucho at six."

Sam followed the directions to the Arce rancho and found it at the end of the dirt road through a breathtaking canyon, passing several ranchos on the way. Scores of black, brown and white goats were around a watering hole fed by a tiny waterfall. He was greeted by Gerardo and introduced to grandma Marta who was hanging her last tied-off cheese-cloth bundles of fresh goat cheese from the wooden palapa ceiling of her home.

She, of course, offered him food and coffee which was basic Rancho hospitality and he accepted only the coffee. TommyLynn came out looking like he'd just awoken from another nap to say that Dani was still sound asleep. Sam shared that the FBI agents should be arriving tomorrow and TommyLynn seemed a little stunned. "I guess that will end our rancho visit, but I know we're still at risk, so thanks for setting this up Sam. What do you think will happen next?"

"I think they'll want to get Dani's statement about the kidnapping and being held prisoner and they'll probably want to get her back to the US where they can put her in protective custody. I think the same will go for you, but its hard to be sure with the Mexican Federales involved also. I think you're a real hero in this story TommyLynn and I hope you get treated as such."

"I just hope Dani gets the medical care and protection she needs. She's been through hell and I think she's going to want us to stay together through this next phase. She doesn't really have anyone else and I want to be sure she's okay."

Sam said his goodbyes and that he'd likely come back with the agents when they got in.

At six o'clock, Sam and Juice were having dinner with Presedente Rodrigues. The FBI agents had left a message for Sam that they wouldn't arrive until twelve-thirty the next day. Chucho said, in his perfect English, "The INAH official is Luis Echeveria, and he should arrive in about an hour. He'll call me when he is here, and he asked to see the silver bar. I told him you had found one, but hinted that there might be more on the site.

"As I told you before, my friends in the agency told me he is not trustworthy and has been suspected of stealing and selling artifacts that have gone missing, but he is now the highest ranking official in Baja Sur. His uncle is apparently a State Senator from La Paz. He may even have connections to the Sinaloa cartel, which scares me.

"It looks like we have to deal with him, but we should tell him as little as possible. Let's show him the ingot you have that has been cleaned up and ask him to verify its provenance and analyze the metal.

"Since you told him there may be more ingots, he'll ask you to take him out to the site, but you explain about the cave. I don't think he'll want to dive into the cave, but he might want you to pinpoint the area so he can take a GPS reading. We could put him off until he has the bar analyzed, but he might insist on going out there. You may have to decide if you want to show him where it is or put him off, but I think we'll have to deal with him sooner or later."

Friday, October 14, 2005

RICARDO's men had spent the night driving south on Highway One, stopping at every bus stop at every town along the way. They'd arrived in Loreto at eight in the morning and had finally gotten lucky when the bus station worker at the counter recognized the photos of Dani and TommyLynn. They were told that the two young gringos had arrived about the same time the day before, but he didn't know where they'd gone from the bus station. They immediately called Ricardo, who began to mobilize his re-sources to locate the two fugitives in Loreto. He told his two men to ask around town to find out where they might have gone.

Sheila and Bella broke camp at the petroglyph site, and after a breakfast of machaca burritos and strong ranch coffee (poured through a sock-like filter that looked like a small butterfly net), the expedition guides saddled the mules and they set off on a mellow downhill ride that would take them to another cave painting site.

Juice and Sam again put in Juice's boat at the marina and waited for Luis, the INAH official to show up. They had met with him and Chucho the night before, and though Luis was very friendly and offered to buy them drinks, he insisted that they take him out to the site the next morning so he could see the evidence for himself. They had explained the difficulty of the narrow cave and the large boulders that blocked access, but he said he was an experienced diver and at least wanted to see where the silver bar they had shown him had been found.

Luis had also asked them if he could take the bar with him so he could send it to Mexico City for testing at their main INAH lab. They had tried to put him off the dive until the bar was returned and the test results known, but he said he needed proof of the site before he could have the testing done. They reluctantly agreed to take him to the cave.

Chucho would hold the ingot until they returned and he told them again, after the meeting, that he still didn't have a good feeling about this guy, from what his friends had told him, but they didn't seem to have another option to pursue finding the crate of more silver bars.

They saw Luis walking toward the marina talking on what looked like an expensive satellite phone, and Sam said, "I don't know about this guy. Hey, the FBI agents are supposed to fly in at twelve-thirty. You sure we can get back here to meet with them Capitan?"

"Just the one dive, yeah, we should be back in time." Juice thought, I don't have a great feeling about this trip, either.

Ricardo was talking to El Jefe at their new warehouse operation out near the airport. "My men have found the trail of our two problems in Loreto. I'm not sure why they went to Loreto, but maybe the Puto has family or friends there. He looks like he could be Mexican. I'm flying to Loreto on Mexicana Air at ten-thirty and taking a man with me. I have men on site there also so I hope to find them soon, Jefe, and lay this matter to rest."

"Good work finding where they went, Ricardo. You know that everyday they are alive, we are at risk. I hear the FBI are still here following up leads, and the Federales were pissed that we were tipped off. Loreto is a small town, so you should be able to find them there. I look forward to hearing from you soon."

Ricardo's men in Loreto had been up all night and were in need of sleep, but the twenty-five thousand peso reward for finding the young gringos was motivation to keep at it. They had already stopped at a dozen cafes and restaurants and shown photos, but had not gotten lucky yet. They were now in the zocalo, where there were another dozen or so restaurants and taco stands, and when they came to Cafe Ole, one of the women seemed to recognize the photo.

The lead man quickly offered her five hundred pesos for any information and she remembered that Gerardo Arce had picked up the couple in his old red Ford pickup truck on Hidalgo Street, nearby. She knew and liked the Arce family, so decided not to mention who it was, but she did tell the men that the couple in the photo were picked up by a man in an old green Chevy pickup, but she didn't know who the man was or where they went. They gave her the five hundred peso bill and she smiled, intending to warn the Arce family that these men were asking around about the couple Gerardo had picked up.

TommyLynn and Dani were on horseback again, with

Gerardo in the lead carrying an ancient twenty-two caliber Ruger rifle in case they ran into a pack of wild dogs or other predators. They had covered the main canyon and a side canyon of the rancho by nine that morning. Already eighty degrees, the sky was so blue, Dani smiled at TommyLynn, feeling closer to heaven than ever before.

Dani rode along side TommyLynn, "This is so beautiful! I don't want to leave. I wish we could have one more day."

"I know, I'd love to stay longer too, but the longer we're here the more chance they could find us. I don't want to have my family caught up with the cartel. I've already put them at risk."

"Of course you're right. Maybe if we're in witness protection or something we could go to school and have a chance to follow a dream. I had a lot of time to think alone in that dingy room the last few weeks and mostly I thought about getting out of the sex work business, maybe going to school, living a slower, more normal life. That used to sound boring, but now its all I want."

Wispy clouds formed all manner of abstract shapes against the blue and the canyon was resplendent green, dotted with yellow and red flowers at the end of hurricane season. They had found three stray goats, so they had earned their keep, and Gerardo had fired over the head of a coyote to scare him away. Dani had only once been camping with the family of a friend and rarely escaped the city, so was profoundly moved by the natural beauty and sweet sounds of wind, trickling water, birdsong, and the cries of baby goats.

Grandma Arce greeted them with a heaping plate of burritos and TommyLynn joked, "Looks like we have second breakfastses." But nobody got the Hobbit reference. While they were eating, Gerardo's phone rang and Angela, the woman who worked at the Cafe Ole, warned him of the two men looking for their guests. She told him she had given them false information, but since they were offering money, someone could point them his way, and they seemed like bad men to her.

Gerardo hung up and a serious expression overtook his face. He immediately addressed his sister in Spanish. "That was Angela Davis" (Davis was a common name in town, linked to an English sailor who had settled there generations ago.) "Some bad men have come to Loreto and are looking for these two. They are offering money to people to tell them where we are." Grandma Arce, always smiling, now had a grave countenance as she thought for a couple moments before answering. "We should radio Jorge's wife Ana to watch for them, and leave to go to the mountain cabin soon."

Gerardo nodded. TommyLynn had understood some of the conversation, so he turned to Dani, his face etched in concern. "It looks like they have come to Loreto to look for us." Gerardo again nodded and said, in English, "We are lucky Angela has warned us. We will radio the family with the rancho closest to the highway to keep a look out for them and call us if they come. We should pack immediately and move to our mountain cabin far above here, where they cannot find us easily."

TommyLynn looked stricken. "I'm so sorry to bring you this trouble, abuelita y tio (grandma and uncle)." He stood up and said, "We should leave right away and find somewhere else to stay." Gerardo translated for Grandma, who shook her head. He then answered, "No, Mijo, you are safer to stay here and go to the mountains. They will not find us easily there, and we have escape routes. We will go by horses and mules, and they will not be able to follow in their cars. Let's get packing, we need to hurry."

Luis, the INAH official, boarded "La Aventura" and Juice motored out of the Loreto marina. It was a hot, windless October day, the sea was eerily calm with equal parts blue, green, and silver. The sky was a pure blue that Sam seldom witnessed in Sacramento, except right after a good long rainstorm. Luis was companionable, thanking them for taking him out, but all three of them felt a tension under the surface. Very little was said on the way to the backside of Carmen Island.

Juice anchored where they had before and they suited up for the dive. Juice turned to Luis. "Have you ever dived in a cave?" Luis considered, then said, "I've dove in cenotes in the Yucatan, which were definitely in caves." "Okay, but the cenotes, were very large caves, right?" Luis nodded. "This is nothing like that. This cave gets progressively narrower, down to less than four feet in diameter. I can tell you from experience, you could become extremely claustrophobic, and if you panic, you won't be able to turn around and you could drown."

"There isn't room to show you into the cave past the halfway point, so we will tie a rope to your ankle and pull you out when you signal with your flashlight." Luis nodded confidently. Juice explained to Luis about the octopus and the wolf eel and what he'd found at the end of the cave, and the crack above the rock where he had seen the crate. Juice instructed Luis to follow him, and Sam would tail along as a backup.

Diving conditions were perfect, and they made their way to the underwater ledge without incident. Juice gave the thumbs up and turned on his flashlight. Luis and Sam did the same. Juice dropped over the ledge to the dark hole and disappeared inside. Luis waited until Juice gave the okay, then squeezed through, followed by Sam. The wolf eel was not there to greet them, so they continued into the cave. Sam tied his rope to Luis' ankle and Juice pointed into the narrowing cave. Luis face looked suddenly much less confident, but he nodded and set off into the tube.

Luis moved very slowly and tried not to stir up too much sediment, but his tank bumped the top of the cave several times until he found the right buoyancy. He had gone about twenty feet when the cave narrowed to the point he would not be able to turn around. He froze in water, which was hazy with sediment. He tried to will himself to move slowly, but fear gripped him in place. He took deep breaths as he felt his heart beating in his ears. He'd never felt this claustrophobic before. He thought about giving the signal to pull him out, but resisted, waited for the water to clear, and moved forward.

Juice looked at the rope, then at Sam, who nodded and shrugged. Luis should have made it to the end of the cave by now, but was only about halfway. Then they saw the rope playing out again.

Luis was moving in earnest, now. I need to get the fuck out of here. He saw the large rock filling up the cave ahead and shined his light at the top, where he saw the cave angle upwards, and the crack Juice had mentioned. He moved closer and shined the light directly into the crack. Instead of a crate of silver bars, he was repelled by a moving creature of some kind, inside the crack. He almost dropped his light, but pulled his dive knife and tried to poke through the crack at what must be the octopus they had mentioned.

Thankfully for the octopus, it had cleared away by then, and his knife dinged a silver bar in the crate. He heard the muffled ding and looked to see the edge of the crate and the corners of two bars through the small crack. Madre de Dios! Incredible! (Mother of God! Incredible!) He quickly pulled his GPS device from his vest pocket and took a reading of the location. He then signaled with his light and tried to relax as they pulled him backwards, out of the narrow part of the cave.

They were still about thirty feet underwater, kicking to the Aventura, when Juice spotted another large boat that had pulled alongside of his. What the fuck are they doing? He would find out very soon.

The cave painting expedition was on its fourth day. Shelia and Bella felt like veteran mule riders by now, and the mild downhill that morning was much easier than the first few days of rough going. There had even been a slight misty rain on their trail, for a while. They came later that morning to the next cave painting site, which was more modest than the previous sites, but had some artful giant fish that looked like halibut and a large sea turtle. They set up camp for the last night in the incredible San Gregorio mountains and took advantage of some mild hikes in the area.

The FBI agents Juan Morales and June Black were seated at the Mexicana Airlines gate in the Tijuana Airport, awaiting the boarding of their ten-thirty flight to Loreto. They were also waiting for Captain Moreno of the Mexican Policia Federales, who had asked to accompany them on this trip. He arrived just after the first group had boarded the flight, and agents Morales and Black were glad to see him. They all shook hands and boarded the Mexicana jet.

Captain Moreno was squeezing through the aisle in first class when he saw the large figure of Ricardo taking up two seats. He didn't think Ricardo saw him, or at least, Ricardo gave no indication that he recognized Moreno. Moreno recognized him, though. He knew Ricardo was a henchman for Moreno's nemesis, El Jefe. That asshole is a step ahead of us again. Shit! He's going to Loreto to find the same people we are! If we can find the kidnapped girl first, the U.S. will charge him and possibly extradite him for kidnapping and sex trafficking.

The captain took a seat next to Agent Black and told her who he'd seen in first class. She said, "I noticed him at the gate, and he was with another man who is also in first class. Look!" She pointed with her chin and Moreno looked to the front to see a man leaning over Ricardo's seat. The man was nodding, then turned to look in their direction, so they both looked down.

"Did he see your badges or anything that identified you as agents?"

"No, but he and the other guy were checking us out pretty closely, so they may have guessed we were cops."

Just before the jet took off, Captain Moreno pulled out his cell phone and made a call to the office of the State Police in Loreto. He asked them to send two plainclothes officers to follow Ricardo, who would be hard to miss when they landed. He wondered if he should just arrest Ricardo when they landed, but decided against it. The three agent's guns had been checked onto luggage, per protocol.

Ricardo could probably slip away while they were waiting for their baggage.

Moreno talked in a low voice to Agent Black. "This is good news. They haven't found the young victims yet, so we are in time. We need to find them first and get them to safety. I have state police officers meeting us at the airport and bringing us a car. I'll have them follow Ricardo while we go to the State Police office to see if we can arrange for more backup."

Gerardo led the way up the steep trail on his palomino horse, followed by Grandma Arce on a mule, then Dani on her mule, with TommyLynn on a beautiful chestnut mare, bringing up the rear. They were loaded down with enough supplies to stay in the mountains for several days, if necessary. Dani's arm ached in its cast and her head was pounding, but she was game, climbing the mountain trail and looking out over the rancho and arroyo several hundred feet below.

They rode up the switchback trail for over an hour until they came to a small verdant arroyo with a few old trees, a worn wooden palapa (palm frond roof) and a burbling spring. Behind the hidden oasis, the mountain soared steep and rugged and the spring was flanked by a thirty foot tall, flat ridge with cardon and cholla cactus, that was a perfect look out. They unpacked their supplies and let the animals drink their fill. Gerardo lead Dani and TommyLynn up to the ridge while Grandma unpacked her kitchen and began to set up camp.

Up on the ridge, Gerardo showed them ancient manos and metates (flat grinding rocks and smaller rounded grinding stones) that were scattered around. TommyLynn thought of ancient Guayacura women sitting on this ridge, enjoying the view and grinding the seeds and flour for their meals. They looked over the trail and down to the arroyo at the bottom, all of which remained deserted and peaceful.

Gerardo was looking up the mountain when he gave a "pssst" to TommyLynn and pointed with his chin. TommyLynn followed his line of sight up the mountain to see a large puma climbing a steep cliff, and he grabbed Dani to point it out. They all watched as the magnificent cat stood very still and turned to look at them before bounding into an area of large boulders. TommyLynn smiled at his uncle. "That is a good sign, Tio. No?"

"I believe it is a very good sign mijo. Your animal spirit watches over you."

Juice didn't rush to the surface. He stopped at a depth of twenty feet, and when joined by Sam and Luis, he pointed to the large boat next to the Aventura. After hovering for a couple minutes, Juice pulled off his vest and oxygen tank, deflated the vest, took his last breath, and let the weight of the tank pull his vest to the bottom. Sam and Luis rose to the surface while Juice, with mask and snorkel, kicked for all he was worth to the Aventura. He rose to take a breath and listen.

Sam and Luis were greeted by two Latin men looking at them over the side of their sleek racing boat, pointing automatic weapons at them. They commanded the two divers in Spanish to come to their boat, and one of the men put down his gun and helped them aboard with their equipment. Sam pretended not to understand Spanish, so Luis took the lead, asking the men what they were doing, and saying he was a government official. One of the men took Luis into the boat's cabin at gunpoint while the other one kept his gun pointed at Sam who was dripping wet and stunned by what was happening.

Juice heard the men command the divers to come to their boat, and when he peeked around the Aventura's stern, he saw the end of an automatic pistol pointed at his friends. Shit, this is not good. His mind was racing over possible scenarios.

Maybe if I can board without them seeing me and get to my radio, I could call for help. He managed to pull himself up and over the side using the pilot cabin for cover and peeked across at the other boat, where he saw Sam looking at him, a gunman hovering over him.

Sam had been subtly looking for Juice and happened to be facing the Aventura. He saw Juice climb onto the boat, and just as the gunman started to look that way, he stood up and diverted the guard's attention by asking for some water, in English. The gunman pushed Sam in the chest so he fell back into a sitting position, and he put his hands up to signal, take-it-easy. "I'm just thirsty."

Juice had a problem. He couldn't get back into the cabin without being out in the open. Maybe I can create a diversion. Just then, he heard Sam tell the man he was thirsty, and saw that Sam was already causing a diversion, so he jumped up from his hiding place and rolled onto the deck and into his cabin. He grabbed his radio, only to find that it had been pulled apart and disabled. Shit! I'm unarmed. We're screwed.

Luis appeared from the racing boat's cabin and was

pushed into Sam by one of the gunmen. Then the gunman who seemed to be in charge put his gun to Sam's head and, in English, said, "Where is your friend? I know there were three of you diving." Sam said, "I don't know what you're talking about." The guy punched Sam in the stomach and told his partner to search under their boat and aboard the Aventura. He yelled, "If you don't give yourself up, your friends will pay."

Juice stepped out from the Aventura's cabin and was ordered to the other boat to sit with his companions. He looked at Sam and they exchanged knowing looks, like they could still, after all these years, know what each other was thinking. They both turned to Luis, who shrugged, still pretending he was on their side. Sam thought, With a friend like this, who needs enemies?

The Mexicana jet flew over Carmen Island and looped toward the runway at the Loreto Airport. The agents were awed by the natural beauty of the island and surrounding water. They saw the runway and small Palapa building that served as a reception point, baggage claim, and boarding facility.

Quaint little airport right on the beach of the Gulf of California, Agent Black thought as she turned to Capitan Moreno and asked, "What's our play with these guys?"

"I have plainclothes officers waiting in the airport. They have orders to follow Ricardo wherever he goes and to report to me when he stops somewhere. We will go to the State Police headquarters, they are armed professionals, the local police are amateurs, to warn them about Ricardo and put together a posse to get to the Arce ranch before they do. Arce is a very common name here, and there are many ranches with Arces, but I was able to get the names of the brother and sister who run the rancho we want. They are members of an ejido (clan-based land owner co-operative), so I was able to look them up. TommyLynn's mother is still listed as a member also."

The jet landed, and Ricardo and his accomplice made sure they were the first ones off. They hurried into the Palapa, apparently had no luggage, got the green light at customs, and emerged out in the waiting area before the agents were at the bottom of the jet's staircase. They were escorted to a black Hummer right outside the front door by one of his men, who had been in Loreto the past two days. His partner was driving their sedan, parked behind the Hummer. The State Police officer, whose partner was in their unmarked SUV in the parking lot, saw them and immediately exited the building and jumped into their car.

The three agents had to wait for their luggage and weapons, and were picked up by another federal officer in a black and white Federal Police car about ten minutes after Ricardo had left. They quickly drove to the State Police office and met with the lead officer, who offered to take them to the arroyo where the Arce Ranch could be found. While there, the State police called Moreno and told him that Ricardo was in a black Hummer and had stopped at the Rodeo Bar to talk to the owner. He explained that the

Rodeo Bar was a strip club and house of prostitution at the edge of town.

Ricardo spoke to the manager of the Rodeo, who worked for El Jefe and was expecting them, but she was still stunned to see so many of El Jefe's people from Tijuana. This looks like big trouble. She was a local who knew most of the families, and had gotten the information they asked for about the location of Gerardo Arce's ranch. The two men who had been in Loreto for a couple of days had found someone who saw Gerardo pick up the young fugitives. The strip club manager told them to take Highway One north and turn left at the thirty-three kilometer marker, and explained that the Arces were the last ranch at the end of the arroyo.

The State Police were in the lead in a black and white SUV, with the Federal police car and three agents following. They were racing at top speed to the military checkpoint on Highway One at kilometer twenty-eight. Ricardo had his traveling companion in the Hummer, followed by his other two men in the sedan, and they were only minutes behind the police cars.

When the police cars arrived at the military checkpoint, they parked across both lanes of the checkpoint and asked to speak to the commanding officer of the platoon of about a dozen soldiers, armed with dated AK-47s. They asked the commander if a black Hummer had passed, going north. Then they told the Commander what was happening, and that the men in the Hummer were probably well armed. The commander quickly told the two or three waiting cars to drive through, and deployed his men behind military vehicles and inside buildings. The state police and federal agents, U.S. and Mexican, had guns drawn behind their vehicles.

Ricardo and his team were at kilometer marker twenty-five, and his two men, who had driven down to Loreto from the north, had brought weapons and told him about the military check-point they had to go through to get to the arroyo.

Ricardo knew the police were close, but probably behind them. He had told his men to approach slowly, but if the soldiers asked to search the car, they would try to blow through the checkpoint before the soldiers could get a shot off. He placed a call on his satellite phone to Santa Rosalia, about a hundred miles north, where El Jefe had stationed a helicopter, and gave them his position and directions to the arroyo.

When the Hummer turned the corner on the Highway and Ricardo saw the checkpoint a couple hundred yards away, barricaded by police cars, he didn't think twice, and ordered his driver to find a gap and drive through as fast as they could. He knew the Hummer was bullet-proofed and that his men in the sedan probably wouldn't make it, but he had told him to follow close behind the Hummer no matter what he encountered.

The police and military force were ready. They watched the Hummer approach, then accelerate about a hundred yards away, and at fifty yards, the commander gave the order to fire. A fusillade hit the Hummer, but the bullets just pinged off as it rocketed toward the barricade and changed lanes, aiming for a small gap between the smaller Federal Police car and the side of a hill.

The sedan behind did not fare so well, as a hail of bullets tore through the windows and sides and killed the driver and passenger, whose car rolled through a hay bale barricade under a palapa, knocking out a post so the palm frond roof fell on top of it.

The FBI agents and Captain Moreno saw the Hummer bearing down on them as they fired at the windshield, to no effect. They jumped aside to the cover of the police SUV as the Hummer clipped their car, spinning it around. Then the Hummer's left tires climbed the slanted hillside to pass by the checkpoint and career back onto the highway. It sped the last four kilometers to the arroyo and turned off before the police and military vehicles could catch up.

The Hummer bounced and flew through the arroyo in fifteen minutes, and Ricardo saw the rancho at the end of the dead-end canyon. He ordered his man to search the rancho and find the two young gringos. "I'll take the Hummer and block the road at that narrow point between the trees." He pointed to the nearby gateway of the rancho. "We have a helicopter coming in about twenty minutes. If the police and soldiers follow us, we'll see them coming and I'll hold them off here. Hurry! Find those putas!"

His man returned, after searching for ten minutes, to

report that he found signs that the two gringos had been here until very recently, but it looked like a party of three or four people had ridden horses or mules from the back of the main structure up a steep mule trail into the mountains, probably in the last hour or two.

"Shit!" yelled Ricardo, who had a murderous look in his eyes. The man cowered. "Did you see a place up there where a helicopter could land?"

"Si, Si! (yes, yes) hay una lugar circa las chivas atras la casita (There is a place near the goat pen behind the house)."

Ricardo was thinking hard. The fucking helicopter better get here soon. El Jefe will probably have me killed anyway, even if I can get out of here. I'm fucked either way. He told the man, "Stay in the Hummer and hold off the police, if they come. You'll be safe in here while I signal the helicopter where to land. When it lands, leave the Hummer to slow them down and run up to the house. We'll fly out of here." The man lowered the two side windows and readied his automatic weapon.

Ricardo jogged up to the house on the rise and found the area to signal the helicopter to land. This looks pretty protected from below, where the Hummer blocked the road. Where the fuck is the copter? Then he saw the cloud of dust rising back at the entrance to the arroyo, and his heart skipped a beat. "Shit! Shit!" he yelled out loud, watching the rising dust cloud get closer and closer until he could see a large armored military vehicle roaring up the arroyo at the head of a convoy of vehicles, with red lights flashing, only a few miles away.

He was on his satellite phone with GPS, trying to reach the helicopter pilot, and just when the pilot answered, he saw the copter buzz over the convoy and head towards his location. He told the pilot to land behind the house on the ridge, and when the chopper got close, he waved his arms frantically. The helicopter slowed and began its descent as the goats scattered, bleating in panic, amid swirling dust.

The man in the Hummer watched as the long convoy of military and police vehicles charged forward, ever closer. Then he saw the helicopter swoop in and breathed a sigh of relief as it hovered over the rancho and began to land. He thought. I should go to the helicopter, but Ricardo said to hold off the police. He'll be pissed off if I run now! He fired on the convoy, but it was over a quarter mile away, badly out of range. After emptying his gun to no effect, he jumped out the other side of the Hummer and ran towards the helicopter, which was uphill and a hundred yards away.

Far up the steep incline above the rancho, Tommy-Lynn, Dani, and Gerardo, with his ancient twenty-two Ruger rifle on his shoulder, kept watch on the arroyo below as the drama unfolded. They had first seen the Hummer fly up the dirt road like it was in the Baja 1,000 Race. They had let all the animals free, but still feared that these gangsters might shoot animals and burn the rancho when they found no-one there. TommyLynn looked at his grand uncle and said, "I'm so sorry, Tio!"

About fifteen minutes later, the convoy of military trucks and jeeps, followed by police vehicles, charged up the arroyo, and they felt some relief that help was on the way. They were surprised to see a helicopter enter the fray, coming in over the military convoy, and assumed it was on their side, but then watched as it hovered over the rancho and began to land. Dani said, "Oh no! It looks like they're going to get away."

Ricardo had run into the structure for cover when the helicopter set down nearby. Now he bent low under the blades as he ran to the copter and climbed in on the passenger side. He yelled to the pilot, "You got here just in time." But the pilot had on headphones and couldn't hear him. He looked out to see his man running up the hill only fifty yards away and the convoy not far from where the Hummer blocked the entrance to the rancho. He grabbed the pilot's arm and yelled, "Go! Go!" pointing his thumb upward.

The pilot was at first confused, assuming they were waiting for his other man, but he saw Ricardo's face and deftly moved his foot pedal to make the copter rise slowly. They were hemmed in on three sides, and the pilot wanted to keep as much space between them and the armed military vehicles as possible, so they quickly rose hugging the side of the steep mountain.

Just as his man made it to the structure and the helicopter began to rise, the massive armored troop carrier leading the convoy slammed into the side of the Hummer and kept pushing forward, knocking the heavy vehicle on its side over and over again, clearing an entryway for the rest of the vehicles.

Next inside the compound was a "Rat Patrol" jeep with a large machine gun mounted on the back and manned by a helmeted soldier in desert camouflage. The jeep pulled its front tires up the small hill to give the gunner a higher trajectory, and the machine-gun fired up at the rising helicopter.

The two young friends watched all the action from their vantage point high above as the helicopter rose toward them. "Get down, Get down!" yelled Gerado as he sat down, balanced his rifle on his knee, snatched a bullet from his breast pocket, and slid back the bolt to load his weapon. They heard the crash of the collision below as they dove for cover, TommyLynn on top of Dani behind a large cardon cactus. Then they heard the machine gun firing as the chopper rose closer and closer to their position.

Small tufts of smoke followed in a line up the mountain as the machine gun rounds chased the helicopter, but only slammed into the rocks. The gunner in the jeep slid down until his butt was touching the floor. He yanked the gun up as high as it would go and fired one last volley. The last couple of rounds found their mark, and a small plume of smoke started to emanate from the tail of the chopper just as it came up to the level of the Arce's oasis.

The chopper began to slow its climb and now hovered only a couple hundred feet away, Gerardo watched the pilot working the instruments as the engine sputtered. He aimed his trusty Ruger rifle like he was shooting a wild dog trying to eat his goats, let out a breath, and pulled the trigger. The copter hovered in place and the pilot somehow stopped the flow of smoke right before the twenty-two round sped through his open side window and tore into his neck.

Ricardo saw the smoke, felt the engine sputter, and yelled at the pilot to do something. He watched the pilot struggle with the controls as the chopper stopped climbing. Looking out the pilot's side window, he saw an old vaquero (cowboy rancher) sitting on the mountainside, aiming a rifle at them. The pilot suddenly slumped forward as the engine stopped sputtering.

The chopper veered downward and everyone below at the rancho and on the mountainside watched it slowly arc back across the arroyo over the rancho, where the soldiers opened fire again until it crashed and exploded against a vertical cliff on the north side. Fire and heavy metal rolled down the slope while blue and black smoke rose into the crystal blue sky, defiling the peace and beauty of the arroyo.

A cheer rose up the mountain from down below as TommyLynn, Dani, and Gerardo got to their feet and looked over the edge at the amazing scene of scattered goats and soldiers, military trucks and jeeps, police cars, lights flashing, and the Hummer on its side. TommyLynn exclaimed, "It looked like you got him too. Great shot!" Gerardo turned to them, smiled and shrugged.

When they climbed down to the oasis to see if Grandma Arce was okay, she turned, smiled, and said in Spanish, "Ready for lunch, yet?" They all laughed, and TommyLynn asked in a loud voice, "Didn't you hear all the shooting and crashing Grandma?" She laughed, thinking he was joking. "I might have heard some firecrackers or gunshots."

Gerardo said to the young couple, "I know she isn't hearing so good anymore, but we better have her checked out." They ate quickly while Gerardo saddled the mules and horses. TommyLynn looked at his uncle with admiration. "Shit, Tio, your old rifle took out a helicopter. You're a hero!"

Gerardo smiled again, "They got what they deserved, attacking puma mountain like that. We must ride down to help with the fire."

They rode down the steep switchbacks, anxious to get back to the ranch and check on the animals. TommyLynn and Dani discovered they had to lean back in the saddle and put more of their weight on the stirrups. Dani's thighs and calves still ached from her climb down the chute, so she grimaced with every step of the mule, her good arm braced on the horn of the saddle. But she hoped fervently, maybe this nightmare is almost over. God I hope so!

When the riders came to the last long downhill stretch, they saw a fire truck putting out the flames on a copse of trees near the bottom of the north side of the arroyo. More Federal Police had arrived, placed the one prisoner in custody, and were driving away with him, in the back of a police car. Most of the soldiers had returned to the checkpoint, but the large lead truck that had knocked the Hummer out of the way was too damaged to move. A tow truck was already working on it.

Captain Moreno was directing his Federales from the rancho's house and saw the four riders come down the hill in back. He called for the two FBI agents, who walked back to meet the riders. They recognized Dani and TommyLynn from photos and smiled up at them as they approached. Agent Black said, "Dani Blue and TommyLynn Watson-Arce, I presume?"

The two young riders looked at each other and nodded. "I'm FBI agent June Black and this is agent Juan Morales, from the San Diego FBI office. We've been looking for you, and are glad to see you're safe." TommyLynn then introduced his uncle and grandma.

The agents addressed Dani, "I know you've been through a lot, but we'll need to place you both into protective custody as potential witnesses in order to prosecute the people who held you. As you know they are very dangerous"

Sam and Juice were now on Carmen Island, at the spot where they thought the lava tube ended. The gunmen had threatened to hurt them if they didn't tell them where the tunnel with the silver was located. Luis was still pretending he wasn't in cahoots with them, but it was clear to Sam and Juice that when he met with the lead gunman inside the boat's cabin, he had given them his GPS coordinates and told them there was no way to get the silver from underwater, and there must be a place on the island where the lava tube ended.

The two friends had decided to just show them where the tube surfaced. There was no way they were going to get down to where the crate was without some heavy duty equipment, anyway. They were allowed to change out of their wetsuits into t-shirts and shorts. One of the gunmen stayed with the boat while the other ferried Sam, Juice, and Luis to the island, with pry bars, shovels, tarps and ropes, in a dinghy. It became obvious that Sam, Juice, and Luis were now going to be put to work digging into the tube.

Luis tried to kid with them like they were good buddies, but his entreaties brought him only hard stares and fake smiles. "This treasure thing has gone downhill fast," Juice whispered to Sam as they stepped foot on the island, "from glamorous treasure finders to slave laborers." The armed guard told them to shut up, in Spanish.

They were given some food and water to bring with them, but the day was hot and the sun searing. They began removing rocks the size of melons at the top of the tube, and this went pretty well, but as midday approached, it got hotter, the rocks got larger, and the hole grew deeper. They had cleared about five feet of rocks, and it was clear that this was the tube.

Now one of them had to be lowered down by rope to load a large heavy rock onto a kind of sling they made with the tarp and rope, and two of them would pull one or two rocks out of the hole.

The tide had been low but now was rising, and by early afternoon, there was a foot of water at the bottom of their hole, getting deeper by the hour. Luis was younger, maybe late thirties, but Sam and Juice were both pushing fifty, and were not used to this kind of hard labor, so progress had slowed. At one point, when Luis was down in the pit, trying to roll a rock onto the sling, Juice whispered to Sam, "I have an idea. I'm going to tell the guard I have to crap over there." He pointed to an indentation in the cliff about fifteen feet away, on the other side of the large mound of rocks they'd removed from the tube. The steep walls of the cliff made it a dead end.

"If he comes to watch me, I need you to create a diversion. If he stays sitting, I'll divert him, and if I think its safe, I'll take his weapon." Luis looked up and saw them talking. "What's up, amigos?" The guard looked up from his sandwich and pointed his gun at them. "I just need to take a crap. I'll be right back," Juice said to the guard, and pointed to where he was going.

The gunman had managed to find some partial shade, now that the sun had moved, so he felt put out by Juice's request. He sighed and motioned with his weapon for Juice to go, and he got up to follow him. Luis was having trouble with a large rock, so Sam pointed to a smaller one and said to Luis. "If you can do that one, I think I can lift it out." Luis moved the smaller rock onto the sling and Sam began to pull.

Juice didn't really have to go, but was grunting and sighing behind a bush. The guard positioned himself with his back against the cliff, where he could see Juice on his left and the tube on his right. Sam was exaggerating his strain trying to lift the rock, but had almost gotten it to the edge of the hole when he let the rope slip through his left hand and yelled, "Watch out!"

Luis had squatted down and was trying to sit and rest at the bottom when the rock dropped six feet and glanced off his shin as he moved his foot out of the way. He screamed, "Chingada! What the fuck are you doing! My leg! Get me out of here!"

The guard rushed over and pushed Sam out of the way to look into the tube. Juice had started moving, catlike, when Sam yelled. He was right on the gunmen's heels with a rock the size of an apple in his hand, deftly watching where he stepped, to make as little noise as possible. The guard heard Juice coming and started to turn just as Juice launched himself, swinging the rock towards the guard's head.

They heard a sickening thud and the guard teetered on the edge. Sam reached over and grabbed the barrel of the automatic pistol as the guard collapsed into the hole on top of Luis. He almost pulled Sam down with him, but Juice grabbed his friend by the belt and pulled him back from the edge. By some miracle, the gun hadn't fired, and Sam handed it to Juice, who immediately pointed it into the tube to stop Luis from screaming, but Luis appeared to be out cold. The guard unconscious on top of him.

FBI agents Black and Morales were talking to Captain Moreno about arranging for a safe house for their potential witnesses until they could be transported back to California. TommyLynn and Dani were in the middle of a tear-streaked goodbye with Gerardo and Grandma Arce. They had collected their few things, thanked them for everything, expressed the sorrow they felt for bringing this evil upon them, and promised to return as soon as possible for a more relaxed visit.

Captain Moreno advised the elderly brother and sister to go away and stay with family somewhere safe, but they had their animals and the ranch to take care of, and said they needed to stay.

Agent Morales said to Agent Black, "I totally forgot we were supposed to meet with Sam White at noon. Have you gotten a call from him?"

"No, I'll call him as soon as we get out of this arroyo and get cell service."

The two agents were soon in a Federal Police SUV being driven by Captain Moreno with TommyLynn and Dani on their way to a safe house in Nopolo, about eight kilometers south of Loreto, where there was a Federal Police station. "Sam White isn't answering his phone.," TommyLynn heard Agent Black tell her partner. TommyLynn said, "Sam told us you'd be coming today, you made it just in time. We were warned this morning by a friend of the family that the gangsters were coming for us. That's why we were up the mountain."

Agent Black responded, "We were lucky because a couple of the bad guys who went to the rancho looking for you were on our plane this morning. Captain Moreno here recognized one of them and we had to race them to find you. You were lucky you left the rancho when you did."

TommyLynn, Dani and the two FBI agents settled into the comfortable accommodations at the Nopolo safe house. Captain Moreno had arranged for a small plane to take them back to Tijuana the next morning. They were afraid to take a commercial jet that the cartel could infiltrate and try to threaten or kill their witnesses. The agents had tried to call Sam several times, and mentioned his role to Captain Moreno.

Captain Moreno had also gotten a call from Chucho Rodrigues, President of the local college, who was concerned about Juice and Sam. They hadn't returned by noon, as planned after their dive with Luis,. He told the captain about the Spanish silver they had found, and that he'd contacted INAH, but had been warned about Luis. The captain ran a check on Luis with the cartel task force and found that he was suspected of having ties with the Sinaloa cartel. He then contacted the small naval station near the Loreto marina and asked them to check on the Aventura, which should be on the backside of Carmen Island.

It was late afternoon, and the sun had dipped below one of the saddleback peaks of Carmen Island. Juice and Sam were hot, sweaty, and exhausted from their hard labor and the lack of any breeze to cool them off. After Juice's plan had worked, they had two of their three captors in the pit, unconscious for now.

Juice had immediately checked to see if the other gunman on the boat had seen what happened, but he didn't hear anything or see the other man on deck. "We were lucky. The other guy doesn't seem to know what's happened. Since we're armed, it's kind of a stand-off, but I'm worried he might do something to my boat, or he could call for reinforcements." Sam nodded. "What do you want to do, Lieutenant Fierro?"

"Let's finish the guard's water and food first and rest a few minutes, though I'm worried Luis might wake up and start screaming. We should probably tie them up and gag them, and I should check to see if the guy's still alive. I tried not to hit him hard enough to kill him, but I had to hurry, at the end. I don't think its smart to swim or take the dinghy to my boat, but after we deal with them, we should move the dinghy somewhere so he can't shoot it. We might need it. We'd better hurry. He might call over here at any time."

Juice lowered himself down the rope into the pit. He gagged and tied Luis first and found a knife in his pocket. He then checked the guard and found he was breathing, though his head wound was still slowly bleeding. He bound him, and Sam gave him a hand out of the pit. They sat behind the pile of rocks they'd made so they couldn't be seen from the boat, ate and drank the rest of the food and water, and felt much better.

Before they could move the dinghy, the other gunman yelled over to the island from the boat. They looked at each other, not understanding what he said. Juice whispered, "Let's keep him wondering. He might bring the boat over to check things out, and I could get a shot at him." Sam nodded while the gunman got a hand-held megaphone and said, in Spanish, "What's happening, Ramon? There is a big boat coming."

"Did you get that?" Juice asked Sam.

"Yeah, there's a boat coming. Is that what you heard?"

"Yeah!" Juice peaked around the rock pile and saw the large, heavy-metal, dark gray boat he recognized as the local naval vessel. "Its the Navy, and they're coming close by here." He saw the gunman quickly pulling up his anchor and then heard him blasting again in Spanish, with his megaphone, "Ramon! It's the Navy! If you don't answer, I'm leaving, but I'll come back for you."

Juice balanced his weapon on top of the rocks and told Sam, "Get down and cover your ears!"

Juice heard the big inboard engine of the boat turn over and he pulled the trigger, emptying the magazine of the automatic pistol. His intention wasn't to hit the guy. He just wanted to make sure the naval vessel was alerted to their presence on the island, but he did hit the boat with a few of the rounds. The gunman bent low behind the wheel and sped off into open waters at high speed.

The Navy captain was more focused on the shooting coming from the island, and pulled the boat up to within a couple of hundred yards of where he had seen and heard the fusillade, not far from the Aventura. He ordered his men to combat positions. His voice blasted from his built-in amplifier in Spanish. "Drop your weapon and step out in the open, or we will fire."

Juice threw the automatic pistol to the edge of the island and stood up with his hands high in the air. Sam followed in kind, and they waited while the Navy launched a large dingy from the boat, with four armed sailors. Juice yelled that there were two men injured who could use medical attention.

The sun dipped below the Sierra Gigante mountains to the west, creating an amazing light show of rainbow colors that was typical of Loreto sunsets. Juice was under armed guard, piloting the Aventura to the marina, followed by the Navy gunboat which held Sam, Luis, and the gunman, also under guard. The captain didn't know who to believe, as Luis regained consciousness and demanded to be released as a government official.

The Naval captain had radioed ahead to Presidente Rodrigues and to the Federal Police, so they were met by Chucho and Captain Moreno, who vouched for Juice and Sam after hearing the captain's report of what happened. Luis limped badly, but refused medical care and was released, as it was hard to prove he was involved. He immediately demanded that they give him the silver ingot, as historic artifacts were his jurisdiction, but they refused to turn it over, agreeing that Chucho would retain possession of it, for now.

President Rodrigues finally reached his friend Pancho Navarro in Mexico City, who was a high-ranking INAH official, and he reported what had happened with Luis. His friend Pancho was livid, and said he would bring a team to Loreto within the next few days to take over the search for Spanish silver, and the Navy was asked to guard the site until the INAH team arrived.

After pulling the Aventura out of the marina on its trailer and parking it at Juice's compound, Sam and Juice took quick showers and dressed. They were beat, but Captain Moreno took them to Nopolo to see TommyLynn and Dani. They were soon sitting around a large table eating "Pedro's" Pizza" with TommyLynn, Dani, FBI agents Black and Morales, and Captain Moreno, listening to the story of the battle of Rancho Arce. Juice and Sam just shook their heads at the incredible tale.

Sam said, "You guys have had quite the adventure. I hope this means you have a safe place to live for awhile?" Agents Black and Morales explained that, starting tomorrow, they'd be in a safe house somewhere in California, in protective custody for the foreseeable future.

"Sheila will be sorry she missed you, TommyLynn. She comes back from her mule trip tomorrow."

"Oh yeah, she was going to see some, like, ten thousand year old cave paintings, right? Please thank her again, for me!." TommyLynn said to Sam. "You guys didn't know me that well, and you took a chance on me, bringing me to Tijuana in time to find Dani."

Sam and Juice then told their story of finding the silver and being forced into slave labor at gunpoint most of the day. It was the agents' turn to shake their heads in wonder. "Juice is a retired marine lieutenant and special forces badass," Sam explained. "He disarmed the guy guarding us, and then the Navy showed up, thanks to Captain Moreno here and Juice's friend Chucho Rodrigues who is the president of the local college."

There were questions about the possible treasure, how much silver there might be, and who could have possibly buried it in the sixteenth century. Captain Moreno, who'd been a history major at the university in La Paz, said, "There were a number of Spanish explorers who came to Baja, starting in the 1530's with Fortun Ximenez, who led a group of mutineers to La Paz after escaping a Cortez-organized expedition. Cortez himself came soon afterward, and there were others. Though, since your silver bars are marked, the Spanish may be able to trace them back to a certain ship and captain."

Sam and Juice could barely stay awake, so began their goodbyes. Sam hugged TommyLynn and Dani. "You better stay in touch. It sounds like we won't be able to reach you for awhile. So sorry all this craziness and pain has happened to you, Dani. Both of you have proved your courage and resilience, and should be proud of overcoming some serious evil forces. Take care of each other!"

CHAPTER SEVEN

TONS OF SILVER LINING

Saturday, October 15, 2005

Sheila and Bella had driven back to Loreto with Trudy early in the morning, and met Sam and Juice for a late breakfast at Cafe Ole. It was another warm, clear, blue-sky day, and it also happened to be Sam and Sheila's sixteenth anniversary. She and Bella brought out their cameras, excited to show the men their amazing photos of the cave paintings and mule ride.

The two old friends marveled at the photos and adventures the women described, and held off on their own stories until Bella asked, "What have you guys been up to? You are way too sunburned. Did you get drunk and fall asleep on the boat all day, or what?" Sam and Juice laughed and launched into their diving adventures.

Sheila, speaking for them both, said, "You guys expect us to believe another treasure story? Good try, but we're not that gullible." Juice and Sam had expected this reaction. Juice reached into his daypack, pulled out the silver bar, and passed it across the table. The women were blown away, holding it and feeling its heft. Sam then offered them his copy of the morning paper, which had a front page photo of the helicopter burning at the bottom of the arroyo cliff at the Arce Ranch. He explained what had happened with TommyLynn and Dani while he and Juice were being forced to work at gunpoint on Carmen Island.

"I feel exhausted just hearing your story. You two are lucky to be alive," Bella said, her voice choking and tears welling. They were soon all teared up and wiping their eyes, a bit embarrassed by their public display of grief and relief. Sheila shook her head looking at Sam. "You and your treasures are a pain in the ass!" They all went from crying to laughing, and were sure the breakfast crowd at Cafe Ole thought they were lunatics.

TommyLynn, Dani, Captain Moreno, and the two FBI agents were flying over the Baja peninsula in an old Cessna 441 Conquest II (Cessna's first turboprop), that was piloted by a Federal officer. The young couple had never flown before, and felt like VIPs sitting at their window seats. They took turns pointing to dazzling undeveloped bays on the Gulf of California, then small lakes, like jewels, across the mountainous spine of the Baja Peninsula. The agents smiled at their wonder and went over the plans to get them across the border.

They landed safely in Tijuana, then Dani, TommyLynn, and the two agents were whisked away in a black unmarked Land Rover. Captain Moreno took the lead in a Policia Federales black and white, with its red lights strobing, as they drove directly to the border, crossing at Otay Mesa. They used the emergency vehicle lane and crossed the border in record time. Agents Black and Morales went over the contracts they would have to sign to enter witness protection.

They would agree to testify against El Jefe, particularly Dani, who had seen him and been forced into a sexual act with him. They would assume different identities and could live together or apart, and their activities would be very restricted. They, in turn, would receive paid housing and income, and twenty-four hour protection and assistance finding work or entering school. They agreed to try to live together, and were very excited by the prospect of beginning work on a degree.

Sam and Sheila had their anniversary dinner in the early evening at Picazon after kayaking the five miles from town. After a sip from his large and very tasty margarita, Sam asked Sheila, "Well, we have a full week left before we have to drive home. What else do you want to do?"

"Well, I know you guys want to be part of the treasure hunt when the INAH team gets here. How long do you think the digging will last?"

"I don't think the digging will take more than a couple of days, once they have some heavier equipment. But I don't want the treasure search to take all our time. I don't need to be there for everything."

"Okay, I still want to drive up to San Javier to see the other Mission and to hike a bit, but mostly I want to kayak camp on the back of Danzante Island, like we did the first time we came here. Its the thing I remembered most from earlier trips. So peaceful and beautiful." Sam nodded and held up his large margarita glass. "Happy anniversary, Sheila Bright!" "Happy anniversary, Sam White." They clinked glasses and kissed, while Alejandro and the table next to them applauded.

Juice and Bella came by to join them for a drink and to pick them and their kayaks up. After an anniversary toast, Juice told them, "It looks like the INAH team flies in tomorrow and hopes to get started on the dig the next day. They offered to rent my boat and services while they're here, and I agreed."

The four friends made plans to drive up to San Javier Mission the next morning. Sam told Sheila, "Tomorrow, I'll get a permit at the marina for our camping trip for three days from now."

Monday, October 17, 2005

THE morning sun was already hot, but there was a bit of a breeze, and pink cotton candy clouds hung in the clear blue sky. Juice had piloted the Aventura across the glassy water with Sam and the four members of the INAH team to the back of Carmen Island, and they were suiting up for a dive into the cave. Pancho Navarro, the team leader, was the same age as Sam and Juice, with movie star looks, longish curly black hair, and the physique of a much younger man. His team included three younger men in their late twenties to early thirties who looked like college wrestlers and turned the heads of women wherever they went.

Pancho wanted to dive into the tube with an underwater video camera to film the cave and the crate. Juice told him what to expect, including their sightings of the octopus and wolf eel. They were impressed that Sam and Juice had explored the tube without knowing what to expect. Juice, Sam, and Rogelio, from the team, would accompany Pancho on the dive.

The dive went smoothly, with perfect conditions. The guardian octopus was near the mouth of the cave, where Pancho got excellent footage of the beautiful creature changing its colors before it fluidly swam out the mouth of the cave. Pancho was an expert diver and videographer, and documented the underwater treasure (what little they could see) brilliantly.

When they were back on the deck of the Aventura, he excitedly showed his footage to the group and then reported, "There is clearly at least one case of silver bars, but I predict that there probably are more than one crate at the site, because someone went to a lot of trouble." This news was met with nodding and smiles, but they all knew there was much work to be done just to find out.

The party then paddled to the island in a rubber raft to look at the pit. They developed a plan to return the next day with a small crane, chains, and motorized pulleys they would rent from a business that dug water wells. Juice helped them put together a plan for other supplies like food and water, awnings, heavy-duty metal crates, folding chairs, and tables, they would bring back to this site the next day.

The INAH team, with Sam, Juice, and Chucho, had a meeting that night at the Palapa Restaurant, over dinner and margaritas. "I have contacted Spanish authorities regarding the silver," Pancho informed the team. "I have worked with them before on a number of Spanish ship-wreck extractions and other finds. My contacts there are fair, knowledgeable, and trustworthy.

"They may send someone to monitor our extraction, but probably only if there are more than one crate of bars. I also received word that the bar found by Señores Fiero y White has been received by our lab in Mexico City."

The team had not been to Loreto before, and marveled at its beauty. The word 'tranquilidad' (tranquility) kept popping up in the conversation. "Chucho explained that he and a group of prominent ecotour providers like Trudy, fishing excursion captains and local government officials, had been organizing to apply to the federal government for a National Marine Park designation for the waters and islands within the greater Loreto Bay and region. This would protect them from commercial fishing, which was, by most accounts, depleting the fishery, turtle and sea mammal populations.

"There seems to be a consensus that we need to do this,

and we have submitted our application and started a campaign to get the designation. I hope you might be able to help, since you live in the capitol city."

Pancho added, "Between the natural beauty of this place and its historical significance, the first California Missions, the beginning of the El Camino Real, and perhaps now this find, I think you have an excellent chance of receiving the National Park designation. When we get back to Mexico City, we will attempt to help."

TommyLynn and Dani were settling into their new home, which was a small but cute little gray house on a cul-de-sac in the Claremont hills of San Diego. They were meeting with their new tutor the next morning to begin studying for the GED, and a special dispensation was arranged by the feds so they could immediately attend San Diego Mesa Community College. They both missed the beauty and quiet of the Arce Ranch, but for the first time in a very long time, Dani felt safe and hopeful. She still had the cast on her arm, and she still had headaches and felt extremely tired, at times.

TommyLynn was on the phone with her parents, who had talked with their family and were assured that she and Dani were safe. They were shocked when they heard about her adventures and their move to Witness Protection. TommyLynn could not tell them anything but that they were safe and in California, but the Feds had agreed to set up a supervised visit with she and Dani and TommyLynn's parents at the Los Angeles FBI headquarters in the next week. They had already been given their new identities, after having chosen from a few possibilities.

Dani Blue was now Sally Wakefield and TommyLynn Watson-Arce was now Linda Cielo (Beautiful Sky) in Spanish. They were also starting their relationship anew in this cocoon of relative comfort and safety, away from the chaos and dangers of the streets and its predators. TommyLynn felt safe, again, to dress as a woman, and they very much enjoyed each other's company. They had separate rooms, and were close friends telling each other everything. They snuggled at times and kissed like brother and sister, the sibling they never had.

Dani wanted to take it slow, and didn't want to lose this precious friendship. TommyLynn was also happy with the friendship, and wanted to be there for Dani as she healed from her physical and emotional trauma. Dani still had violent dreams at night, and sometimes awoke with a cry or a scream. Dani also had mood swings from her trauma, and could be silent and withdrawn, at times; then judgmental and cross with TommyLynn, but he gave her space and understanding, trying not to take it personally.

Tuesday, October 18, 2005

SAM and Sheila had been gone for ten days, and with all the excitement, they hadn't thought much about the organizations they managed back in Sacramento, that usually took up much of their waking hours. They both called into their respective jobs the first thing in the morning, to talk to the managers they'd left in charge. Sheila talked to her long-time friend and assistant director of the Care For All Health Clinic.

"Sheila, is that you?" "Yeah, your long-lost Director, just checking in."

"Great to hear from you. I hope you are enjoying yourselves?"

"Its been a wonderful time, so far. I loved the week-long mule trip into the mountains, where we saw ten-thousand-year-old cave paintings and amazingly beautiful, rugged, isolated country. I took lots of photos, so we'll get together as soon as I'm back. Sam has had a little too much excitement, but that's a long story."

"Things are good here at the clinic. The board is concerned about the budget but what's new?" They talked awhile longer. Sheila thanked her for covering, and promised to check in again, in the next week.

Sam called The Village and spoke to Sister Julie. "Hi, Julie, everything okay back there?"

"Hi, Sam, good to hear your voice. I was getting a little worried, since we never actually talked. I hope you're enjoying yourself and are getting recharged."

"Thanks. I've had an amazing time with my old friend, and its good to have Sheila back, after her mule expedition. It's been more excitement than I bargained for, and I wanted to update you on the saga of TommyLynn and Dani."

He told her about what happened to them while in Loreto, and that they were back in California in protective custody. He left out the silver discovery. Julie replied, "Wow, I'm so happy they survived all the craziness. Poor Dani! She finally caught a break."

"So, how is everything at The Village?"

"The big news is that we are receiving the proceeds of a bequest from a man who recently passed away, and he left us a number of properties here in Sacramento and Washington State. We aren't sure of the value, but it might be several hundred thousand dollars."

"Wow, that's great news. That takes a little pressure off the usual budget anxieties."

Julie said, "By the way, it looks like the opening of the hospital-funded shelter is going to be the first day you're back, so I'm glad you"ll get to be there."

"Well, I wish it would have opened by now. Will you go with me?"

"Sure."

They talked a bit longer about a personnel issue, then said their goodbyes.

Juice and the treasure search team had spent the morning loading all their gear onto the navy ship, which had agreed to help the INAH effort with their larger boat. Juice and the team, along with Sheila, Sam, and Bella, were following the Navy vessel out to the site on Carmen Island. They set up their camp with awnings, tables, chairs, ice chests, and water stations, then had lunch.

After a fine lunch of frittata, ceviche, papaya, and limonada (lemonade), they assembled the crane the Navy men had transported. It was almost two in the afternoon when they finally started lifting rocks out of the pit.

Pancho had shown Sheila and Bella his video of the tube, and they looked at Sam and Juice, shaking their heads with expressions that said, "What were you thinking, diving into this cave? Are you two crazy?" Sam and Juice shrugged and started laughing as the women's heads shook again. Sheila said, "That octopus was even larger and more beautiful than we imagined. I'm glad you didn't have a return visit from the wolf eel."

Pancho's team was making quick progress, now, and the two couples had returned to the Aventura. Their work was done, and it was happy hour after all.

"This feels like vacation!" Sheila raised her tequila shot and the other three raised their beer. "Salud" (to your health), said Bella as they all took a sip and the two women waved at the two sentries they could see on the naval vessel.

Then there was a cry from Pancho, and a cheer went up from the men on the island. They listened for more, and Pancho yelled, "You'd better come see this, amigos. Bring some tequila with you, too."

They were back on the island in minutes, with a bottle of tequila and shot glasses for everyone. A couple of young men from the INAH team were down in the now twelve-foot pit with snorkels and masks, brushing sand from something flat that was underwater and definitely not another large rock. Pancho exclaimed, "We have already found the first crate, with another fifteen feet to the one at the bottom."

The men finally cleared all the rocks from around the crate, which was four feet under water at low tide. With a small pry bar, they pried off the wooden slats at the top of the crate. Then they pried up three of the heavy bars that were blackened from tarnish and put them in a sling that was lifted by the crane and winched up to the waiting party.

Pancho told them to measure the crate and come up out of the pit for a toast and a rest. They were all soon shooting tequila and whooping like kids. "I have to notify my boss and let the Spanish authorities know what we have found, so they can join us for the rest of the dig and start research on the probable ship they were unloaded from in the sixteenth century. We will need to upgrade to twenty-four hour security for the site, so I will ask the Navy if they can provide additional help."

They did the math on how many crates were likely to be in the pit. "Twelve to fifteen crates, at least," estimated Pancho. "Since each bar is about fifteen pounds, that means each crate is close to eight hundred pounds. We may have five tons or close to 5,000 kilograms of silver bars!" They all whooped again, and high fives went around the group. Another round of tequila was poured. "To the treasure of Carmen Island and the Red Monkey Rock!" Pancho yelled, and the shots went bottoms up.

After their celebration, Pancho, in a more sober tone, got everyone together. "We must keep this a secret! We don't know for sure how many crates are in the tube, and if word gets out before we bring them up, the silver will be at risk and we will be at risk. I think our INAH team should take turns camping out here with the naval guards, but we should downplay the discovery to the Navy and others. The press will swarm this place and interrupt our progress, too, if word gets out." Pancho radioed the local naval captain and was assured that the Navy would provide twenty-four hour security of the site as long as needed.

Juice added, "You know that Sam and I have already been kidnapped at gunpoint and had to fight our way free over this silver. We can't get complacent or underestimate what criminals will do for this kind of treasure. We may be in danger already, whether we're camping out here or in town, so I'll be asking the local and state police for protection in town, wherever we're staying."

The INAH team spent an hour photographing the scene and documenting the first crate to be salvaged. Pancho's team cleaned the tarnish off three of the bars to bring them for further study, and to send photos as proof of the find to the Spanish officials. The bars seemed to have similar markings as the first two they had found and cleaned.

They were bouncing over whitecaps on their way back to town on the Aventura. An afternoon wind made the ride choppy. Pancho yelled to Juice, over the noise of the engines, "You have found what appears to be a four-hundred-year-old treasure, my friend."

Juice smiled and yelled back, "I guess you could call me lucky, but we'll see if its good luck or bad. I've already had my life threatened, so probably it's mixed, at best."

Pancho nodded. "I assure you that you will be recognized for this find. The Spanish are good about paying finding fees - usually ten percent. If there are a dozen or more crates down there, you may be looking at a big payday." "I'll believe it when I see it, Pancho." Juice slowed the Aventura as they approached the marina.

━━━━━━━━━━━━━━━━━━

TRIXIE paced rapidly back and forth in the yard of the Sacramento County Women's Jail, trying to stay out of the way of the other forty to fifty women who were congregated in the yard. The inmates got forty-five minutes outside once a day, unless they were in lockdown. Trixie spent the time alone, moving around wherever she could to get some exercise.

A group of three latin women inmates walked into her path, and she was forced to veer out of her makeshift track close to another group of four latin women. One of these women kicked out at her back leg as she went by, and she stumbled. Another stocky woman who looked like a kick boxer whirled and landed a roundhouse punch to the back of her neck, which planted her face into the cement slab and knocked her out. Both groups of inmates surrounded her and viciously kicked or stomped her once or twice in every part of her body.

The orchestrated attack happened in seconds, and by the time one of the woman guards sounded her shrill whistle, the group of attackers had scattered. Ten women guards were soon on the scene, and began clearing the yard. Within a minute, another dozen guards had entered the yard with a medical worker, who tended to the bloody, broken, unconscious Trixie.

El Jefe was inside his heavily fortified compound on the top of the tallest hill in the exclusive Tijuana neighborhood where he lived. He had doubled his guard after learning that Ricardo had failed him and been killed. He had just finished dinner and was on a scrambled phone, talking to his uncle, a high ranking member of the Zeta cartel. Uncle was none too pleased with El Jefe's handling of things, given the Federales were breathing down his neck and might come for him at any moment.

"Let me get this straight. You traded for a white puta from California Norte, and another fucking puta helped her escape? Then you let them slip through your fingers, and they didn't even cross the border, but went further south into your territory, to Loreto? Then Ricardo was killed, and your man got arrested trying to get them? Now they are back in the US and in witness protection?"

"Yes. I am sorry, Uncle. Please get me out of here. I am afraid to leave my place, and my sources tell me the U.S. may try to extradite me. I have dealt with the woman who traded the girl to me, who was in jail, so they have only this huera (blonde girl) and her puta friend, but I need to get out of here quickly and disappear."

Juice, Bella, Sam, and Sheila had dined at Domingo's Restaurant with Pancho and his one team member who wasn't camping out on Carmen Island that night. Pancho told them he had requested police protection for himself and Juice, which meant there would be more frequent patrols coming by Juice and Bella's house and the Oasis hotel, where Pancho's team was staying.

Sam and Sheila had moved to the Damiana Inn and were exhausted after the long day, so they retired early and were soon fast asleep. Juice and Bella returned to their compound, which was surrounded by eight-foot walls with ornamental metal spikes on top. They had their various boats and expensive diving gear to protect.

Wednesday, October 19, 2005

JUICE was restless, despite their long day with beers and tequilas. The prospect of a serious treasure find and an eventual big payday had his mind whirling with possibilities. The bedside clock read one-thirty. Bella was fast asleep. Juice climbed out of bed to walk around outside to try to clear his head. He slipped into sandals and stepped out to their second floor patio, which looked out over the sea and a portion of Carmen Island.

He was greeted by a red-orange full moon that had risen far above the Island, then blazed an orange river of reflection parting the glassy black water and flowing straight into his eyes, subtly changing and ever-moving. He was on the north edge of town on Calle Davis, where there were few neighbors and no streetlights. A municipal police car drove slowly by their house and around the block.

Suddenly, he noticed a sliver of shadow on one side of the moon. *An eclipse, my god! I've been so busy, I didn't see or hear this was coming.* He watched the red shadow progress across the cratered orb. *It looks like a full lunar eclipse. It's been a while. I should wake Bella up.*

He loved the night sky here - how the sun and moon rose over the water and set behind the Sierra Gigante range. *This planet is so beautiful, maybe we should travel to our bucket list of amazing places while we can still dive and hike the adventures we've only dreamed about. South America, Australia, New Zealand, India, China... we could take a year off, once I get my finders fee.*

He saw a truck approach in a cloud of dust coming from town. It wasn't unusual to have young people drive by on their way to the beach where they could party late or park with their sweetheart. This truck was big and black, and slowed as it came to their place. He felt the hair on his neck rise, and had a bad feeling about this truck. He didn't see the police car anywhere.

Hmm, I better go to plan B. He kept a loaded pistol in his safe that was legally registered.

He quickly ducked inside the bedroom and woke Bella as he headed to his safe in the closet. His guard dog, Pepe, was at the gate barking as all four doors of the truck opened. Bella was groggy and whispered, "What's the matter?"

"We have visitors. Lay on the floor of the closet, here." He was entering his combination and had his Marine-issued 45 in his hand as Bella crawled into the closet and the bedroom window exploded at the same moment they heard the automatic fire.

Thank god for these cement block walls, he thought as he ducked under the windows on his way back out to the patio, which was ringed by a four-foot block wall. He checked that his gun was loaded as he heard more automatic fire, then he peeked over the wall. One gunman was firing on his gate, but his gate was heavy-duty metal, with two bars across the back, and was holding up, so far. Another gunman started strafing the upstairs again and shattered another couple of windows.

He rested his gun hand on the top of the wall and returned fire. One of the gunmen crumpled to the ground. The others fired wildly as they regrouped, taking cover behind the truck. He saw one of them light something on fire; a flaming bottle. He shot the thrower as he stood up to lob a molotov cocktail over the wall into his compound. Luckily, it just missed his boat, and flaming gas spread across the rock walkway to the front door.

Juice heard sirens, and from his upstairs patio, he could see police cars coming up Calle Davis from a half mile away. The gunmen jumped into the truck, leaving their partner on the ground, and sped off, but not before Juice shattered the side and back windows of the truck with his remaining shots.

He saw the truck heading north, flying over the dirt road as the two police cars braked in front of his compound, raising more dust.

He ran into the bedroom to find Bella, who was safe, still curled up in their closet, which had cement block walls on three sides. She asked if he was okay and he nodded, looking her over. "I'm okay, just shook up. Our poor house is shot up, though." Juice kissed her forehead as he helped her up. "I've got to get our fire extinguisher. Watch out for all the glass on the floor."

Juice ran downstairs, grabbed the fire extinguisher from the kitchen, threw open the front door, and was assaulted by heat and smoke. He pointed the extinguisher and the fire flashed out quickly as he coughed. He saw his dog was whining, but safe under a boat trailer, then opened his gate to tell the police that four men in a black truck had attacked his place and had just driven north on Davis. The police were standing over the man in the street, and one pronounced him dead with a hand cutting across his throat.

One of the cops called for backup and a fire engine while the other drove north to look for the truck. A fire engine arrived, but there wasn't anything left for them to do. A shooting was a big deal in Loreto, as there was very little serious crime and minimal cartel presence. Juice and Bella's place was crawling with state and local police and forensics for hours, and they got very little sleep. The truck had disappeared, but they had found more blood where the truck had been parked, so it looked like Juice had wounded another of the men.

El Jefe's wife and kids had been living at their Villa in La Jolla in San Diego. He had warned them to go into hiding. He had packed his most important papers and possessions into eight heavy-duty plastic boxes that were assembled on the roof of his sprawling four-story Tijuana compound. Painted on his flat roof was a large red circle, lighted for helicopters to land. He looked out over the brown hills east of Tijuana as a red sun rose into the hazy pink/gray sky.

He stood with his two armed guards, waiting impatiently for a helicopter to land and take him to his uncle's place in Monterey, Mexico, by way of Mexicali. The quiet early morning suddenly exploded with gunfire and what must have been hand grenades. His guards ran to the roof wall that overlooked the front of the compound and found a line of police vehicles on the private street below, which was obscured with smoke. The black and white cars and trucks, including two armored vans, had red and white lights flashing, but were silent.

El Jefe joined them at the wall. "How the fuck did they get through the bottom gates without an alarm sounding?" His compound wall was at least ten feet tall, so they couldn't see the many SWAT police gathered at his walls, waiting for the heavy metal gate into the compound to be blown with C-4 explosives. He'd had two guards in turrets above his front wall, who had used automatic weapons to fire on the two armored vans that were the first to arrive, but the turrets were now in flames.

We only have four more guards downstairs, now. Shit! Where is the helicopter?

"What are you waiting for? Why aren't you shooting?" he yelled at the two guards, who started firing at the vehicles in the street. Then a huge explosion blew the heavy metal gate back into the compound, smashing into his Mercedes SUV in the driveway.

Their ears were ringing as tear gas filled the air below, followed by helmeted police with gas masks, who swarmed into the compound. The two guards and El Jefe were knocked back by the force of the explosion but recovered and rained fire down on the attackers, but they couldn't aim at specific targets through the thick smoke, and were soon out of ammunition.

El Jefe heard a helicopter and looked east again. He stared hopefully for several very long seconds and saw it approaching. Finally, my rescue! He picked up two red flags and started waving them to signal the landing. No! Its two helicopters that I'm hearing.

He turned to see a black and white helicopter hovering over the police vehicles, looking down at their position on the roof. It was turned sideways so a sharpshooter could fire on the two guards. One guard went down immediately and the other jumped behind the boxes, which were the only cover.

El Jefe then looked back to see his rescue plans dashed as his uncle's helicopter turned a quick one-eighty and retreated. Smoke was everywhere, and plumes rose high into the morning air. He stood in shock, not even able to find cover as more automatic fire shredded the boxes and took out his other guard. He spread his arms as if to say Shoot me, please! But Captain Moreno was in the chopper looking through binoculars, directing his shooter to spare El Jefe. I've got you El Jefito (little chief). Who's laughing now?

Captain Ortega of the Sacramento Police's Major Crimes unit tried to call Sam mid-morning, but couldn't get through. Next, he called Sister Julie at The Village.

"Hi, Sister. Captain Ortega here."

"Hi, Captain. Good to hear from you, I hope."

"Yes, I call with good news. I assume you've heard that TommyLynn and Dani Blue are safe in protective custody?"

"Yes, Sam called yesterday to let me know. I'm so happy they came out alive and well."

"Well, the other news is that Trixie, the Madame of the sex workers who was involved with Dani's kidnapping, died last night at the jail's medical ward, from wounds she received from an attack by other inmates. It seems the Tijuana cartel has quite a long reach and is probably responsible. Trixie's girlfriend, who laundered all the money from the sex trade into real estate and other investments, is also now in protective custody and is turning state evidence."

"My goodness, the plot just keeps getting thicker," Julie replied.

"Lastly, I was just notified that the cartel boss in Tijuana who had held Dani and ran an international sex trade operation was captured earlier this morning by the Mexican Federal Police. The FBI is attempting to extradite him to the U.S. on charges of international sex trafficking, and with TommnyLynn, Dani, and now Trixie's partner testifying, it looks like they have a solid case. I wanted to thank you folks at The Village for your help, again. Please pass this on to Sam."

"I will, Captain, thank you for keeping us informed. Sam still has another week before he returns, but I'll talk to him soon. Take care." Sister Julie hung up and called Cat at the Teen Center to let her know the latest.

Juice and Bella went back to bed, exhausted, at about five that morning. "I was on my way to tell you about the lunar eclipse when the truck drove up, and then I forgot all about it." They slept fitfully until about ten o'clock. Juice got out of bed and woke up Bella. Bella rubbed her eyes and chuckled. "This was all a dream, right? We're going to find everything like it was before?" Then she saw the gaping bedroom windows and shards of glass they had missed earlier. "I guess not."

Juice came back from the bathroom and sat on the bed with her. "It doesn't look like its safe here." He stated the obvious. "The Federales have a safe house in Nopolo that I've been to. Its right by their local headquarters and is nice, but we'd still have to be in hiding indefinitely. Sorry about all this, honey! I just wanted to dive and spend time with my old friend, but the silver has turned into a shit storm!"

Bella teared up. "Its not your fault, Juice. I'm thinking I need to go see my family in North Carolina. I know you want to finish the treasure dig, so maybe in a week or so, when that's over, you could come join me. We can figure out what's next, then."

Juice teared up also as she spoke. "That sounds like a plan. If you pack up, I'll make a flight reservation for you tonight from La Paz to somewhere in the States, and I'll drive you to La Paz and watch you board the plane. I don't think its safe to wait for the flight from Loreto to LA on Saturday." Bella nodded and they embraced for a good while. "Please give Sam and Sheila hugs from me. They don't even know what's happened, but I'm sorry to not be able to say goodbye."

Sam and Sheila had been up at six that morning to finish packing for their kayak camping trip to Isla Danzante. They had already loaded their kayaks and gear in the Subaru the day before and had finished packing their food and water, which they hoped would get them through three days and two nights on the island. The water supply would be tight as they had to manage the weight in the kayaks. They were soon in the Forester, driving south on Highway One for over twenty kilometers, hoping the glassy surface of the sea would last for their crossing.

They parked on the beach at Ligui, which had been a

site of one of the early missions (now disappeared) and was straight across from the south end of Danzante Island. They were soon in their kayaks, which were loaded down and low in the water. They were headed around the south end of the island to Primitive Camp Number Four on the back end facing southeast with views of Carmen, Monserrat and Catalina Islands. They had camped here once before about five years earlier, and remembered it as one of their favorite kayak camping adventures.

It was only a couple of miles to the island, but the currents and swells could cause problems at a moments notice. They lucked out with flat water and only a slight crosscurrent slowing them down. They made the crossing to Danzante smoothly, and about a half hour later, they spotted their campsite. It was at the mouth of a steep canyon dotted with towering cardon cactus and amazing rock formations along the beach, including a natural arch nearby.

The next camp, a quarter mile away, was empty, and the only sign of civilization was an occasional panga or large yacht or sailing vessel in the distance. They set up camp with their tent and kitchen area in the partial shade of an overhanging cliff. The morning sun was intense on their camp, but around noon, they'd enjoy the shade. The only other discomfort were the many large, yellow, but slow island wasps which craved fresh water and liked to land on skin or kayaks.

They had learned a trick to divert many of the wasps,

which was to leave an open jar of fresh water at the edge of their camp, but otherwise you had to relax and be calm when they landed on you. Their little beach was partially protected from the north wind that often came up in the afternoon, and they snorkeled during the day to cool off. They had no idea that Juice and Bella had been attacked, and they thoroughly enjoyed the peaceful, natural beauty of the island.

Juice was pretty wiped out from his long day of recovering from the attack and driving Bella to La Paz. The taking of a human life always weighed on him, but he'd had to put that aside, for now. He and Bella both teared up as she boarded an Aeromexico flight to Las Vegas. He had then driven back to Loreto, about a three to four hour trip each way. He had put a carpenter friend of his to work on their house before he'd left, boarding up windows, cleaning up, and adding security. A police car was parked outside his compound when he got home, so he decided to sleep at home that night with his pistol.

Thursday, October 20, 2005

Two Spanish government authorities had flown into Loreto the day before, and joined the INAH team in organizing more equipment for the treasure dig. They had begun research on the recovered silver bars and had narrowed the probable dates and origins of the bars to a period of time between the years 1570 and 1580. They hoped to be able to pinpoint the actual Spanish galleon that the silver had arrived upon, and were excited to get to the dig site that morning.

Juice dragged himself out of bed, drank some coffee, and met the team at the marina with the Aventura. They had heard about the attack on his home, but they hadn't really had a chance to talk. The Navy had beefed up their security detail and the police had provided the team and Juice with 24-hour security, in town.

Juice was able to get some more sleep on his boat that morning while the team went to work documenting and uncovering one crate of silver bars after another. They had arranged to load their treasure on the larger heavy-metal naval vessel.

Each crate weighed in at approximately eight hundred pounds, and the old wood disintegrated as they were uncovered, so it was back-breaking work moving each bar into an aluminum container and winching each full container, by small crane, onto a barge that was towed to the navy boat and winched aboard. The job was made more difficult by the rising tides that meant that team members took turns being lowered into the pit to load the bars while connected to air hoses from above.

The good news was that the pit was full of crates, one atop another, and they appeared to go to the bottom of the tube. The team was buoyed by the success of the venture, and by the end of the first day, they had brought up eight crates, or what appeared to be about half of the treasure.

The two Spanish archeologists marveled at how protected the silver was compared to the usual scattered treasure
they painstakingly recovered from sunken boats in deeper
sand and water.

Juice' enthusiasm had been dulled by the attack on he
and Bella, and their home. He knew his dream life in Loreto might never be the same, but it didn't stop him from
shooting tequilas with the INAH team and Navy sailors
while looking at the huge load of recovered silver at the
end of the day.

As they motored back to town, the sun dipped behind
the huge shark tooth, many-named, peak of the Sierra Gigante Range that loomed in clear sight no matter where
you were in the greater Loreto area. Called Loreto Peak,
Lolita's, Sugar Mountain and Las Parras, the list went on,
as did the daily light show at sunset.

Sam and Sheila felt really relaxed after a quiet night in
their tent with only the sound of the breeze and the tidal
swells. Over camp coffee at the water's edge, they began to
reminisce about their vacation and past Baja trips.

"I love this place! Do you think we could live here when
we retire?" Sheila wondered.

"I was just thinking the same thing. We could look at
housing costs here before we leave, maybe talk to a realtor.
Juice and others we've met would help," Sam answered.

They looked out on their little bay towards the natural
arch on the north side, and both saw a big bat-ray jump
three feet out of the water and flip over before slapping

the surface. They both "Oohed!" at the same time. Then another ray jumped, and another, sometimes two or three jumping at once. They flew out of the water, enjoying two seconds of unfiltered sun reflecting off their black, green, or dark-gray wings.

Sam and Sheila started to applaud and give olympic scores to each jumping ray. "Nine point five! Its a ten!" The jumping went on for hours, and late afternoon, they walked along the beach to get closer and marveled at the massive party of rays swirling and dancing underwater, jumping and probably mating.

"Magical! It's a Ray Rave," Sheila whispered to Sam. "Its going to be hard to go back tomorrow, but I'm so glad we made time for this," Sam whispered back, and they kissed as the rays applauded by jumping and slapping the water. "Quite a send off!" kidded Sam.

Friday, October 21, 2005

SAM and Sheila were having lunch at the PachaMama Cafe on the Zocalo, with Juice. They had reluctantly paddled back to Ligui earlier that morning, and had returned to find out about the attack on Juice and Bella. They had packed their things in the Subaru to start the drive back north to Sacramento. This was goodbye to Juice, but before leaving, they would walk over to the Loreto Mission Museum to see the display of six tons of Spanish silver bars.

"Thank you for everything, Juice. This has been the most memorable vacation of them all," Sam said, smiling and looking his old friend in the eye. Juice chuckled. "Hey, I'll try to make it more exciting, next time. Seriously, I'm really happy we reconnected. I missed you, brother. We made up for lost time, though, didn't we?"

It was Sam's turn to chuckle. "I love you, Juice, but I'd be happy just catching more fish and sun, next time. I'm so sorry about your place and the changes you and Bella are going through. We knew it would be a mixed bag, but all this shit is so sudden. Hang in there, Brother!"

Sheila added, "Please give Bella a hug from me. We really became close on our challenging mule trip. Great to make new friends, and so sorry for what's happened to you both. Please stop in Sacramento on your journey north, and if you start your world travels like you talked about, we'd love to meet you in some exotic location."

Loretanos were proud of their history, and families were flocking to town from the ranchos and fishing villages, some by mule and horseback, to view the treasure. It was like a holiday, which Loreto seemed to celebrate almost every week. The three friends waited in the long lines waiting to see the treasure until one of the INAH team spotted them and explained to those waiting that these were the people who found the treasure, then ushered them inside.

Juice had seen the exhibit already, but Sam and Sheila were in awe of the massive mound of silver bars that were on display. Word spread through the crowd that the ones who found the treasure were there, and they were instant celebrities. They met the mayor, and mothers, fathers and children smiled at them and shook their hands as the line went by.

Needing to get on the road, Sam and Sheila said their goodbyes to Chucho, Pancho, and his team and Trudy, who had come by. Juice walked with them back to where their cars were parked and Juice said he had a surprise that would just take a second. He walked briskly to his car and returned with a bag that looked quite heavy. He reached into the bag and handed Sam one of the two original bars they had found. "Pancho said we could each keep a bar, but he added that we didn't get them from him."

Sam looked at Sheila. "I guess we'll have to sneak this over the border when they ask us what we've brought back from Mexico." Juice hugged Sheila, then the two child-hood friends hugged tightly and tears welled in their eyes, spilling down their cheeks.

Too choked up to say anything else, Sam and Sheila got in the car and waved as they drove off. Juice wiped his face and watched them turn the corner.

Monday, October 24, 2005

SAM and Sheila both had busy first days back to work after driving more than twelve hundred miles over three days for a late arrival home the night before. Sam met with Sis-ter Julie first thing, that morning. She'd taken notes on is-sues that he'd have to follow up on, and they went over everything. He filled her in on the saga of TommyLynn and Dani, though she'd heard some of it from Captain Ortega.

Sam met next with Reverend Don and Jake Winters in Dignity Park. Don and Jake reported that the hospital dumping had slowed to a trickle, but Jake had found out about more patient dumping incidents involving hospitals in the state of Nevada.

Don explained, "We passed Jake's information on to Monica at the Bee, and her article got the State Attorney General involved. The A.G. subpoenaed Nevada hospital records, finding hundreds of these dumping incidents from Nevada to cities all over California. Last week, they filed a lawsuit."

"Nice work, Jake, Don. You guys rock! I wanted to invite you to the new respite shelter opening at five tonight."

Jake said, "Finally! Thanks, but I'm going out with family."

Don begged off, too. "I can't stomach some of these wealthy suits after being with homeless folks and their suffering all day. We'll let you do the dirty work, Sam." Sam smiled. "Its good to be back at The Village."

Sam had managed to escape most of the media circus surrounding the silver. The Baja treasure find had been an international story covered by press all over the planet. He had seen the photo of Juice with Pancho standing behind the huge pile of silver at the Loreto Mission Museum in the L.A. Times. He hadn't told anybody but Sheila's two younger sisters, and he planned to keep it that way for awhile, at least.

━━━━━━━━━━━━━━━━━

DANI and TommyLynn, now Sally and Linda, were study-ing in their living room to take their GED tests. The dean at San Diego Mesa Community College had made an ex-ception to allow them to enroll in classes as long as they passed their GEDs by the end of the semester. They had part-time jobs at the community college already, assist-ed by the Federal Marshals. Dani worked in the campus child care center, where she loved being an assistant with the two- and three-year-olds, and it was great experience for a future teacher. TommyLynn had a job as a crisis-line worker at the campus counseling center, and was learning a lot from his licensed social worker supervisor, who had also taken her under his wing.

Dani took a break and was staring at her friend, smil-ing. "What?" TommyLynn asked when he noticed her looking at him.

"Can you believe that its been a month since we met, and so much has happened. I keep wanting to pinch my-self, afraid I'll wake up from this dream.

"When I was sick and held captive in my cell, I thought my life was over. I imagined I'd either be killed or made into a sex slave. My head pounded when I was awake, I was so nauseous I couldn't eat, and I couldn't do anything but sleep." She began to cry. "I couldn't even imagine that my life could be so good, so soon. Thank you for changing my life, TommyLynn Arce!"

TommyLynn got up and walked over to her, put his arm around her shoulders, and began to cry, as well. He kneeled down to be at eye level with her. "When I got shot and was at the hospital and got the news that you'd been kidnapped and Jethro was shot, I felt like I'd failed you and gotten my best friend almost killed, and couldn't do a fucking thing about it. I felt so helpless, and I'd gotten so close to you, only to have you taken in just a few days.

"It's still hard to believe that I found you, and things have worked out so well. Thank you for changing my life, Dani Blue!"

———————————————

It was five o'clock, and Sam was with Sister Julie at the Salvation Army shelter a block from the Village, negotiating a crowd of hospital administrators, local elected officials, media, shelter staff and homeless activists. He saw State Assemblymember Kalen Jones talking to Scott of the Hospital Association, and the County Health Director, so they walked over and all shook hands, smiling at the well-equipped new hospital respite shelter.

Sam and Sister Julie thanked everyone profusely and gave a couple of media interviews. There was a long press conference with too many speakers. Sheila and Carly showed up near the end and they all decided to go out for drinks. Later, Sam and Sheila, Kalen and Carly, and Sister Julie were at Frank Fat's restaurant/bar on 'L' Street, sipping drinks with little paper umbrellas. Sheila showed photos of her mule expedition and the amazing cave paintings.

Kalen asked, "So Sam, Sheila mentioned that your Mexico vacation was a lot more exciting than expected. Something about the young couple who were shot and kidnapped here showing up in Baja?"

"That's not the half of it, but yes." He went on to describe the events concerning TommyLynn and Dani showing up in Loreto, the battle between the police and the cartel, and the "happy ending" with them being placed in protective custody. "I just found out that the Tijuana cartel boss involved in the human trafficking ring that held Dani has been extradited to the U.S. and charged with sex trafficking"

After Sam finished, Kalen was shaking his head and Carly offered, "Remind us never to go to Mexico with you." Everybody laughed, and Sam looked at Sheila. "Yeah, next time, we'll just sit by the pool and drink margaritas."

"Yeah, right!" she replied, shaking her head.

EPILOGUE

New Year's Eve - Saturday, December 31, 2005

ON CHRISTMAS DAY, Sam and Sheila received a letter from Juice and Bella that was sent from Sydney, Australia. It included two round trip tickets to Sydney for Sam and Sheila and a check for twenty thousand dollars made out to St. Frances Village. Juice had included a note that said he had just received payment from the Treasury of Spain in the amount of eighty-thousand dollars, with a note from the King of Spain thanking him for finding their missing silver (a copy of the note was included). He wrote that the silver had been valued at one-point-six million dollars and that the ten-percent finders fee had been split between Juice and the Mexican Treasury.

Juice's letter also explained that even though Sam had refused to accept any of the money, Juice insisted on making this contribution to The Village. Sam had told him he hoped to hire TommyLynn to be a service coordinator for LGBTQ homeless folks at The Village, so his donation was intended to be seed money for this new program.

TommyLynn and Dani had finished their semester at

San Diego Mesa, but in their last week of school they were informed that the cartel jefe had hung himself in prison, their testimony was no longer needed and their protective custody would end at the end of the month. They had decided that they would always be friends, but Dani had a boyfriend now and she wanted to move in with him. TommyLynn had moved back to Sacramento and was staying with his parents. Sam had kept his promise to offer TommyLynn a job at the Village, so he would work part-time while also attending Sacramento City College.

Sheila's and Sam's flight to Sydney left on Monday, and they were taking another ten days off. They decided to have a New Year's Eve party with forty of their friends and family. Now it was close to midnight, and everyone was in the best of spirits. Kabu, their chocolate Labrador, had been the star of the party but was fading, now laying on her fluffy dog bed. The Slingshots band had been jamming in the back yard for a couple hours, and Sam sat in on harmonica with Mota and Cat. Almost everyone had been dancing, but now they were all looking for something to drink as midnight approached.

Sam went to the microphone with Sheila. "First, I've been keeping a secret, and I want to get it off my chest." The alcohol-infused crowd oohed in unison, then laughed. He had their attention.

"In October, while we were on vacation in the town of Loreto, Sheila left on her week-long mule expedition to ancient cave paintings and I went scuba diving for a few days with my old childhood friend Juice Fiero, who is a retired Marine and master diver. To make a long story short, we found an underwater cave, and Juice found two Spanish silver ingots dating to the sixteenth century."

With a flourish, Sheila now removed a scarf that was covering the heavy silver bar she was holding, and everyone oohed and aahed. Sam continued, "It turned out that we had found a long-buried treasure that weighed in at six tons of silver ingots just like this one. I should say again that while I helped, it was really my friend Juice who found the treasure and deserved the credit.

"The Spanish government finally reclaimed the silver with our help and the help of the Mexican government, and researched its origins. They now believe that this treasure was buried by the famous English admiral Sir Francis Drake after he had plundered it from a Spanish galleon, La Señora de la Concepcion, around 1578."

Sheila walked the silver bar around the back yard for people to see and touch. People were looking at each other, but it got quiet. "You aren't kidding, are you? Most of us saw the story about the silver treasure found in Baja," Kalen said loudly, continuing. "It wasn't enough to find 49ers gold right here in your neighborhood? Now you're an international treasure hunter?" Folks laughed as Sam extended his arms out to his sides, palms up, and shrugged.

A few minutes later, Sheila went to the microphone. She and Sam raised their glasses. "We're very thankful for this past year, and friends like you are the real treasure. Happy New Year!"

"Happy New Year!" echoed the partiers as the end of year countdown began. "Ten, nine, eight…" Sam pulled Sheila into an embrace. "Sorry, I couldn't wait." They kissed until it was well into 2006.

Character List:

- TommyLynn Watson-Arce - 20 year old, homeless intersex person
- Dani Blue - Prostitute for Trixie, TommyLynn's friend
- Sam White -Director of The Village of homeless services
- Sheila Bright - Sam's wife, director of Care For All, Health clinic
- Sister Julie Baldwin - Director of Day House - Women's center at the Village
- Jake Winters - formerly homeless, assistant Director of Dignity Park
- Cat - Oretha Johnson, formerly homeless, works at Teen Center
- Mota - Moreno, formerly homeless, plays in the Sling Shots, Cat's partner
- Trixie - Madam for a large prostitution ring with her partner Ginger
- Markus - Trixie's muscle/pimp
- Captain Ortega - Sac. Major Crimes unit
- Juanita Arce - TommyLynn's Mexican cousin
- Reverend Don Hood - Director of Dignity Park
- Kalen Jones - State Assemblyman and friend of Sam
- Carly Johnson- Lawyer and Kalen's close associate

- Jesus (Juice) Fierro - Sam's childhood friend, former Marine and Dive master with Diving business in Loreto
- Bella - Juice's wife who goes with Sheila on Mule expedition to Cave Paintings
- Trudy - Ecotours business owner who leads Mule and kayak trips from Loreto
- Jefe - cartel boss of the sex trade in northern Mexico, tied to Zeta Cartel
- Ricardo - Jefe's #1 muscle
- TommyLynn's grand uncle Gerardo and grandmother Marta, Loreto ranchers
- FBI agents - Juan Morales and June Black from San Diego office
- Capitan Moreno - Leads the Mexican Federales case against El Jefe
- Jesus (Chucho) Rodrigues - Presidente of Loreto college
- Luis Echeveria - crooked INAH official from La Paz, tied to Sinaloa Cartel
- Pancho Navarro - high ranking INAH archeologist who takes over the Treasure Search

Acknowledgements

Thank you to the Loreto Writers Collective for your review and feedback on my early manuscript, especially our founder Paula Brook-Saltzberg. Baja Silver was inspired by the history and people of Loreto, Baja Sur, Mexico and by the amazing board of directors, staff, guests and volunteers of the not-for-profit Loaves & Fishes, Sacramento, California - providing a village of hospitality and services to our unhoused brothers and sisters for nearly forty years.

Author's note -

While there is no definitive proof that Captain Francis Drake landed his ship The Golden Hinde on present day Baja California. He would certainly have sailed up the Pacific coast of this magnificent peninsula and very possibly into the Gulf of California on his journey to present day Northern California. His landing at Cabo San Lucas and the burying of silver on Carmen Island was completely my creation, but the rest of my prologue was taken from a very patchy written history of his historic circumnavigation.